NOTHING THE SAME, EVERYTHING HAUNTED

NOTHING THE SAME, EVERYTHING HAUNTED

THE BALLAD OF MOTL THE COWBOY

GARY BARWIN

RANDOM HOUSE CANADA

PUBLISHED BY RANDOM HOUSE CANADA

www.penguinrandomhouse.ca

Random House Canada and colophon are registered trademarks.

Page 333 constitutes a continuation of the copyright page.

Library and Archives Canada Cataloguing in Publication

Title: Nothing the same, everything haunted : the ballad of Motl the cowboy /
    Gary Barwin.
Names: Barwin, Gary, author.
Identifiers: Canadiana (print) 20200268171 | Canadiana (ebook) 20200268198 |
    ISBN 9780735279520 (hardcover) | ISBN 9780735279537 (EPUB)
Classification: LCC PS8553.A783 N68 2021 | DDC C813/.54—dc23

Text design: Andrew Roberts
Jacket design: Andrew Roberts
Image credits: (cowboy) © MoreMass / Shutterstock

Printed and bound in Canada

10 9 8 7 6 5 4 3 2 1

In memory of *my cousin,*
Isaak Grazutis
who walked into thin air
and returned en plein air

and my grandparents
who carried it with them

The facts are sonorous but between the facts there's a whispering. It's the whispering that astounds me.

—CLARICE LISPECTOR

———

the future is already over . . . that doesn't mean we don't have anywhere else to go.

—BILLY-RAY BELCOURT

✥ PART ONE ✥

Poets are fakers
Whose faking is so real
They even fake the pain
They truly feel

—CHARLES BERNSTEIN (AFTER PESSOA)

I

VILNIUS (VILNA)

JULY 1941

Motl. Jewish cowpoke. Brisket Boy. My grandfather.

As usual, he was bent over the kitchen table, his mottled and hairy nose deep in the pale valley of a book, half-finished plate of herring beside his elbow, half-eaten egg bread slumped beside a Shabbos candlestick. His old mother was out shopping for food while she still could.

So, this Motl, was he a reader?

If the world was ending, he would keep reading.

The world *was* ending. He was still reading.

So, what was this book he had to read despite everything?

One of the great westerns of the American frontier, of course. Even though he knew that Hitler adored them.

"The master race should be brave as Indianers," *Der Führer* had said, and sent boxes of Karl May's Winnetou noble savage novels to the eastern front to inspire his troops—those same manifest destiny soldiers crossing the country with orders to kill Motl, his mother and all the other Jews.

Did Motl intend to do something about this?

Yes. He would sit at the table, his shlumpy jacket turned up at the collar, his hat like a shroud of mice askew on his sallow head, and read.

Was Motl a man of action?

"If parking his tuches all day and all night on a chair doing nothing but reading is action," his mother would say, "he's a man of action. Action, sure. Every day he gets older and more in my way."

Why was he still reading this western?

Because Motl, this Litvak, this Lithuanian Jew, this inconceivable zaidy, my grandfather, this citizen of the Wild East—that brave old world of ever-present sorrow, a sorrow that had just gotten worse—had chosen the life of the cowboy.

He would be that hombre who sits on his chair and imagines being calm and steady and manly, speaking only the fewest of well-chosen words, doing only what he wanted and what he must under that vast, unpatented western sky.

"And why not?" he would say. "Should my life be nothing but the minced despair and boiled hope of an aging Jew, too thin to be anything but borscht made by Nazis? I choose to think myself a Paleface chuck line rider of the doleful countenance, a Quixotic Ashkenazi of the bronco, riding the Ostland trail. Like my mother said when I told her I wanted to be a doctor, 'Mazel tov, Motl. Nothing is impossible when it's an illusion.'"

He would say, "What's the difference between a Jewish cowpoke and beef jerky? It's the hat. And feeling empty as a broken barrel. Jerky don't never feel such hollowness, least not by the time it's jerky. But the cowboy, the cowboy keeps riding. He don't look back. Eventually, if he's lucky, he too becomes leathern and feels only what jerky feels."

Motl. Citizen of Vilna. Saddlebag of pain. Feedbag of regret.

At forty-five, he had a history. As a Lithuanian Jew, he was pickled in it.

But though neither he nor his mother knew it at the time, something had changed. Somewhere, deep down in the overworked mine shaft of his imagination, it had been determined that he would set out on a perilous adventure, this time of his own choosing. He would get up on his horse and ride.

And he would have a child.

At his age.

And avoid being killed. Sometimes you have to save your own bacon, when you're a Jew.

The next day, he went to the barber's. Even a grown man will cave in to his mother's demands that he groom if she won't make food for him. Eyes closed, a Texas reverie floating through his mind like the scent of campfire, Motl lay back in the red chair and awaited his shave.

But then:

"Under a hot towel, a cowpoke can think big thoughts, but to act he must stand up," he said.

He stood up.

For a moment, the towel hung from his jowls, the Santabeard of a Hebrew god. Then it fell away.

"Barber," Motl said. "I must seize these last days while the possibility of life remains."

The barber said nothing, wet blade held between trembling fingers.

"The kabbalists speak of repairing the world, healing what is broken. It's my time," Motl said, looking round that hair-strewn palace of strop and whisker, that little shop of Hebrews. "Barber, I thank you, for I have learned much under your towel."

Shave and a haircut.

—Did the barber, Shmuel, expect payment?—

Two bits.

Did Motl toss him these two coins before his impromptu departure?

Having had neither shave nor haircut, he only waved, then hightailed it into the bright sun of Shnipishok, that region of Vilna whose name sounds like scissor blades. He ran through its streets, feeling open to possibility and getaway.

Did Shmuel chase him with his blade?

Let's say it was a close shave.

This day, as the towel fell from his bristly chins, Motl saw beyond his scraggy self and straight into his crimpled yet resilient heart. He understood that it could become pink and new as the callow fundament of a child. How? He recalled that there remained a means by which he could become procreator and thus begetter. In this time of murder and loss, to make new life would be to make life new. It would be a salve for the broken world. He could say, both to his child and to himself, "It is worth being born into this world. It is worth being born."

And this fathering, would it involve the usual squirming ministrations known since our ancestors first began to beget?

It would not.

But first, he had to retrieve his old saddle of a kvetching mother and get them both the galloping Gehenna out of the *Einsatzgruppen*ing hell that Vilna would soon be.

The cavalry were coming, or—raised as they were on Karl May—they'd more likely imagine themselves Aryan elves of the plains, Rhineland braves with bellies like six-packs of strudel.

Noble cabbages.

Coming to lead their band of Lithuanian Lakota against the godless yellowstars, locals happy to have the excuse for an anti-Semitic whoop-up.

Besides, if a boychik cowpoke was going to ride off in quest of new life, who else to bring but his mama?

But first, before he even retrieved this mama, we must go back nearly twenty years and speak of the family jewels because, in the end, that's where all roads begin.

2

SIBERIA

AUGUST 1915. TWENTY-SIX YEARS BEFORE

The First World War. Blood, fire and rising smoke. Like many Litvaks, nineteen-year-old Motl and his family were exiled to Siberia, far beyond the Pale. Chaos and dismay on leaving. Litvaks in shtetls and town were given orders to be gone by daylight, or else be shot. The panicked packing. The search to find wagons. Everything stacked into rented peasant wagons. Motl was sent to rescue Torah scrolls from the study house, from the synagogue. Torahs were wrapped in the coats of dead relatives then buried under the exiled family's possessions. Hand-wringing. Weeping. His mother lamenting, wringing her hands. Lamentation from every house. Finally, at the train station, they were loaded like premonitions into cattle cars. Disease and starvation on the journey. Children, the old. Parents. Their houses burned down behind them.

"Sometimes I think it'd have been better if we Jews had never been born," Motl would say. "But who has that much luck— maybe one in a million?"

Welcome parties on arrival: pogroms.

But some survived. Motl survived.

The Ural Mountains. The edge of Siberia. A thousand miles to the east. Motl and his family lived in an incapacitated shack, sleeping together in a gap-toothed single room as if in a cabin on the prairie. Motl, his mother, father, his sister Chaya, his cousins Hershel and Pinchas, his aunt Anya. Each morning, his grandparents Abe and Faigel hacking awake with blood and phlegm, sputtering their Model T lungs.

"Oy, Gott, if you're punishing me, at least remind me why, so I could enjoy the memories," Abe said.

Other cabins crowded round and only squirrels outside, the wind inside, cold blades slicing through the slats. Not the lonesome prairie, except far from home.

Motl, gangling and uncertain, sits in the sun beside a wending river, reading a western. A village youth wanders by, lifts a thick stick from the stick-covered ground, raises it behind Motl's head, intending to acquaint Motl's brain with the outside air.

A shadow crosses the page. A circling vulture? An editor's too-late hand? Motl twists in time to raise his own hand, the stick a downward blur snapping into his open palm. Motl stands, turns, wrests the stick from its owner, loses his balance, topples toward the youth, knocks him down. Motl, falling, thrusts his arms out to catch himself, and the stick, still clutched between his hands, spans the villager's spindly throat, a one-finger cutthroat sign.

Motl, finding himself part of this deft accidental choreography, pratfall as martial art, gazes into the youth's eyes, surprised and fearful, recalls the hero's droll words from the western, now toppled in the grass like an injured bird: "A warrior should suffer pain in silence. But you . . . you may scream if you'd like."

The gasping villager was unable to exercise the option. Then, from the path, a soldier in a greatcoat.

"Jew?"

"Yes . . . I . . ."

"Litvak?"

"Yes."

Single words, unless spoken in the throes of passion, seldom result in happiness.

"Stand. You go see Golubkov now."

Motl rose and brushed the dirt from his debilitated trousers. Was he to be hobbled or hog-tied only to be scranched and boot-hilled in a lock-up by these Czarist brutes? He left the young villager with the stick now delicately balanced across his skinny gizzard. Dead? Unconscious? Only the vultures knew for sure.

The soldier led Motl along the riverbank to a squat stone building, outside of which sat a Russian captain, drinking tea at a small lace-covered table.

"Who is this?" the captain said.

The soldier saluted then muttered a few words at close range into the captain's fleshy ear. Then he pushed Motl forward.

"Golubkov," the captain said, introducing himself to Motl. The patronizing greasiness of his voice made Motl feel the urgent need to wash. Golubkov lifted a teacup to his fuchsia lips, his dainty slurps like the death throes of a drowning fly.

"Perhaps I will send you where the peckersnot will freeze in the spout of your little Hebrew samovar. Or perhaps," he said, placing the teacup on its saucer with a clatter, "you could be useful. We don't like Jews to create trouble. Unless we ask them to.

"So," he said, pausing to lift the lid of a squat silver sugar bowl, silting up the liquid of his cup with heapfuls of sugar. "In two weeks, enemies—enemies of Czar Nicholas and of our Mother Russia, enemies of this necessary war—will gather in a village far from here to hiss and mutter. They will attend a secret socialist conference to plot the demise of Europe. Secret except our intelligence reaches even into the mountains. They will meet in Switzerland—in Zimmerwald—in the shadow of the Alps where robins and skylarks sing. These execrable Marxists will pretend to be ornithology enthusiasts attending a conference of birds. You will travel there and kill who you can. There is Vladimir Ilyich Ulyanov, known as Lenin, and there is Trotsky."

"But what do I know of killing? Why choose me and not a soldier or spy?"

"You're not important, so I have nothing to lose," the captain said. "Except money. I have staked money on a little wager. Last night at the officers' club, I bet that anyone, anyone at all, even a Jew, could assassinate one of these Bolshevik eggheads—they're more manifesto than man. And you, my friend, are just the kind of anyone I was looking for. The private here tells me you handle a stick with surprising expertise. I'm counting on you to be successful so I win my wager. And so is Mother Russia. But of course I sent others this morning. Many hunters and one goose guarantees a good supper.

"Understand that we are very interested in these socialists. We are very interested in having them shot. And know this, my young comrade," he said. "If you're not successful, we'll murder your entire family."

Again, the fuchsia suction as Golubkov raised the slurry of tea to his lips and waved them away.

3

SIBERIA TO ZIMMERWALD

AUGUST/SEPTEMBER 1915

By that afternoon, Motl was on a train travelling west across Russia carrying imperial-issue cheese, Cossack pickles, an extra pair of Czarist underwear and the soggy western, which he'd been allowed to retrieve from where he dropped it by the river. After some days' travel, the train neared the border at Tarnopol, only recently captured by the Central Powers. Three greatcoated men, each with a moustache like the overgrown pelt of a shaggy marmot, entered the car and loomed over the passengers in the seats near Motl. They gazed with mild yet meaningfully unrelenting eyes until everyone but Motl left. Then they sat down.

"We sit down," they said, as if to claim reality for themselves.

From inside one of their greatcoats: vodka. A silver fish-embossed flask was passed from one thick hand to another ("To Czar Nikolai!" they toasted) and then to Motl, who had no option but to splutter down a compliant snort of the blistering solvent.

There was silence until the train slowed and stopped between stations.

"Stand," one of the men said, and Motl, vodka-fuddled, did his best to comply.

"Follow," said another and, as one, the four men strode to the door.

"Jump," they said, and Motl jumped. The three men hopped down onto the track gravel behind him, then plunged into a nearby stand of woods, where an automobile lay camouflaged by branches. Only once before had Motl seen such a large and impressive car, and that only a few hours before as their train had pulled out of Kiev. He clambered over the running board and was instructed to crouch in the back while a blanket was thrown over him. It had the foul goulash stench of hopelessness and farts.

A hacking and shuddering as the engine came to, then the crunch of branches, rocks and gravel as the car found the dirt road.

After some hours of turbulent darkness, heat and regretful breathing beneath the blanket, the car stopped. Motl heard an unintelligible exchange of what might have been German between a voice outside the car and the driver inside. Then two gunshots. A call-and-response of blasts.

The car lurched forward, shuddering over the bumpy road and cornering fitfully. After a few minutes, quiet moaning. After a few more, one of the men said, "Vodka." A multi-voiced grunt of assent then subsequent expressions of satisfaction as the flask made its rounds.

After many more hours, Motl was uncovered with a flourish of light and air, and he sat up. A splotch of blood on the arm of the driver's greatcoat resembled the rust-coloured shape of Texas, blood dampened by vodka to sterilize the wound. The man stared straight ahead, impassively, both hands clutching the leather-bound wheel. Motl had read about such men, overcoming fate and bullets through sheer self-reliance, pluck and tenacity. And the duplicitous courage of drink.

They had arrived outside a train station of imposing scale.

"Stuttgart," the driver said, and told Motl he was to board the train for Switzerland here. "You'll be met inside the station by a Polish woman, Urszula. She'll have a loaf of bread wrapped like a baby."

"Thanks," he said, and the men nodded. This, his only conversation with these three shaggy-lipped sherpas.

As instructed, Motl rendezvoused with Urszula. Her dark hair was tied under a red floral kerchief and, Motl noted, she embraced a loaf of bread, wrapped like a baby, in distinctive blue cloth.

"Michal—my nephew?" she had said loudly as she approached him, so that others around her could hear. "I didn't recognize you. You've grown so big."

Motl blushed as if he were actually this woman's nephew.

They climbed aboard the train to Bern and sat near the back of the car. They whispered. Or rather, Urszula whispered and Motl leaned uncomfortably against the window.

"The end may justify the means as long as there is something that justifies the end," she said. "And the end we'd like to see is the bourgeoisie's as we kick 'em out their easy chairs."

These weren't the words of someone on the Czarist side. Was this a test, the failing of which would cause Motl's pale skull to be separated from his two-faced brain? Was Urszula trying to root out his allegiance? But she had shared the loaf of bread and Motl couldn't argue with what she said about how the rich took "from each Jew according to their abilities, from each Jew according to their needs."

"So, maybe I'm a Bolshevik," she said. "And, if so, I've found the best place to hide: right under the Romanovs' onion-domed noses. And without knowing it, they're funding me to build a Bolshevik network all through Europe. To be revolutionary is to be good at turning your back on those who pay you," she said. "So maybe you'll turn with me?"

By the time they'd arrived in Bern and transferred to a horse-drawn coach for Zimmerwald, Motl was also quoting Trotsky. "There are no absolute rules of conduct, either in peace or war. Everything depends on circumstances."

As far as Golubkov, the Czar and his stuffed Golubtsi know, Urszula said, she was on her way to Switzerland with Motl to assassinate Lenin, or Trotsky, or both. She'd been recruited as an imperial operative years ago, but not before she was already working for the other side.

"But don't trust anyone," she'd said. "Especially someone who tells you so. Everyone involved in this business holds a mirror in front of another mirror. Try brushing your hair in such a place and you lose an eye, if not the revolution and your life."

4

ZIMMERWALD

SEPTEMBER 1915

It was the morning before the delegates were to arrive. Motl had never seen so many mountains. Or mountains of such size. They made the sky seem larger and farther away. How else could it contain objects of such immensity?

Beyond the village, at the foot of these Alps, sat a grand house inside of which was a Russian count, apparently protected by the bewildering turmoil of the lederhosen-inspired architecture of the half-timbered upper storey. The count lived surrounded by pots of caviar, silverware, caged birds and his wounded yet resilient entitlement. His dacha had been torched in the 1905 revolution, increasing the likelihood that he too would soon be noble barbecue, and so he'd left Russia. Though he was an aristocrat, he was a capitalist first. And a capitalist with debts. So, he would host this incendiary conference of revolutionaries in his new home—he who pays for the balalaika calls the tune, and the Bolsheviks would come armed with rubles. He'd hold his aristocratic nose and accept them.

But none of them knew that a small team of monarchists, both professional and amateur, had also gathered, sent by Golubkov and his cronies. And there were also, like Motl and Urszula, some counter-counter-revolutionaries, who had turned from the work they were supposed to do and who intended to eliminate all the monarchists they could find.

The following morning, forty revolutionaries assembled on the lawn of the great property for breakfast. The plan was this: while Urszula kept an eye on the dining delegates, ensuring that they weren't assassinated by those still loyal to the Czar, Motl and a few secret comrades would start by knocking off the near-Romanov count.

Motl and his allies felt a tremor through their bodies as they stormed the grand house. They entered from the kitchen, each scooping a pastry as they stomped past. Each now with a comma of jam curling from the corner of their lips, they burst into the library, much to the surprise of the count, who was quietly reading about the taxonomy of birds.

Kingdom, phylum, class, family, gentry, serfdom, species, gout. A classification for people as well as birds.

They burst through the familiar order of class to lift their guns and their prospects.

The count stood, startled as a duck before hunters, and squawked his astonishment.

"Serfs up," said one of Motl's new comrades as he shot the count through his book of birds, piercing the coloured breasts of swallows and swans, and then the petulant pumper of this hereditary lord and landowner. The books around them were beautiful. A leather forest. Flights of like-coloured volumes bound by bands of gold and brown. Walls of dark shelves punctuated with glowing sconces and portraits of self-satisfied gout sufferers dressed in lace and velvet.

Motl froze. Though it had been the plan, he hadn't expected that murder would result in death. At least not right in front of him. Then he quickly pocketed the count's small volume—evidence? history? a connection with the mysteries?—as one of his hot-headed companions hurled a lamp against the wall, lamp oil dripping down between broken glass and bursting into flame. The revolution would be a firebird, rising from a fire fed by the roasting aristocracy. Personally, I'd have kept the summer houses and palaces and only cooked their soft landowning insides. But brazen revolutionaries can't resist braising hell and so they torched everything.

Afterwards, it was chaos. Curtains, kitchens, bedrooms, cherrywood cabinets and dining room all on fire. Servants, a contessa, little dogs and puppy-like wigs, horses, chefs, maids, children running wild into the fields and gardens. Socialist delegates on the lawn looking for water, not quite able to agree on the best way to coordinate a bucket brigade. Motl and his comrades mad with exhilaration and second thoughts and filled with wine from a well-stocked cellar ran from the weeping and yawping and the scent of roasting wealth. Motl made it to the end of the elaborate OCD gardens, hedges trimmed like the moustaches of a dandy. Then up the rising slope of an untrimmed mountain. Motl found the suggestion of a path and plunged up, leaving the conflagration of revolutionary progress behind. He ran until he could but walk and then walked until he was so lost he could not find himself. Deep in the breathless thicket, all he could find was his own cow-hearted terror, his own shaking hide aiming to become verb.

He had no choice but to continue up, an adolescent Sisyphus dropping his revolutionary rock and running. The crackle of his boots on the forest floor. His still-ragged breath. It began to snow and so he wept, his face a sludge of snot and tears. He was a whippersnapper who had lost his way fleeing from his first foray into history. A revolutionary only because he felt he'd spent most of the time running in circles.

What about his family? Golubkov threatened to kill them if he didn't succeed.

The fire.

There'd been a fire. It wasn't his fault. What could he have done?

He kept running until he found himself in an icy valley beneath a grey-white sky. He was on a glacier slid between two peaks.

A voice, as young as Motl's, from the pines. "Hands up and drop your guns." But Motl was a gunslinger without a gun. He had only the text on ornithology. He would subdue his challenger with a wounded disquisition on the manifold varieties of passerine, with talk of beaks, endothermic vertebrates and the delicate rustle of feathers as the night wind blows. Where to begin? Perhaps at the beginning: with the egg.

Unless it was the chicken. He'd cross that road when he came to it.

He had no knife to bring to this gunfight, but he could repeat a gunfighter's words.

"I will not perforate your pine-scented chicken-pocked lady-balls with lead," he said, "if you stop hiding like a girl and show yourself." The best defence is a strong imagination, the illusion of the possible.

Silence.

"Does your heart pump your mama's chicken soup?" he shouted. "Do you have the parboiled spätzli of a mouse between your scrawny legs? Come out or I'll make red doilies of your weasel-guts."

A shot from the dark woods. A bullet entered a tree a hundred feet behind Motl.

Then another.

"Show yourself!" the voice said.

Silence.

"I'm not moving," Motl said, though in truth, he quaked. "Not even to jump into the path of your runty bullets so you can kill me."

A confident nothing seems like something.

Then the voice said, "Samy. My name is Samy Rosenstock. I've come from Bucharest."

Motl had exhausted the script. How would this scene unfold?

"Samy," he said. "Come out. Let's both stop shooting and I'll not repeat the name Rosenstock to no one. Then I won't need to tell them what name to write on your grave. Or that we walked away in peace."

Silence.

Then another gunshot from the woods.

"Oh!" said Samy.

Between Motl's legs the heat and fire of a volcano.

Then another shot.

"Oh!" said Samy.

Motl folded over a glowing magma of pain.

"Sorry!" said Samy.

And so Motl's two vital cobblers were shot.

Off.

As Motl fell, he saw his testicles roll a man's length over the glacier and into a crevasse where they would freeze solid—two fetal mammoths, hairy and still, waiting for the future.

———

"An accident," Samy called, appearing at the edge of the woods. "I didn't mean to. I'm a *flâneur*. I was trying to put the gun away. Anyway, I'm changing my name. It's Tristan Tzara. I'm a poet." And with that, he ran off.

Motl lay motionless for a while, moaning and bleeding. Then he sat up and packed his pants with ice. "Sometimes you're cauterized with loss," he muttered. "And sometimes you need to be frozen."

Unable to stand, Motl was sure he would die, a desperado felled before his first real shootout. It's only a duel if both cowboys know it is. And if they both have guns.

Motl fallen in snow, on the frontier between vision and oblivion. The lonesome howling of angels. A golem playing harmonica late into the night.

The afterlife? Motl thought. It's the heavenly day after—after the tin-cup coffee, the bedding down with blanket and saddle, a red fire flickering against the vast black night—the next morning when the sun grapples its pink fingers over the horizon, like a man trying to pull himself up a cliff face, ready for the edgeless light of a new day.

A few hours later, disoriented and frozen half to death, Motl woke. It was a new life.

5

.

"I never can recall that day without doubling over," my grandfather Motl would tell me. "Though I knew my seed lay frozen. Blue balls biding their time."

And his quest these two decades later?

The mystic *tikkun olam*: repairing the world, healing what was broken. Motl had decided he would travel to this distant Swiss snowcap to retrieve his two prodigal dumplings and return them to civilized company where first sperm extraction and then impregnation could occur. And thus, history and his heart could defrost and the future begin.

But before this seminal event occurs, we need to talk about books and death. First, as always, books. Why? Because books tell us how to die.

Unless we die in the middle of one.

Then they tell us that we should have read faster.

VILNIUS, APRIL 1941

Sometimes the mortal soul requires nourishment and so, some three months before he ran from the barber's, our brisket boy had ambled to Yankel the Butcher's for a piece of meat. He'd wandered along *Žydų gatve*—Jewish Street—half-shut eyes filtering out the slant rays of warm spring sun. Were those cacti or his spiky-voiced neighbours kvetching? A stagecoach heavy with strongboxes or a piled-high potato cart? Soon, he'd be riding the dusty range beside purple sage. Now, the smoke of brushfire curled his nose. Something in the tiny garden surrounding his home was burning.

His mother, Gitl the Destroyer, illuminated by orange flame, skin glistening, eyes flickering in grim delight, stood over a pyre of books, crackling, their black type and yellowed pages released as smoke into the shtetl air.

"Why all the time you read of these rude *grubers* running with cows, punctuating themselves with guns, picking fights with Apaches?" she said. "Your head's soft enough already. Read the Torah or the newspaper like a regular boy."

Gitl, Destroyer of worlds. She had gathered his collection of westerns, poured lamp oil over the pile, then snapped a match into flame and ignited the musty butte of them.

What to do with these lariats of fire, this bonfire of fantasies? Motl, bucketless, panicked, unbuttoned his fly, ready to extinguish the flames, relying on such inner resources as he had.

As he did, the meat he had bought at the butcher's fell from his coat pocket into the fire. "So finally these books have some practical use," his mother said. "A real cowboy cookout."

Motl plucked a charred book from the fire, its crooked black pages like broken slate.

Part of a horse, part of a cowboy and part of an "Indianer" remaining on the dark, almost-night cover: a half-burned copy of Karl May's *Mutterliebe*. Motl, gripping it by an intact corner, held the title up to his mother, needing to say nothing more than this.

He tucked the smoking book under his arm, did up the buttons of his pants, then went inside.

What to do?

You can burn a book or a library, but to really destroy a story you have to destroy the language and its people. Or write another one.

He went to his bed and slept, the smell of burning books entwined in his skin and clothes.

Rustlers, having discovered some whiskey-shickered cowboys camped in a night poked through by stars, took a torch and set fire to the cowboys' bedding, their blankets, the saddles they used as pillows while the men slept. Only Motl was awake, having gone down into the coulee to cool himself in the crick water. What to do now that everything was on fire? He examined the face, the clothes, the shape of the rustlers and their horses, the way they moved through the short grasses, the things they said. How they tied the wranglers with their rope. How they shot one in the back. How they didn't notice him watching from behind a tree on the coulee bank. How they rode off whooping and hee-hawing, stolen horses tied to their own. How their voices echoed off the distant range. The sound of the other men wrapping their dead partner in his singed blanket, clearing their throats instead of speaking or weeping.

Gitl shook him awake.

"Eat now. You're hungry. Wishing for things to be different makes you hungry." She held out a plate of the fallen meat, chunked on kasha, flakes of paper stuck to its dark, wrinkled surfaces. Motl picked at it, pulled a flake of story off and read it. "'I'm lone-some,' . . . hollered . . . the Stetson . . . his Colt . . . a bitter wind over the horizon."

Motl and his mother in their little kitchen, late at night. Silent save for Motl's steady chewing and his mother's surveillance.

When he was a toddler.

A small boy.

A teen, a young adult, a man in his thirties. Now.

She'd watched him on the train as they'd been sent to Siberia. Before his father had died of tuberculosis. As they celebrated and ate and got fat. When they were thin and he ate the only food they had. The food she'd given him.

She'd watched.

"Don't worry about me," she said. "You're a growing boy. And too skinny. Besides, I lose my appetite watching you eat."

6

KAUNAS (KOVNO)

LATE JUNE 1941

We've spoken of books, now to speak of death. It won't be a challenge. There's plenty to choose from. A week before his trip to the barber's, Motl attended a funeral a few hours away, in Kaunas.

Though not a professional mourner, Motl was sometimes paid to pray. He'd add in weeping at no extra charge. Someone said that eighty percent of life is just showing up. So the other twenty percent must include some kind of existential monkey business where you also show up alive. In the case of a Jewish funeral, unless it's yours, showing up is even more important, because ten Jews are required so that there can be prayers.

Motl, having proven himself good at remaining alive, derived some of his income by being so. He was often paid to be the tenth member of a *minyan*.

"This being alive," he'd say, "it's a living."

Of course, each one of the ten was required to be a man. But in such situations, there was no inventory of the contents of one's

trousers, and Motl with his patchy beard and perennial skirtless-
ness appeared as much their idea of a man as any. Who knows
what someone isn't hiding beneath his clothes?

Besides, it was no one's business except the circumcising mohel's.
And it was too late for that. Also, he wasn't not a man. He didn't
know what he felt. A steer, a gelding or something else than that.

And since the German invasion on June 22, no amount of money
could buy enough mourners for all the dead. Besides, the mourners
were the dead. And so here Motl was, mourning without pay.

It was Mendel the Carpenter's funeral. He was a cousin once
removed. And now he was removed forever.

Because all of life—everything—is, ultimately, like a book—
even if that book is only a commentary on the book beside it—of
course, it was raining. Bitterly. Ironically. Because it didn't
know what else to do. Motl pushed between *minyan* men five and
six as they stood around the grave, the collars of their dark coats
pulled up around their bent necks. The rabbi leading the chanting of the mourners' Kaddish.

Yisgadal v'yiskadash sh'mei rabbaw.

Glorified and sanctified be God's great name, the mourners
chanted.

They didn't say how Mendel, the dead man, had died. So
many had been murdered these last few days. By German soldiers. By Lithuanians taking advantage of the opportunity and
encouraged by Nazis. It was Lithuanians who had found Mendel
walking a road around the north of Kaunas trying to escape a
pogrom in Slobodke, the Jewish suburb.

They had brought Mendel back into the centre of Kaunas, to
Lietūkis Garage at 43 Vytautas Avenue. Mendel dragged to the
front of the gas station with other Jews.

Horse dreck everywhere, the garage also used as a stable.

Twenty Jews surrounded by armed Lithuanians. A crowd watching. Children on the shoulders of their fathers. Women standing on boxes.

"*Norma*"—move it—the Lithuanians shouted, and hit the Jews with iron bars until they fell to the ground and were made to crawl in the abundant shit of cart horses scattered everywhere. The Jews were forced to gather the shit with their bare hands. The Lithuanians continuing to beat them until finally the Jews stopped moving. The dead and the dying. A hose snaking on the ground, turned on to wash blood into the gutter.

Then a young man leaning on a club thick as a human arm, tall as his chest, raised his hand. Thirty more Jews in a line behind him.

A casual wave from him and one of the Jews steps forward. The man raises his club and beats him. With each blow, the assembled crowd cheers. Assistants pile the fallen onto the heap of already dead Jews, and the young man motions for another to come forward.

Mendel steps forward.

As he had to.

He was surrounded by Lithuanians with wooden clubs, rifles, handguns, iron bars. Every tiny compliance was another second more. A chance the future might change. A statement of belief that this couldn't be true. That the world would wake from this dream. That he would.

When all fifty Jews were in a pile, the man put down his club, went over to a small black case and took out an accordion. He put the straps around his shoulders, unfastened the clip holding the bellows together, climbed on top of the heap of Jews. He placed his right hand on the keyboard, his left on the little buttons that were the bass notes, and began playing. This man, later called the Death Dealer of Kovno, blond, about twenty-five. He played the Lithuanian national anthem. The spectators sang.

Motl, standing at Mendel's open grave, chanted with the other mourners.

B'allmaw dee v'raw chir'usei.

In the world which He created as He willed.

Mendel's widow, Chiena, and Rochel, his teenaged daughter, standing on the other side of the newly cut earth, the naked casket awaiting its spadefuls of soil.

Chanting and trying to understand why. How can this be what He wanted?

And He had to include an accordion?

A neighbour had run across Kaunas to find his wife and daughter, who had been staying with cousins in another part of the city while Rochel went to school. Everyone running around him, thugs pushing victims into the River Vilija, shooting those who didn't drown. Houses burning filled with screams, Lithuanian "freedom fighters" blocking firefighters trying to help.

When Rochel reached the garage, the cement was slick with blood, and water was still pouring from the hose, though no one remained alive. She approached the dead with horror and panic and fear. Tried not to look or notice anything, tried not to recognize or imagine. Then she saw her father's thick red carpenter's hand stretched out over his broken face. Of the rest of him, only the shoulders of his dark suit, soiled and torn, were visible from beneath the dead. The neighbour helped her drag his body into an alley and wrap it in a sheet, then haul him, like a heavy carpet, into a borrowed car. They drove away, their set faces holding in their grief and horror, praying not to be discovered. Arriving at the cousins' house under a moon obscured by clouds, Rochel opened the door quietly, found her mother waiting, worried her husband had not yet returned.

7

VILNIUS

JULY 1941

Now we talk of leaving. In those days, the world having given up most of its spin, heavy as it was with dust and ash and the blood-soaked boots of war, Motl told me he would often dream he was a person of size, horse-wide, chesterfield-rumped, full as the pink bosoms of a cow, grown great from happy satisfaction and an intimate familiarity with cherry pie. Why? Because it would mean his story would have been one of ease and bounty. Of bounce.

"But to tell you the truth," he'd say, "I was impotent and scrawny as a crack in the dried-up earth or a witch's crooked finger accusing the world.

"Still," he'd add, "I commend my heart for continuing to pump through those times. And while I could have rode out to where the sky was but a clot of buzzards in the pitiless heat, hankering in a circle for my weak nerves to expire so's they could pick the historical flesh from my unfortunate spine, while I could have rode there and laid upon the inflexible earth of Lithuania, waiting for my story to be done and the satisfactions allotted my wispy soul to be spent and evaporated, I did not so lay for my heart continued its drumming, and it I did not wish to disappoint."

And so instead, after he'd scuttled from the barber's, he scurried to the clapboard house he shared with his mother in Vilnius.

His mother. Gitl the Destroyer. The source of an entire genre of jokes.

If she gave you two sweaters, a red and a blue, and you came to the table wearing the red, she'd say, "It's so cold in here you need a sweater, big man?"

She was that thing beyond old, not a witch exactly, but a bristly gnarl of sheer stubbornness. Time and the world could not be allowed to think they could get the better of her. Not without her putting up two twisted dukes and fighting back.

"Also," Motl said, "I needed her. It wasn't as if I was going correct myself. At least, not properly."

When he arrived home, the door was bolted from the inside.

"Mama," he said, knocking at the door. "Mama."

"Who's that?"

"It's me. Who else calls you Mama?"

"Maybe it's a trick. How do I know it's you?"

"Ask my opinion. When I'm wrong, you'll know it's me."

She opened the door and looked up into the face of her only son.

"This you call a shave?"

"Mama, there's no time. The Nazis are heading this way. We must leave."

"Looking like *that*?"

———

Gitl could not conceive of leaving before Motl had a proper supper. And a decent night's sleep. And a proper breakfast. Would there be food in the outside world? Would there be sleep?

And so they left as the dawn moon was setting in the cloudless sky, shadows crawling along the curving Vilnius streets, their hoss's hooves clopping on the cobbles as they travelled under archways, over the bridge and across the Neris. Motl and his mother, setting out for the lonesome hinterland of Lithuania and the uncertain southeastern border.

The streets silent but for the wind and, through the windows, old men on their backs in bed, open-mouthed and sighing, not knowing enough to hold their breath while history came to town. Motl and his mama had hidden their possessions under the straw of their little cart, hitched up their hoss and left in the pale dark. So long, little home where discouraging words were not exactly seldom heard.

"Gee up," Motl had said, and shaken the reins. And so his quest had begun.

What they carried.

Two silver Shabbos candlesticks, once Motl's great-grandmother's, in their shroud of wax.

His late father's prayer book, worn soft as a glove from the touch of his hand. Did Motl believe the words it said? Had his father?

"Depends how much I need to," his father had said.

What else? A knife. Matches. A bottle of schnapps. When finished, they could use it for water. In the meantime, it was a valuable salve for contusions, both inside and out.

In Motl's pocket, some lint, a bent screw and a single clandestine book, the western *Di Virginianer* by Owen Wister, recently sent from America by Frank, his Cleveland cousin.

His mother had wrapped herself in shawls and, beneath them, her own mother's good white tablecloth.

There were some apples and some oats to feed the pony. His father had called their first hoss Rasputin, because it seemed inextinguishable. Turned out it was as extinguishable as he was. Motl acquired another after they both were gone. Four days after trying out several bronco names—Silver, Trigger, Coco, Loco, Buttermilk, Blackjack and Champion—he named it Theodor Herzl, because, old paint that it was, it was rarely willing to go in the direction asked, but instead insisted on a path of its own choosing, which Motl imagined might be toward Zion.

They carried several loaves his mother had baked because, as she said, if they catch us and we have to die, then at least we won't die hungry.

They brought no money. Why provide for the kerchief-faced Lithuanian varmints who would hold up the familial caravan only to shake shiny bits from its sacks? Don't fill your pockets with salmon when you're walking between bears. Besides, the saddle-skinned heroes of his westerns never carried money.

"And to be honest," Motl said, "I had no money. Both my heart and wallet were empty."

He'd decided they'd travel toward the border with Poland, then on to Minsk, in Byelorussia. The Germans had not yet invaded. And the Russians? When it's a choice between a devil and a scoundrel, you choose the one who is not killing you yet.

Then, when he'd found a safe place to stow his mother, he'd head for Zimmerwald, to the glacier, to new life.

———

They turned south, clopping over the cobbles behind their old pony, wending their way between others who were also in the streets, leaving, or wandering, unsure what to do. Behind them, rising above the city, the Hill of Three Crosses. A giant could sashay across Vilnius, using churches for stepping stones, not ever touching ground, but that selfsame brute could also spit his chaw most any direction and slather a rabbi *brocha*-ing in prayer at any of a hundred synagogues of this Jerusalem of the North.

At least, for now.

They'd just passed the baroque frou-frou of the Church of St. Casimir when his mother held up her parsnip-root hand. "Stop," she said. "Take me back."

"But the Germans," he began.

"Soup," she said. "I left the soup on the stove."

There were few as bullheaded as Gitl when she got a notion.

"Motl," she said. "Now."

Between their lives and the soup, she favoured the soup.

"Haw," Motl said to Herzl, and steered him into an alley to turn around. The great Zionist nag stopped and stuck his big face in the leavings around Abe the Grocer's door.

Then, a gunshot.

Herzl bolted. All they could do was hang on as the cart buffeted against the alley walls. Motl wrenched the reins, but the hackles in Herzl's horse brain were urging his bones to outrun his skin.

Run, the hackles said. A horse is safest at full speed.

And so Herzl galloped along the alley until they burst out onto the wide road.

And sent a Nazi soldier flying, *Einsatzgruppen* over *Schutzstaffel*.

Then Herzl stopped.

Gitl looked over the side of the cart at the soldier. He lay on his back, gazing senselessly at the sky, apparently not quite certain what had occurred. Her dried-apple face, furrowed like the bellows of a mummified accordion, loomed into view.

"Bread?" she said, holding out a loaf.

Knee by knee, the soldier got up, brushing and rearranging, patting himself down, taking inventory, assuring himself of the tangible presence of his own body. *Ja*. It was there and missing no pieces. He found his hat a few feet away, his rifle beneath him. Blood dripped from a nostril. He wiped it with his buttonless sleeve. He returned his hat to his head, righting his rifle, which he held like a baby. Then he remembered the story and his face hardened. Blue eyes like two rifle sights.

He was a young man, fresh-faced and innocent. Apparently, having been stripped of his lederhosen, mountainside and goat, he'd fallen into the crucible of war and couldn't tell his alp from his valley.

"Heil Hitler," he snapped and, with predictable choreography, thrust a hand upward in salute and clicked his boots together. He was preparing to Anschluss the living Österreich out of both of them.

"Bread," Gitl said again, and pushed a loaf toward him.

He stepped back, avoiding it like a knife.

"Mama," Motl said, pulling on her arm. "Officer," he said. "Mama and me are regretfully sorry for this mishap. Our hoss, you see . . ."

But then in one deft motion his mother tore the bread in two. The German raised his eyebrows and smiled. He was a boy again. Greedy. The inside of the loaf was stuffed with a thick stack of paper money.

"Bread," Gitl said, and handed both halves to the soldier.

"Go," the soldier said, "*schnell!*" and waved them away.

Motl flicked the reins. "Gee," and they continued down the wide road, joining with others hurrying to the famous Gate of Dawn.

His mother's bread was like so many other delicacies: it's the ingredients that count.

Once, there were ten gates surrounding the city, but now only the Gate of Dawn remained, a sacred portal to the south. Once, Our Lady of the Gate of Dawn, an infinitely younger and infinitely more Catholic mother than Gitl, came to the rescue of her people. Swedes had captured the city and the Virgin Mary, golden-beamed radiator of divine mercy, arranged for a few metaphysical God-strings to be pulled to crush the invaders. Nothing like dropping the heavy iron Gate of Dawn to spatchcock some Swedish soldiers on its sharp ends to make a point.

"Mama," Motl said as they trotted in the direction of the Gate. "What about the soup?"

"Go faster," she said. "Soon that Kraut will discover it's only a few rubles on either side of a stack of old scrap paper."

8

VILNIUS TO KAUNAS

Motl and Gitl, outside the Gate of Dawn, ten minutes down a side road leading away from Vilnius. Now Gitl insisted they turn round, head for Kaunas.

This was meant to be Motl's quest and he expected to be able to call the route, but already with Gitl it was the cart before the hoss, telling the cowboy where to go.

"Ma," Motl protested. "The only safe road is out."

"Anya, my sister. Her daughter, son-in-law. Her granddaughter, Hannah."

"But Kaunas?" Motl said. "No reckoning the blood in that Nazi-poxed hole."

"You want we rescue her from somewhere else?" Gitl said, black eyes squinted to obsidian. An invitation to make the right choice but also a challenge. To re-evaluate his devotion to family. To his mother.

He pulled on the reins and turned Herzl around. His bollocks could wait.

"Kaunas," Gitl said definitively, and for once even Herzl didn't argue.

They wouldn't go back through the Gate but would travel the perimeter of the city.

"Let's keep quiet and mind our own business," Gitl said.

"What business do I have to mind?"

"I didn't want to be the one to say."

Everywhere was movement, flowing away from Kaunas. Families in carts, in cars, trucks, on horseback or walking. Parents anxious and already exhausted, holding their small children's hands, moving briskly, even smaller children in arms—mother, father, sister, aunt. Bundles, bindles and suitcases, trundle carts. Gitl thought it was possible they could avoid attracting attention, two travellers in a chaos of travel. Did they look Jewish? They kept as far away as they could from Nazi soldiers or troops of White Armbanders—nationalist Lithuanians. When the Germans had arrived, the streets of Kaunas had been lined with Lithuanians throwing flowers and gifts and waving flags. What were they celebrating?

That Germans weren't Russians. The Russians were Bolsheviks and the Bolsheviks were Jews. With the Germans here, Lithuania could return to independence. To greatness. With a bit of murderous spit and Fascist elbow grease, it would become *Judenrein*, not just clean, but Jew clean. "The Jew shall die though every dog in Europe bark in his favour," they said, not that many dogs were currently barking.

After half an hour of troubled silence, Gitl said, "So, Mr. Cowboy. You have a gun?"

In truth, the idea of a gun filled Motl with fear. His groin ached hot and cold at the thought, and his head ached more. They could hear gunshots echoing from inside the city, as if the sound came from the lights, the windows, the cars and storefronts. From invisible hands and from nowhere.

Where would he get a gun?

He could think of only three options.

Wrestle a Lithuanian. Kill a German. Pray.

And how to do any of those things with either skill or confidence? He knew how the West was won, one's hinterland plonked on a horse, what it looked like from under a Stetson, or, at least, what it looked like in words. But now this rawhide maverick might be called to do more than squint and marvel at the bigness of sky, the nearness of stars.

"Why would I have a gun?"

"What are you, a schlepper? A real cowboy has a gun when they shoot."

Travelling toward Kaunas was like descending level by level to the centre of Dante's Inferno, finally to arrive at the lake of ice, the fate of the most treacherous.

Halfway there, just outside the town of Kaišiadorys, they came across a woman in a black dress, red flowers on the scarf she dragged behind her. She was muttering, wandering unsteadily on the side of the road. Motl stopped Herzl, and Gitl helped the woman into the cart.

"They threw them into the river. Bayla tried to swim, so they shot her," she said.

Gitl gathered up the scarf and wrapped it twice around the woman.

"I was so scared," the woman said. She had been upstairs and so had hidden in the attic when the partisans came and pulled her sister and frail parents out the door. She wanted to save them, to do something, but could only watch from the window, helpless. She'd been walking the road from Kaunas since dawn the previous day. She'd heard horror stories from others.

The Nazis and their special platoons of Lithuanian volunteers had gathered many men and women and forced them to walk into the forest. They'd made them dig their own graves. Then they shot them. Entire villages. Thousands of them.

"My Anya? Her granddaughter, Hannah?" Gitl asked. "They live together in Slobodke. In Kaunas."

"They were having lunch," the woman said. "I was so scared. They were having lunch."

The woman could only repeat the elements of her story and was not able to answer Gitl.

"Eat," Gitl said, and broke pieces of bread from a loaf and brought them to the woman's mouth. But the woman wouldn't eat.

"All right," Gitl said, handing the pieces to her son. "So, Motl, you eat. You could hide behind a chicken's shmeckelbone and still there'd be room for a homeland." He ate.

Motl flicked the reins and they began moving again. The woman made to step out of the moving cart. Gitl tried to hold her back, but the woman resisted.

"So, we let her go," she said. "Maybe wandering is as safe as going somewhere."

Motl pulled Herzl to a stop, and the woman climbed down.

9

The sun slung low in the sky, a weary red.

"This is Kaunas. Slobodke district," Gitl said.

"Yes, Ma, I know."

The place looked deserted. Theodor Herzl's hooves plodded over the worn-flat cobbles of Sajungos Plaza and then down Linkuvos Street. Shutters and doors were wrested closed on the fronts of the wooden houses, except where they were hanging or smashed in.

"My sister's house. It's down this street," Gitl said with a great heaviness.

"Yes, Ma, I know."

They trundled between the steep-roofed and homely bungalows, toward Jurbarko Street and the yeshiva on the corner, and stopped in front of Anya's house. The shutters on the three windows were closed. Four steps led up to the half doors, both heaved open. Blood was on the steps and threshold.

Gitl jumped from the wagon, and Motl followed. The door was unlocked. It was dark inside, chairs tossed on their sides, the table overturned, silver Shabbos candlesticks in twin pools of spilled wax as if light had hemorrhaged and congealed. Motl lifted the candlesticks and put them in his pockets. The Lithuanians would be back. They had left these valuable things as they struggled to remove Anya, her husband, Moishe, their grandchild Hannah.

The room darkened further as Gitl went to stand in the front doorway.

"*Gey gezunterheyt.*" Go in good health. See if I care.

"Who are you talking to, Ma?" Motl asked. Was it God, her sister, those who broke into the house?

Motl slipped around her and out into the street. At the neighbours', he hammered on the front door, calling, "What happened? Where are they?" Then, "It's Motl, nephew of Anya and Moishe."

"They don't take them to the beach for ice cream," Gitl said.

Motl hammered again. No response.

"Bluma. Lev," Motl pleaded.

Finally, as if from deep underwater, a male voice. "They came this morning. We hid in the basement. Hannah was at camp." Despite Motl's further entreaties, Lev said no more.

"If Hannah is still at Pioneer Camp," Motl said to his mother, "maybe she's safe."

Gitl climbed into the cart. "What we can do, we do," she said. "We will find her. And my sister."

Gitl directed them a few streets over. Gee. Haw. Gee.

Whoa. They stopped on a cobbled lane bounded by small houses.

A city slicker once asked a grizzled old rancher, "Surely it's hard to live so far from civilization?"

And the old rancher replied, "Surely it's hard to live so near."

Motl longed for the boundless prairie, its inexhaustible horizon, longed to unhitch Herzl and ride away. But for now, he had to stay put.

"This is the house of the Chief Rabbi of Slobodke, Zalman Ossovsky," Gitl said. "He came to your bar mitzvah."

"I remember."

"He's a wise man. He will say where are Anya and Moishe. And what to do. And how to get Hannah."

Gitl unfurled her legs and clambered down. An ornate iron fence, waist-high, enclosed the small garden. "It's a display. His brother the blacksmith makes them," she said. "Schmancy things for goyish graves."

"Christians visit the rabbi to order goyish fences? Or Jews come looking for a Christian funeral?"

"If they were Christian enough to be buried a goy, then maybe they'd be Christian enough not to be killed."

The house was hushed and dark. Gitl knocked delicately. "Maybe he sleeps. I don't want to wake him too quickly."

No answer. Gitl pushed on the door, which opened, and stepped forward slowly, as if entering a tomb.

A shadowy shape, like a small bundle of rags on the thread-less carpet.

Gitl fell to her knees, placed a gentle hand on the shape. A dim and indistinct pool had formed around it. It wasn't wax.

"Motl . . ." she said. But Motl rushed by her, as if it were not too late. He ran into the rabbi's study. The fireless grate. Like an autumn forest—a Hebrew forest of yellowed leaves—books and scrolls and papers were scattered across tables and chairs and in stacks on the carpets. An empty wine bottle, a broken cup, the worn velvet bag containing his prayer shawl.

In the dim light, he could see Rabbi Zalman Ossovsky leaning over an open volume of the Talmud. He'd been studying. It appeared as if the grizzled rebbe had dozed off for a few minutes, dreaming maybe of floating over a Torah-coloured field, joining a gesticulating and airborne flock of other greybeards, mumbling and admonishing and debating, the small villages of their communities before them, the great mountain of the Promised Land behind them, their children in the field below. But the rabbi was not sleeping. His headless body rested against the open volume of Talmud, his hands flat on the table as if he was to give a sermon, as if he were pleading, but blood spilled across the page, obscuring the words.

Gitl in the hallway not weeping, her hand still resting tenderly on the head lying on the carpet.

Motl motionless, trying to find a way to move, gritting his teeth against the grim memory of the adage, "One studies not only with the head, but also with the heart."

Dusk-lit Kaunas was shadows and ghosts. The streets were all empty. Maybe the persecutors had stopped for supper. Nothing like a pogrom to work up an appetite. Motl and Gitl returned to Anya's house. To be enclosed by walls. To have a world with limits.

"Maybe the half-hitched varmints won't come back," Motl said, hoping they had forgotten the candlesticks. Or had stolen their fill from others.

He pushed the table against the door. Might buy them time to make leg bail out the back door if the Lithuanians returned. Soon, there was shouting in the streets, screams, gunshots. All night Gitl and Motl hid, scrabbling in the sage field of dust under the beds, attempting sleep.

Gitl lamenting or praying. That sound which is both.

"Ma," Motl said during one short lull. "Get some rest."

"Who can sleep?" she said. "You know what the old crones say: if things don't get better—they'll get worse."

Morning. A lox-orange sky. Outside, the street like a juddering film. German soldiers standing beside cars, old men in long coats, a man chased by another who was beating him with a long stick, the first clutching his head, shirt open, tails fluttering behind him, his prayer shawl dragging against the cobbles, his mouth twisted. Torah scrolls were strewn about like hallway carpets. The dead or wounded on top or beneath, nightmare bedsheets of words, the impotent babbling of scholars.

Smoke from the yeshiva door.

The neighbours' home—Lev's home—the door smashed.

Lev stood on the corner, bewildered, disconnected, as if he was standing somewhere else. Or nowhere.

"What has this to do with us?" he said. "Why always us?"

"Lev," Gitl said. "Lev." She spoke quietly, as if to a child woken in the night.

"They leave us nothing but our eyes to weep," he said. "Bluma," he said, and only now looked at the street, at a shape under parchment.

"Come with us," Gitl said, steering him to where Theodor Herzl was tied in the yard behind the house, eating whatever he could.

Motl hauled Lev up onto the wagon bench. He harnessed Theodor Herzl and took up the reins. It was eighty miles to the Pioneer Camp in Druskininkai, where young Lithuanians and Jews could spend the summer outdoors.

An hour later, Lev had fallen asleep in the back of the cart.

"So, Mr. Cowboy?" Gitl said, pulling out a loaf of bread from beneath her shawl.

"Ma," Motl said, flicking the reins, manoeuvring Theodor Herzl onto a side road. "I'm not hungry, but Lev, maybe, when he wakes up?"

"Motl," Gitl said again, breaking open the loaf. Inside was a revolver.

"You think I'm only made of money?" she said.

10

Motl's reverie as they rode. At the crack of merciless noon, Motl knocked back his Manischewitz and swung through the saloon doors. Main Street silent as a ghostless tomb, as if you could hear the sound of what was not being said, the sound of held breath, voices muted in horror and fear. Motl strode forward, his chest pushed out like a rooster's, his two hands resting on the pearl-handled six-shooters given to him in gratitude after he perforated a scoundrel.

More than once.

Until he was scoundrel no more.

Down one end of the street, Big-nosed Fritz, the Nazi gun-slinger, stood motionless, eagle-eyed in the pitiless dust, a storm cloud dressed in black leather.

"Quick, Motl," someone said. "Draw your six-shooters."

"Won't help," Motl said. "No bullets."

"So why wear guns?"

"Style. Didn't think I'd need 'em."

Fritz's ice-blue eyes regarded Motl without emotion. Did he wonder if the guns were truly unloaded? People said Motl only shot blanks, but would his two guns shoot blanks also? No one knew. Not even the flouncy belles dressed in scarlet at the curvy top of the saloon stairs.

"Fritz," Motl said. "Let me explain my philosophy. In my world, all German soldiers are called Fritz whether you have three grandparents who are German, or four who aren't German but speak German and maybe look German. Or maybe because you just look like a Fritz. But let me explain something else."

He repositioned his hands and cocked his head.

"You see, Fritz, it's like this. From where I'm standing, there's only one of you and you're all alone. I reckon if you know what's good for your purebred potato dumpling hasenpfeffer self, you'd better get outta here."

Fritz's hands, pallid as doves, twitched their murderous wings in the direction of his holsters.

Without warning, the silence bled noise, a single gunshot rippling off the face of buildings, the echoes quickly disappearing as if this noon was nothing but dust and expectation.

Fritz stood still as the street itself stood still. Then one of them moved, falling onto the other with a dry and remorseless thud. Gitl's rifle slid back out of view into the alley between what was Zalman's Drygoods and Itzik Fridman's tailor shop.

Motl raised his eyebrow and held it for a minute. As if to say, "I am a philosopher and all of us here have just learned something about the nature of being, justice and style. Especially about style."

Then he returned his eyebrow to its default position, dark scrub across his sweaty brow, turned around and strode back into the saloon.

"Barkeep. Manischewitz. A double."

———

Noon.

"The hoss needs watering," Motl said. "Yonder, there's a home-stead." With a "Gee," they turned down a trail leading to a decrepit cabin squatting on the dirt of a scrubby farm.

"Is it safe?" Lev asked. "Are they Jews?"

"We're safe." Gitl smiled. She had her hand on the gun buried Freud-deep beneath her several skirts.

But something was awry, something about what they heard. Sure, there were birds, the burbling of the running river, the requisite wind in the trees, but it was as if the sounds had been replaced with replicas. Perhaps the entire world had been replaced with a replica. Something certainly was shot to pieces, the clockwork of the world deranged in its maniacal grinding.

Motl got down and led the horse to a dented water trough, and unlike the old saw, it drank.

"Howdy," he called. "Hello." Like too many doors they'd recently encountered, the farmhouse door was open. He squinted around the jamb into the murk of the cottage.

"Hello?"

No one.

But the sound. A frail, birdlike whining. An injured animal? It was as if it came from the cottage itself. Motl pushed the door fully open and stepped inside. In the door light, he saw the small kitchen—turquoise metal stove, rickety table, broken chairs, blackened fireplace. A few cups, some mismatched plates, a jug turned on its side. There was a dark-red couch against a far wall, the stuffing like battered clouds billowed from slashes in the fabric. The wailing became louder. Feeble and desperate. Was an animal nesting in the cushions? A pup in distress?

As Motl approached, he saw the couch like a body, exposed insides covered in blood. There was an iron poker beside the hearth and he used it to carefully push the cushions aside.

The body of a man squeezed inside the frame, below the cut-open batting, wounds in his body corresponding to slashes in the pillows. A bayonet had honeycombed the man.

Wailing. A child, just a baby, lay pressed against the side of the dead man, unharmed. She was very pale, curly blond, her eyelashes translucent.

"Ma!" Motl called, then prised the girl away from her father, wrapping his arms around her. "Ah, little buttermilk," he said. "Come with me and we'll set everything right."

"Once you were this pretty and small," Gitl said to Motl, coming up behind, taking the girl from him and gazing into her tiny, tear-wet face. "But, I ask myself now, were the labour pains worth it?"

Motl found a spade behind the house and thrust it into the ground with a snick. "Might dig right through to Peking itself," he said to himself. "Walk straight through the earth, out the other side." An hour later he didn't have a passage to China, just a shallow chute to the beyond.

Lev came from the cottage with a bottle of vodka. "In the couch," he said. "Under the man."

"In the West they call that 'coffin varnish,'" Motl said. "Though they say a corkscrew never pulled no one out of a hole, it sure helps with putting a body in."

They sat together, leaning against the back wall of the house, sharing the bottle, listening to Gitl around the front, speaking to the little girl: "My Motl, when he drinks, he becomes another person, and the other person wants a drink too."

Finally, Motl and Lev staggered back inside and stood unsteadily to consider the sheet draped over the couch.

"You take the legs," Motl told Lev. "I'll get the other end."

Equal parts lifting and dragging, they carried the dead man outside, Lev weeping as they went. "Bluma," he said.

They covered the man in earth, taking turns to lift and drop spadefuls of dark soil.

Yisgadal v'yiskadash sh'mei rabbaw.

And Motl thought of lines from an old song.

Where a body dies,
someone lies down to sleep,
Where a body dies,
someone wakes.

They returned to the shack. The little girl was now asleep in a half-closed dresser drawer, and Gitl had prepared some food for them, a concoction made of weevily flour and near-brackish water. No point using up the fresh bread.

"Sling your teeth over this," Motl said to Lev. "It's like chewing saddle."

"Next time, learn to boil for yourself some air," Gitl said. "Though you seem good at that already."

After they ate, they sat around the table. There was nowhere else to go unless they gathered on the empty coffin of the couch and its sundered pillows.

"So, what about the baby?" Lev asked. It was clear she shouldn't share their treacherous path toward Hannah. It was already too dangerous. Besides, she would only make it more difficult for them. "We need to find somewhere to put her."

"Where? The moon, a cabbage patch, Christians?" Gitl asked.

"Somewhere she'll be safe. There must be someone who'll take her."

Through the farmhouse windows, the sun shrugged over the red edge of day, twilight merging into night. The fields stretched out black and gloomy. One dim star gloamed uncertainly in the southwest sky. The silence was broken only by a faint pattering of leaves in the night wind. Gitl lit a candle that cast flickering wraiths of shadow about the small cabin.

A small, dishevelled bed was pushed against the side wall. "I don't share anyone's sheets," Gitl told Lev. "You sleep there."

She gathered the wounded pillows and threw them on the couch. From a small dresser she gathered skirts and dresses and smoothed them over the pillows. "I must sleep fast. The baby will wake soon—such a big fresser—she'll be hungry." Then she lay down and covered herself with an overcoat. One quick *oy* of a sigh and she was out.

There was a loft below the gabled roof, actually more of a shelf a few planks wide. Motl stood on the dresser and hoisted himself up. He attempted sleep on piled burlap sacks and rags, but he twisted and tossed. You can be lonesome even when your ears are filled with other people's snores, lonely even when you smell their feet. And so Motl's mind drifted in the dark.

A vast heave of purple uplands, castle-crowned cliffs. A town on the edge of the sand-rimmed wilderness, and therein a village girl with snow-white skin. She plucks goose feathers, plunges ivory hands deep into brine-filled barrels, the hands themselves quicksilver fish. Yet still she is redolent of almonds, braided loaf, raisins. A candle-bright smile, teeth new white as a Shabbos tablecloth. And now the long reach of late afternoon shadow. As the sun sinks, she clangs the dinner bell, hailing ranger-riders for grits and sausage, her father shuffling in from the smithy or yeshiva study house.

Ah, floral-skirted rider of stallions, she who would ride with him through violet sage in the evening's purple shadows, beribboned hair honey-gold as the long light. His Dulcinea, his prairie girl.

And Motl, this song in his head always: Oh, in the drowsy farmyard, the open corrals, the green alfalfa fields, I already love you, would seek for you the places where grief, fear and rage do not rampike my spine with fear, the untried canyons of the fissured heart. We'd ranch in a homestead in the high range, cliff-rimmed and sealed by boulders where through a rock face crack only the cool stream escapes and above birds fly free. We'd sleep within the grove of cottonwoods, concealed from the world and its miseries. I've seen you on the cobbles of Yatkever Street, beneath the arch of Gitke-Toybe Lane. I've dreamed of you bathing in the mikvah or playing queen onstage. Your curls and blushes, your radiant eyes and coral lips. Your rindles, your coulee. I would quest mountains, seek what is bereft, my hope cryogenic and awaiting the future. Together we elide time, we leap past and present, two angels floating above history, our alabaster feathers raised by thermals in a troposphere beyond pain.

Somewhere together in this ardent, angel-feathered sky, Motl passed into sleep and dreamed of nothing until dawn.

II

Half-light glimmered through the cabin, and he was woken by the sound of the little girl wailing. The couch empty, the door open, chairs knocked down. Motl climbed gingerly from his roost, looking carefully around, then slipped his head through the door and surveyed the yard. He stepped outside and made a circuit of the little house. Theodor Herzl was gone to some unknown Zion, as was, likely before him, their cart.

"Ma," he hissed. "Ma!" No response. "Lev?"

He saw one of Lev's boots fallen in the hay-strewn dust behind a tree. A braille of splashed blood nearby. Lev and Gitl had disappeared, the baby, still wailing, left behind.

"Ma!" he shouted, though he knew it was futile. "Mother. Mother. Mother." But he held himself back from panicking. If he began, when would it end?

"It's okay," he called to the little girl inside. "It's okay." Knowing that he had only the ritual of the words and the soothing sound of his voice to make it true. He went back into the cabin and held her and rocked. "First thing we have to do, my little blintz," he said, "is to find you some food."

———

They set off immediately. On foot. He'd find somewhere safe— another farmhouse, a town—or a traveller, someone on the road who looked kind, or at least not murderous. In war, if you're not an enemy, you're a friend. And a friend might as well be family. Someone who would take this foundling. This surviveling. "Look," he'd say. "So blond. She'll bring you safety."

As he walked, he scanned for signs of Gitl and Lev. Of the horse. As soon as he found a place for the baby, he'd find them.

He held the girl under his jacket, as if that would protect her from everything, and he began jogging. But Motl had little experience. Babies aren't books and they wriggle. The girl heaved and wailed and thrashed, then slipped from his embrace and fell onto the stony path.

"Oh my little *pitseleh*," he said as he gathered her up in his arms. "Hush, hush," he said, imitating the young mothers he'd heard in the market.

The pale peach of her head was bleeding and Motl could do nothing but cup his hand against it and keep going. They had already been on their way for help.

Motl came across an old man sitting in a small black car parked by the side of the road. The driver—a Lithuanian named Józef— saw the blood still seeping through Motl's fingers where he cradled the baby's head and found a scarf in his car and offered it. "For the *bublitchki*," he said. The bright-coloured cloth carried the powerful scent of flowers, perfume rising, a field full of lavender and weapons-grade honey—the smell of the old man's lost wife, killed in a German air raid. He was not only giving up something that had been hers, but her powerful presence, which found its way through his nose to the deep parts of remembering. But in truth, Motl thought, if the scarf was anything to go by, her smell billowed through the world like a scented monsoon, throwing everyone to the ground as her memory insisted on survival.

Józef told them that he wasn't able to help but he had a cousin who could. She was alone, her husband was gone, and maybe she could look after the baby. It'd be good for her to have something to do.

But why trust this man, or his cousin?

If he was to search for his mother, for Lev, for Anya and Hannah, if he was to continue on his quest, Motl would need someone to look after the baby. Travelling with her was beyond his abilities, and besides, she had already been hurt in his care.

And this was a baby. You'd have to be more than the usual percentage Nazi to harm a baby, and one that wasn't even Jewish.

12

He arrived in the luminous dark, a sliver of moon, a milk-like spill around clouds. He crept down the long lane, keeping to the line of ragged trees, the little girl held close under his jacket. She'd whimpered for hours, finally falling asleep.

This had better be the right farm, he thought. Else we'll be strung up like Hebrew hogs. He touched more than knocked on the farmhouse door, then stepped back into the shadows, ready to disappear entirely.

A sliver of amber door light, then a rectangle, coffin-large.

"Józef said you'd help," he whispered to the woman who'd appeared there.

She closed the door. Motl waited, unsure if weapons and puncture would be involved in their next communication.

"Here's bread," she said when she came back, passing a loaf to him. "And a sausage." She told Motl to hide in the milk house, down the end of the garden, and then closed the door. Until he had a chance to properly speak to her, he thought it too risky to give her the baby—he hadn't even opened his coat to show her—so he carried her with him into the milk house and they found straw and the remains of an old chair. He settled the baby on the chair and she lay back, her eyes half-closed. He fed her torn morsels of bread, tipped her mouthfuls of water from a bottle.

They slept, the girl on the pillowless chair, Motl bedded down uncomfortably on a meagre pile of humped straw beside her.

The chill of early morning, the sky pink as a cow's nose.

The woman's voice outside. "They're here," she said. "They're in the farmhouse." She pointed to a small window at the back of the shed. "Climb out, cross the brook, hide under the hedge. I told them I would get them milk and some breakfast."

The woman scurried back up the path. Motl gathered the still-sleeping baby, stood on the back of the chair and clambered from the window. The brook ran quickly but was shallow, just a stippling thing. Motl rolled under the hedge, only his boots and pant legs cold with creek water, and kept quiet.

Soon he heard shouts about the farm. The baby still slept and Motl turned to song. Or rather, he imagined his head its own opera house, closed the doors and sang.

don't say nothin'
ain't safe to question now
here in this world
moon jumps over cow

It was a chant, a charm, a place to go. There was death and tragedy, but he understood the tale, could always reckon some kind of sense in the western's cut-a-rust melodies.

He bunked down to wait it out. The sun bright when he woke.

The woman stood on the opposite bank. "They're gone. An hour ago. I waited till I thought it safe."

Motl looked at the baby. Still asleep? She'd hardly moved in hours, her body limp. She was getting worse. "The baby . . ." he said.

"I can see."

He leaned close to the baby's frail mouth, lips red like a windflower, hoping she still breathed.

"Bring her to me and I'll help," the woman called.

"Shh," Motl said, holding up his hand.

He heard nothing, but her small exhalations were warm on his ear. Alive. She was alive. He covered her with his jacket and stepped gingerly across the crick with this small bundle of girl. He delivered her into the woman's outstretched arms.

"*Mergaitė*," the woman said in Lithuanian—little girl—and carried her into the house.

Motl followed her, dazed by sleep and fear. Chickens ran free, their sudden propulsions, aimless pecking and idiotic bawk-bawking some kind of metaphor. Small rue flowers and yellow herb of grace grew around the edges of the yard with bees entangled in their blooms. What was his tale? Where would he go next? The Motl story: His missing mother. His missing balls. His fear and survival.

He'd make sure this nameless baby was safe and then—could he find his mother? Should he attempt to cross the Nazi frontier and make it to Zimmerwald?

By the time he'd entered the slate-floored kitchen, the woman, through some kind of maternal enchantment, had the baby propped on a chair and was spooning cabbage soup and dumplings into her expectant face. Also, since she was not able to say anything beyond babble, the woman had christened her Sofia.

"Look, she eats like a warhorse," the woman said.

"Yes," he said, nodding. Then, indicating himself, he said, "Motl." And then, "But what's your name?"

She was Lena, and her husband had been gone for weeks. He'd left to work at an aunt's farm but hadn't returned. She didn't know what had happened but worried he had stayed away because he'd helped anti-Nazi partisans in the past and was in danger. Maybe he was hiding in the forest.

"Leave this girl with me. Sofia. I will keep Sofia safe."

Lena packed him a sack of food—sausages, a bottle of milk, bread—then told him to go. What choice did he have? She told him it wouldn't be long before the return of the lethal White Armbanders. She could say the girl was her cousin's child. And not Jewish.

He thanked her and left through a field of cows grazing on stubby grass spackled with purple blooms and poppies then plunged into the primeval broccoli green of the surrounding forest. There's never a straight route between trees and so he took the knight's path, zigzagging away from the ravenous *Einsatzgruppen* and their Lithuanian pawns.

13

Strošiūnų Forest

Motl in the forest, creeping uphill between pines. His plan: hide and make a plan. Determine which direction leads away from history.

First, though, he would search for his mother.

He thought of a time before his bar mitzvah, his mother at the table, peeling something. It was dusk, there were candles.

"When a crook kisses you, count your teeth. When you're born, count your days," she said. What was she peeling?

Joy.

Her philosophy was based on excoriation—stripping away the happiness of the present, layer by layer, until there was nothing but the dwindled, scraped and unalterable past. "When I was young, it was worse. It was more difficult. But it was also better, because we knew what was true," she'd say.

The cool damp of the forest air. The sweet, acrid, spongy crunch of pine needles. The green-filtered, perpetual coniferous dusk. Somewhere Lena's husband was hiding with other anti-Nazi partisans. Maybe the easiest way to locate resisters was to pretend to be a Nazi and they'd find him. However, there could be unintended consequences. Death, for instance.

And what was the greatest act of rebellion? Living. Unless first place went to creating life. When found, his Lost Boys would be agents of change. Thunder from the mountain. While Nazis obliterated, he would create. His pearlescent homunculi would leap onto stallions and ride. And soon a skimmy or two would be born, Jewish and alive.

Motl wandered, scanning the woods for geography, figuring a butte or arroyo, cutback or wallow would be the best place to hide if on the dodge. He read the ground for footprints or story as would Winnetou or Hiawatha. There was scat of several varieties. Paw prints. Broken rock and lichens. But nothing legible as human.

Then the sound of a rifle being cocked. He'd found the human.

"Hands up."

"I have no gun," he said. "Only candlesticks."

"Lay 'em on the ground," the voice said. "And slowly." Voices and guns poking out of the wilderness were becoming commonplace for Motl.

Carefully, Motl removed the candlesticks from inside his jacket and set them on the forest floor. The trees were reflected in their smudgy silver and seemed to gather about as if the forest were a room at Shabbos.

From behind the bristle of branches, first the barrel of a rifle and then a red-headed woman appeared, swaddled in what once might have been clothing. She was followed by a squat man, himself bristly as the forest, a patchwork of lichen, paw prints, broken rock and scat.

The man stooped to collect the candlesticks and then backed away.

"I have sausages too," Motl said. And then, in slow motion, drew a gnawed one from a pocket. "And," he said, pausing for effect, "I have bread."

A tableau in the forest. Man holding out half-eaten sausage. Man opposite holding candlesticks. Woman with pointed gun. *A Litvak Mexican Deli Standoff.* The barely discernible flicker in the man's eye as he looks at the sausage. The woman's bread gaze.

"I have more," Motl said. "Also, something else you should know. I'm a Jew."

And so, armed with only the ingredients for a nosh, Motl survived his first showdown, with, it turned out, two outlaws who were Jewish and on the same side.

He followed the couple farther into the forest, where a small group—Robin Hood–like—was sheltering together. A group of odds and sods, driftwood escaped from the tide. There was a scoliotic doorway constructed of logs leading to a low-lying cabin that they'd covered over with leaves and branches. They had been living on food they pilfered from local farms, but because of recent raids by gangs of White Armbanders over the last few days, such forays had become too dangerous. And so these desperadoes were eager to chaw the vittles bagged in Motl's sack. Even their tapeworms were hungry, as the old ranchers said.

They gathered round, sitting on rocks and fallen logs, sharing Motl's small store, and recounted how they'd arrived there. Three of them, Tzeitel, Pinchas and Mordecai, explained that they had been sardine-packed in a trench but had survived.

Sardine-packed: making Jews lie down beside each other, alternating head to foot, so more could be crammed in. Then machine-gunned. Then more piled on like logs. And again. Thousands. Women and girls often made to strip naked. Terrified

Jewish boys ordered to go through the bodies and take gold teeth and rings. Sometimes pulling the teeth before the person died. Boys made to play accordion or violin for the drunken soldiers in between killing, or else their parents would be shot next. The parents shot anyway.

"Everyone was dead," Tzeitel said. "I waited until night and then I crawled away. I became a maggot, a snake, but I crawled away. I crawled away and survived."

"A woman called Lena helped me," Motl said. "I was hoping to find her husband—do you know him?"

"He's over there." Mordecai pointed toward a man, almost obscured by branches, sitting some distance away on a fallen tree. "Matis."

The man said nothing.

"He doesn't speak. He was accused of being a Jew," Mordecai explained as if that explained anything. "They scalped his beard."

Matis's face was fissured like badlands, all red knurls.

"He went to help a relative with her farm and was taken by surprise and attacked by the neighbours as he attended the chickens. After that, he cannot—or does not—speak. He does not want to be alone, but yet he does not—yet—want to be with others. And he won't return home, for his own safety and, especially, for his wife's. He won't even allow us to send a message. So he remains between we Jews and the forest," Mordecai said, then carried some bread and sausage over to Matis, holding it out tentatively to the man, who looked fearful.

"It's okay," Mordecai said. "It's a sausage, not snakes. It's from Lena. She's safe."

Matis took the food, holding it as if a bomb were in his hands and he hadn't decided whether he wanted it to explode. Finally, he ate.

They watched in silence as if observing a deer motionless between trees.

Then Tzeitel stood and began to speak into the forest. "One day, years from now," she said, "when I have lived a lifetime in America, or maybe Africa, one day when I have lived for years far from here and I have become a crone who can only dribble and hobble, totter and leak, on that day I will return with my children and my children's children. I will take them into the forest and I will shout: 'Nazis, Lithuanians. You who were my neighbours and chose to murder us. I have lived many lifetimes and yet I have returned. I have returned with my children. I have returned with my children's children. I have returned so you can see us. An old grandmother with her children and their children. You are nothing now, and I have survived.

"'And I have returned to speak to the dead, also. To tell you that I have lived. I have lived to see my children and the children born to them, and all of us mourn and remember you who are buried in the soil beneath these trees. We live in your name and in the name of your children and their children who were never born. We take you with us always, for without you there can be no future.'"

And then she sat down and took a bite of sausage and tore a piece off the bread. "But here I am imagining that I'll live to the end of today or tomorrow," she said, and took a vigorous chomp on the bread.

"I'll never come back—even if I do survive," Pinchas said. "If I'm lucky—wherever I am—I'll feel like a ghost. And this place itself will seem a ghost. Nothing the same. Everything haunted. As if seen through gauze. Of course, a ghost is all gauze. But gauze makes sense, for everything is a wound and being a ghost is a dressing, a protection, instead of returning with no veil. Haunting would be awful, though not as excoriating as reliving, like a living wound. It'd be like watching one of those films we've heard the Nazis are taking of all of this and seeing your father lying dead in a trench. Or your mother chased down the street, beaten with a stick. And then you recognize yourself fallen to the ground in the main square, clutching your head, keening, hoping to die."

Mordecai went into the cabin and returned with a box that clinked as he walked. "There's a farmer nearby. Grows potatoes, carrots, beets. We were going to do like usual—borrow a few supplies for supper—but he was standing like a murderous scarecrow at the end of his fields with a loaded gun. We could have shot him, but these days a village needs even its idiots—so we took some beer instead. Standing where he was, he didn't see us sneak into the barn. But don't worry, we didn't take *all* of his beer."

"Yet . . ." said Tzeitel.

Mordecai handed each one of them a brown bottle and passed around an opener. "I'd say, *L'chaim*—To Life—but that seems too on the nose."

"I'd rather be with you all than with the best people I know," Pinchas said, raising his bottle. "To our health."

"Our health," they said, and drank for a time in silence.

After they emptied their bottles, Mordecai issued them each a second. Then several more.

"There was this sheriff," Motl began, feeling the beer. "Travelled to the frontier. Didn't start out as a sheriff, but his trunk got lost and he stepped off the train with nothing except a star he'd found beneath his seat. Now, he wasn't really sheriff material. His trunk had been filled with books and a single change of gitch—he'd reckoned on becoming a schoolteacher. He only put the star on his chest because he was frightened when he stepped off the train in a dark, deserted place. The townsfolk found him asleep on the bench at the station next morning, saw the star, figured he was the new sheriff they'd been waiting for. Now, though he was no sheriff, he was no fool. He became not only the sheriff but also the town undertaker. A win-win situation. There turned out to be something strange about Sheriff Elijah—Eli. He insisted on burying every man still wearing his gun. And always in the place they fell, whether outside the whorehouse or in the middle of the main street. After a year or so—this was the Wild West, after all—there were dozens of men buried with their guns all over town.

"Then one dark day a notorious gang, the Mazikeen Rangers, invaded the town. Dozens of motley varmints wearing black bandanas and each emanating some startlingly noxious odours. They drank all the whiskey in the saloon then stood pickled in the main street with their guns drawn, saying, 'This town is ours.'

"Sheriff Eli walked into the middle of the street, cool as a dead man, and took out a little book from inside his vest. He kissed it—a quick little smooch—and then returned it to his pocket. 'Now, boys,' was all he said. And from beneath the ground, all those men buried with their guns began shooting. It was like lightning and thunder from the earth itself. After the clouds of black powder cleared, the townspeople observed not a single Mazikeen Ranger standing. Instead, they lay in the dirt, sweet black smoke rising from perforations in their all too mortal remains."

The partisans looked down at their bottles, whether meditating on the bittersweet triumph of the dead or the sad impossibility of such a story, it wasn't clear. Eventually, half-asleep, they all wandered into the cabin.

It wasn't as shabby as Motl expected. The dank, cramped insides of an old cow, birch logs as support beams. The beds were potato sacks filled with other potato sacks. Mordecai, bearing one of Motl's former candlesticks, led the way, cupped hand in front of the flame as if supporting an infant's vulnerable skull. Tzeitel and Pinchas shared a sackcloth bed, pulling a cartful of rags over them as they settled down. Motl was offered his own hummock of old rags near the door. Mordecai gave Matis, Lena's husband, a revolver and sent him outside to be first watch. Motl must have looked surprised.

"If there's anyone we can trust to keep a lookout, it's Matis," Mordecai explained. "He'll warn us of the sudden appearance of a tree. Or if the moon looks treacherous. And if he uses the revolver on himself, it'll wake us and someone else can take over."

After some minutes, Motl heard whispers and squirming from Tzeitel and Pinchas's corner of the cabin. "When life gives you lemons," Motl's father would say, "find someone to screw." But he hadn't meant it this way. At least, as far as Motl knew. Eventually, he fell asleep to the muffled gyrations of their music. He followed the red frills and satin of buxom women as they ascended endless stairs to a room above a saloon. But then he was on a horse pacing toward the sunset on a clay-coloured prairie. He was sitting backwards, facing the frail woman riding with him. They looked at each other mutely—her blue eyes turning him into a deep pool of cool water, tiny surface scintillations everywhere, wavelets like tremors over his body. Then the sun flashed on the shiny leather of the saddle, the woman disappeared, and there was an agonizing incandescence between his legs.

"Motl," his mother said. "Watch where you're going."

And indeed, he was following a long line of horses into a grim stockade, many thousands of Natives imprisoned within. A Nazi in a wide white cowboy hat stood grinning beside a gallows, eating a bagel shish-kebabbed on a cavalry sabre. Then the earth gave way as in an earthquake, and Motl fell into a deep crevasse with many others, who he took to be Lakota.

He was still falling as Tzeitel shook him awake. "Motl," she said. "Time for your watch. And Matis needs your bed. Don't fall asleep out there, or else you'll never wake. Because we'll shoot you."

The goal of being on watch is to ensure you're looking at nothing and that it stays that way. Motl sat on a stump outside the cabin and peered into the dark trees and the darker darkness between them. A Nazi dressed as a shadow. A collaborator wearing emptiness. He saw no one. The sibilance of an invisible breeze rustled the imperceptible leaves. The footfall of a footless ghost. Squirrels. A night bird. His own snoring.

He tugged his own face to wake himself, stood up and scrutinized the trees, glared into the night. Could his mother emerge from the forest? Where was she? He did and did not want to think about it. His little cousin, Hannah. A picaresque of grief: one scene after the other where someone is lost. All this before the hero comes to town, a stranger with a past so scarred it has formed an impenetrable mantle and he can speak only in close-lipped terseness. And in the distant hills, an Indian warrior whose impressive copper-coloured six-pack and unblinking horizon-gaze demonstrate his immutable resolve in the face of death. Both images binding to the stereotype receptors in the European brain.

Something in the woods. A snapped branch. A grunt. The rustling of . . . a rustler? Motl reached for his holster. But he was a sentry without a gun.

"I see you," he said to the darkness. To the now-silent forest.

He held his breath. Then he heard footsteps. Sniffling. A woman's voice. "What?"

He saw her fall onto other bodies, the two tiny pieces of broken button falling with her.

Her last thought? Surely she'd reached out to him. He was far away, somewhere—alive—in the world. Surely she'd sent him her last insistently loving instructions. *Don't die. Don't die. Don't die. Or else, my kleine, my son, she would say, I'll kill you myself.*

And his sister beside her. Until she'd joined her in line, his mother had thought she was dead. And now alive again, so briefly. Maybe his sister had known her work under the Germans was nothing. She'd soon be discarded. But she could choose her own death. With love and gratitude. With her mother. The final act of devotion. You can't destroy me or my family: we leave the world as decent humans, as Jews, our human being-in-the-world a protection even from the despair of death.

Or maybe she was just scared and needed to be with her ma.

For Motl, this crack in an already cracked world was a crack directly underneath him. If only he could fall through and be lost. Or at least, like some parts of him, freeze solid, awaiting better times.

14

But what now? Grief would turn him to fallen leaves, to mulch. These deaths would take his legs, his bones. So instead, he imagined a long bar and a bottle sliding from the barman. His hand opened to receive it. Whiskey then more whiskey. He'd fill up until his heart was insensate as brined pickles. He'd finish the bottle and turn his brain into a pillow.

But soon, Motl would have to decide. Return to the quest for his two faithful Penelopes, waiting patiently there above Zimmerwald? Join these partisans in their small raids and contingent forest safety? Or take on his mother's duty to find Hannah, if she still lived, if she could be found, if he himself would not be killed as he searched?

Dawn. Matis stoked the fire until the flames leapt.

"He's better in the mornings," Pinchas said. "He fades around noon."

Mordecai, who'd stood the last watch, leaned his rifle against a tree, lifted a kettle of water for tea. Pinchas stirred a drab paste of obscure grain with an old spoon. Tzeitel helped the blanket-wrapped Esther to a place by the fire. She returned to the cabin, came back with two candlesticks.

"Maybe you got these from your mother?" she said softly, and passed them to Motl, who cradled them, infant-like. His mother and sister, extinguished.

Then he stuck them down his pants. "Pinchas, could I get some of that chow? Looks like good glue for guts."

Pinchas shovelled out a glop of the stuff and Motl began negotiating the eating of it.

"So you want to know why I have no hair?" Pinchas said, one palm running over his scalp bare as a prairie oyster, a sallow, pockmarked moon. Motl said nothing, but Pinchas continued anyway. Hiding creates its own form of cabin fever.

"When I visit the barber's, it's more ears and nose than head. Less clip, more polish and shine. My father and his father lost their hair early. And so I was worried, and so kept my scalp furrowed to grip each of my hairs tight. Then one day—I was in a meadow overlooking the sea—I lay with a sweet girl I loved among the flowers and yes I was happy and at peace. And for once in my anxious life I unclenched my body as we lay under the blue sky with the soft wind over our naked skin. And I released my hair, which fell about us onto the green grass, never to grow back. Or at least, that's what I tell everyone."

Motl continued to paste his insides with porridge, nodding to acknowledge Pinchas's presence.

"I learned some months later," Pinchas said, "that the girl was shipped to the Soviet north. She died starving and forgotten on the train. If I had hair, it would have turned white." Pinchas paused a moment then resumed stirring the porridge, as if in its drab depths he could divine something about either past or future.

Mordecai passed cups of tea round to everyone except Matis, who at some point had disappeared into the woods. Esther, still wrapped in a blanket, had moved close to Motl, leaning against him. The small group of them sipped the brackish tea, listening only to the song of wrens and woodpeckers, and, as always, for the sound of footsteps.

After Motl had laid down his spoon, the battle with the porridge finally over, Esther led him through the woods, and dropped the blanket into the leaves. She took his hand and held it against her chest. She looked at him, silently. Then she pulled off her dress.

She held herself against him, ran her hand through the tangle of his copper-red hair and gently touched his stubbled face. Whether she was hanging on or trying to disappear, was attempting to make human what was unreal or had lost her senses, Motl didn't know.

She unbuttoned and slipped off his shirt, but as she made to unbuckle his belt, he stayed her hand.

"Esther . . ."

"Shh," she said.

"Candlesticks," he said, and removed them from his pants.

Then he gathered the fallen blanket around them and they held each other in a huddle in the leaves on the forest floor.

Had Motl ever been with a woman? A man?

"Everyone is given the same life, but collects their own scars," Esther said.

"Mine make it hard to sit down," Motl replied.

"It's okay," Esther said. "We'll be careful."

"I'm not sure I'm able . . ."

Gunshots, shouting, the sound of breaking branches and running. Motl and Esther under the blanket, flattened against the ground.

The White Armbanders or else the *Einsatzgruppen* had found the camp. There was nothing Motl or Esther could do. Gather their scars and be silent. Hope there were no dogs to scent them. They remained hours after it fell quiet, until the sun was a hot fist in the sky and they were baking in the blanket.

"Is it safe?" Motl whispered eventually.

"When has it ever been safe?"

"I mean in comparison."

"We should check on the others."

They got dressed and crept toward the camp. Motl held his breath, listening. If evil existed, did it have a sound? A rancorous ache, hissing through the veins like sleet or steam? But if this were evil and not only devastation or terror or pain, it meant God or punishment or the monstrous beyond the human. Beyond what was broken on earth.

They crawled from trunk to trunk. Once there'd been a border between past and future, between the world when it had been imaginable and when it was not. He was a lost horse on a salt plain, parched tongue unable to speak or swallow. Desire made a mirage in front of him. This could be not real, this desiccation of the chest, nothing inside but broken glass.

Esther was the first to peer around a tree into the clearing. "Turn around," she said. "Leave." Everyone had been shot. A soldier was stationed, waiting for the others to return. Esther and Motl must bolt like a spooked horse, but in silence. Like two elves in a school play, feet cobweb-soft, they crept away through forests. Like Indianers in a book, Motl thought, tiptoeing over trenches, boulder, fissures, fallen trees.

After an hour, they arrived at a rutted wagon track. It was more hole than road except for the parts that were road, which were themselves filled with holes. A man lumpy and uneven as the track sagged on the bench of a wagon, carving a piece of stick.

If greed or murderousness could be seen in the bones, this mostly folded man was clearly harmless.

"What are you making?" Motl asked the man in the wagon.

"A smaller stick," the man said. "We're poor. It's entertainment. In summer, my wife wears the winter boots while I wear the summer boots to market. In the winter, she wears the summer boots while I take the winter boots. Both have holes, but if it weren't for the holes, neither pair of boots would fit."

"And so, too, our lives with holes at either end," Motl said. "Please take us to Ponary." Then quietly to Esther, "I need to find my mother and sister. If they're dead, I need to see it with my own eyes, but it's possible they survived."

"Ponary. It is hell."

"Twenty rubles?"

"Are you Jews?"

"Why?"

"It's dangerous."

"What are the Nazis or the White Armbanders going to do— take us even more quickly to Ponary?"

"Dangerous for me."

"So, thirty rubles, then. I need to find my mother and my sister."

"I wouldn't do it even for twice that."

Motl turned around and made to walk away. Bargaining for beginners.

"But I'll do it for nothing—because of your mother—but maybe, because I'm willing, you'll pay me thirty-five rubles anyway."

Esther and Motl clambered into the clutter of sticks, sacks and old clothes in the wagon's bed.

"Where are your stars?" the driver asked.

"The lucky ones are long gone."

"The yellow ones."

"Only star I'll wear is a sheriff's," Motl said. "Like the deputy who buried an hombre who still wore his gun. Went off in the casket, killed the preacher, so he charged the dead man. Carrying a concealed weapon."

"I know that tale. So you, too, read of box canyons and sharp-shooters chawing through the Badlands?"

"Let's say I've camped my nose in a chapter or two between bookmarked sage and flyleaf coulee. But I left everything behind in Vilnius. I have nothing: books, family, home. My father was a Jew. My mother also. And you?"

"A Christian. Since last Thursday." The man held out his hand. "My name is Jonas. Also since last Thursday."

They shook. "Howdy."

"Esther," Esther said, offering her hand too, since he'd appar-ently forgotten about her. "Howdy."

Then "Yah," the newly Christian Jonas said. His horse, with a disconsolate shrug, began to shuffle forward, the customary direc-tion for shuffling. The wagon followed with a doleful shudder, Motl and Esther nestled amid sticks and clothes.

"It won't be fast, if we get there at all. Not the Pony Express, more of a Ponary Schlep," Jonas said.

"Your horse have a name?" Esther asked.

"Only the one his mother gave him. And I never met his mother."

"At home, we had an old horse called Rivka, poor sad thing with one blind eye. I'm glad she didn't live to see what's hap-pened—she wept enough with her good eye as it was."

They followed the path as it meandered through the woods, Motl and Esther ready to turn their bones into sticks beneath the rags if anyone appeared, the horse stumbling over both holes and road.

"I have forged papers," Jonas said after a while. "A cousin of a friend of mine gave them to me. So it'll take more paperwork before they kill me."

It began to rain.

"This is nothing," Jonas said into the downpour. "My wife and I hid in a hole below a closet for more than a week. Water dripped on our heads the whole time. There was no room. My feet were in my wife's face. 'What should I do, eat them?' she said. But soon she became so thirsty from pneumonia, she wanted to drink her own blood.

"They have many ways to kill us," he said. "Disease, death marches, throwing us out of our homes and then packing us together somewhere else. And, of course, bullets. There's more bullets in Europe than stars above it.

"And Alfy One-ball Schicklgruber said, 'Why should Germans worry that the soil that made their bread was won by the sword? When we eat wheat from Canada, do we think of murdered Indians?'

"And here I am with two Jews and a horse slouching straight toward Ponary as those Teutonic cowboys clear the plains."

15

They travelled through the rat-grey afternoon, the road empty
but for mud and holes. And one rabbit, three squirrels and a deer,
all of which came and left in peace, given that the travellers were
weaponless and unable to secure their mortal flesh for vittles.

As they travelled, the travellers spoke:

"My father was a religious man," Esther said. "He studied at
the yeshiva and wanted to become a rabbi, but instead became a
blacksmith, taking over his father's smithy when the old man
could work no longer. No one, not even his father, was as devout
as he who said a prayer before each prayer, and then one after. He
believed his ten fingers were a *minyan* and that working was devotion, each hammer blow forging glowing red psalms from iron.

"'The tong of tongs,' he'd say. 'My beloved.'

"He was a contented man, a *haimshe* gnome with bulging arms,
face covered in soot, never happier than when clomping home to
family, white linen on a table set with silver candlesticks. His
father, his wife and son, and me, his daughter, waiting for him to
welcome Shabbos into our home.

"Three weeks ago, they came in the night, hammering on the
door. I answered in my nightclothes.

"'Let us in.'

"'I must first put on some clothes.'

"'We've seen the likes of you, naked many times. Open up or we will smash the door.'

"And so these police pushed their way into our little kitchen, led by a local guide as if on a safari. Meyer, a Jew and a drunk, showed them the homes of all the Jewish men in town in exchange for being killed a little later.

"The captain kicked over a chair and slammed his fist on the table, demanding money. The others gathered the men, confused like small children in their underwear, and had them face the wall. My grandfather, and my brother. My father—I thanked God half-heartedly and provisionally at that moment—was in another town that night, having gone to deliver an ornate gate, his specialty, to a church.

"They stomped through the rooms of the house, taking jewellery, taking cash.

"One shook me and pointed a revolver at my head. 'You must have more?' And I gave him a key to a box containing rubles I had saved. My mother had hidden jewellery in her sleeve, and when they found it, they made her stand with the men, then marched them all outside.

"'Wait,' I called. 'I have bread for them.'

"'They'll not need it where they're going,' Meyer said.

"It was the last time I saw them.

"Buildings were burned and the men of the village, and my mother also, were marched to pits already waiting for them. The old, the weak, women and children were all who were left.

"I left our village as soon as it was dawn. I hoped to find and warn my father. But soldiers were marching on the road, and I had to hide for hours in a haystack until the way was clear. I was certain I would not be safe if I were seen.

"My father had come that morning, while I was hiding in the hay. His family, his friends—they were all gone, like rats, as if the Pied Piper had a gun instead of a flute, and alas there were many such pipers. Next they came for the children. I don't know about the old people. I heard all this only later, from Leya Razovsky, the village *shadchan*, the matchmaker—we both escaped from the village, though I fled much sooner.

"Our village had two rabbis. The police seized one along with the other men, tore his beard from his chin, wrapped his parchment body in a Torah scroll and burned him. The other, a young man, his chest smooth as a new apple, had hidden in a room beneath the mikvah and emerged from the burned-out building to find the men gone. My father, distraught and shocked, asked this rabbi if he could kill himself. The pain-struck Litvak, if orthodox, consults the rabbi before acting on impulse.

"The rabbi—may his contemptible and cramped imagination cause him pain forever—told my father that suicide was a sin. 'Suffering proves the existence of God. It's a test. The act of faith, the act of believing that God hasn't forgotten you, sets the believer apart.'

"Easy to say when you're still alive.

"I'd say, in times of war, it's not what you believe, it's what others believe that matters. Except in the most extreme circumstances, what *you* believe won't kill you. You keep on."

"Me, I believe nothing," Jonas said. "Where is it going to be better? In the past? In the future? Unless they can blast me back to when I was studying the *parsha* for my bar mitzvah and I snuck behind the outhouse and kissed Shoshana Levinson. Five years later we were married."

"I don't know where my father went and what he did," Esther continued. "I asked as much as I dared, I searched for news in nearby villages as much as I was able, but then I had to escape myself, else all of us would be lost forever."

It began to rain again. Around a bend, the three travellers encountered three women, two of them carrying babies bundled in rags. A mother and her mother and a sister. The babies' mother was laughing uncontrollably.

"Twins," her mother explained. "One of them is dead."

"We were hiding in the cemetery and they found us. They threw a rock—from a broken gravestone—and it hit her," the sister said. "'We'll let the other one live,' they said. 'So you'll remember.' After they left, she began." She motioned to the laughing woman. "She only stops to sleep, and she sleeps only sometimes."

"She won't let us bury the child," the mother said.

"You have food?" Jonas said, rooting around in a sack behind him. He gathered some near-rotten potatoes and dropped them into the large pocket the sister opened in her apron. "Now, let us help," he said, lifting a shovel from under the seat. "It must be done."

The sister gave Esther the dead twin and held back the mother, who struggled but kept laughing, while their mother held the still-living twin. Esther wrapped the motionless twin in a sack for a shroud. Motl dug a hole in the field by the road and they lowered the little girl in.

"Everywhere a cemetery," Motl said.

Yisgadal v'yiskadash sh'mei rabbaw.

He offered the spade to the mother so she could add the first spadeful of earth over her baby, gone. The blade turned over to express regret, as is traditional, though one is duty bound to return one's family to the soil. The mother continued struggling, continued laughing and wouldn't touch the spade.

"Just do it quickly," the woman's mother said. And so they did.

Jonas found a large rock as a headstone—there was no time to think of the formal end of mourning and unveilings a year away— and Motl used the shovel to scratch, if only temporarily, the Hebrew letter *beit* for *Bela*, the child's name, into it. They stood silently around the grave for a few minutes in the rain and then the three travellers climbed back into the wagon and rode off. The women stood in the field, the mother's banshee laughter tangling with the rain until finally they heard only the rain.

16

They rode for an hour after that in silence and drizzle, no sound but the creaking of the wagon and the steady clop of the horse.

The road sloped down into a shallow dale and just as they were ascending the small rise on the other side, a small man ran into the middle of the road, his tiny black eyes burning at them.

"*Sieg Heil!*" he shouted. "*Sieg Heil!*" His arm shot up in the Nazi salute. "*Achtung! Achtung! Sieg Heil!*"

His blunt-cut hair lay askew across his pale forehead and his moustache was a stunted black brush across his twitching lip.

"*Achtung! Achtung! Sieg Heil!*"

"Holy *Scheisse!*" Jonas said. "It's goddamn Adolf H. Aryan Christ himself."

"*Sieg Heil!*" the man shouted again, and raised his arm as if in spasm. "*Sieg Heil!*"

"What the actual Himmler?" Esther said. "He'll get us shot."

"*Sieg Heil! Sieg Heil!*" the man kept shouting.

"What should we do?"

"If I had a gun," Motl said, "it'd be a gunfight. But since he doesn't seem to have one either, it'll be a very quick showdown."

"We should get out of here."

"*Sieg Heil! Sieg Heil! Achtung! Achtung!*"

"We're dead."

"Look," said Esther. "He's by himself. It's some other delirious house painter who thinks he's only got one ball." She shouted, "Go away. Find a carpet to chew somewhere else."

"*Sieg Heil!* The fate of the German people for the next thousand years depends on me. *Sieg Heil!*"

"If he's Adolf Hitler," Motl said, "then I'm Jesse James." He reached for the imaginary six-guns at his hips. "I'll Poland some living room into his chest. Then we'll see how much destiny is manifested. When his blood's done soaking into the soil, Goebbels or Göring or Old Shatterhand himself can cover up the holes as if they were at Ponary itself."

"History is my struggle! We *Übermenschen* will triumph!" The little man began not quite goose-stepping toward them. Duck-marching.

"I think I recognize him," Jonas said. "He's Yankel Fridman, the tailor from Krekenova, though he used to have a beard then and seemed less . . . Nazi."

"I will blast the Nazi out of that little *schnayder* before I'm done," Motl said.

Esther to Motl: "So many Hitlers, so little time. So do something already."

"The *Herrenvolk! Die Herrenrasse! Sieg Heil! Sieg Heil!*"

"A gunslinger only challenges the vaquero worthy of the duel," Motl said. "I'll not fight this puddin' foot."

"Like the saying goes, 'You're all *kippah* and no cowboy,'" Esther said. "'All Jew and no Jesse.'"

Before Motl could answer her, the pseudo-Führer shouted, "There's only one solution to the Jewish question!" And as if there were any doubt as to what he meant, he raised a Luger.

Without hesitation, Esther reached into her boot and pulled out a gun and pointed it at the ersatz Adolf.

"Wait," Jonas said. "When did it come to Jews killing Jews?"

"When they point guns at us," said Esther.

Yankel-Hitler aimed the gun at his own head and began muttering, again and again, *"Yisgadal v'yiskadash."*

"Problem solved," Esther said.

"No," Jonas called to the man. "Don't give up hope."

"Easy for you to say," Esther said. "You're no longer a Jew."

"Yankel," Jonas said. "Put the gun down. Put it down and we'll talk. There are other ways." He turned to Esther. "Put your gun away also. Or at least hide it."

Esther nodded and set the gun on the wagon floor.

"Since when did you have a gun?" Motl asked, but she only smiled.

Then Jonas called again to Yankel. "Come have a drink with us."

"You have something for him to drink?" Esther asked.

"No, but you have a better idea?"

Yankel had lowered the gun and begun ambling dejectedly toward the wagon, when, without warning, he lifted it again and pulled the trigger. The sound of the shot faded almost immediately. Then Esther clutched her shoulder. As blood seeped through her fingers, Jonas grabbed the gun from the wagon floor and squeezed. Yankel stood as if he were trying to think of a word that was on the tip of his tongue. A red button, like those on a child's clothes, began to form on his pale white forehead.

He fell to the ground.

Yankel on his back, his unseeing eyes reflecting cloud-crowded sky, cumulus wool batting for an endless coat whose warmth is everywhere yet whose buttons are nowhere. Or maybe his bill was vast yet the payment was nowhere. Either way, now he was dead, there was plenty of space for angels to dance on his unused tailor's pins and for poor Yankel to go through the eye of the needle to the other side. No need to be Hitler or Jesus or Karl Marx. Like smoke from an extinguished fire, his fear hissed away into air.

Jonas jumped down from the wagon and approached the fallen tailor with trepidation. He'd read enough westerns to know that you could be killed even by a dead man, especially if they weren't as dead as you thought.

Motl was solely focused on Esther. He tore off his shirt, and ripped it with his hands and teeth into strips.

"Motl, there's plenty of rags. Why use your shirt?" Esther said.

"Mmmhhh," Motl mumbled, ripping more of his shirt with his teeth. He tied several strips together and wound the long bandage around her shoulder. As the cloth reddened, he felt close to a swoon, but when his senses cleared, he found that he'd wrapped even more of his shirt around her and that the flow from the wound had eased.

Jonas had pocketed Yankel's gun. Now he began rummaging in the man's pockets. In time of tragedy, the dead teach us many lessons, their pockets in particular. A watch, a pocket knife, a photograph and a small black edition of *Mein Kampf*, pages cut out to hide a roll of rubles.

He took the watch, the knife and the money, and heaved the book into the field. The photograph was of a large family picnicking on a blanket, a horse and a black car in the background. Bread. Cheese. Fish. Wine. Apples. A bearded father, a stolid mother still in her apron, three young women, clearly sisters; Yankel the Tailor, smiling and proud, and, scattered about him, assorted children, all cut, as it were, from the same cloth.

"Jonas," Motl called. "Esther is wounded, and night fast approaches. It could be life or death. We must reach some friendly house soon, for there's no moon to guide us."

"It's the middle of the afternoon," Esther said. "Of course there's no moon. Besides, the bullet barely broke the skin. It's just the shock—your shock."

"We need to bury him," Jonas said. "We can't just leave him."

"And Motl," Esther said. "Next time you're thinking of acting the brave cowboy, take my gun so you'll have an actual gun not to use."

They buried Yankel with the photograph of his family—*Yisgadal v'yiskadash sh'mei rabbaw*—got back in the cart and kept on. Soon Jonas turned the horse onto an even smaller, muddier path, "rutted as Fascist pizzleskin left in the rain," he said, and hopefully free from entire Nazis, either imagined or real.

Motl said, "We need a safe haven, a dwelling place. I see a feeble light winking through the trees."

"Hopeful as a yellow star," Jonas said.

"A star of hope," Motl said.

"Motl." Esther put her good arm around him. "Motl."

The wagon trundled on over the corrugations of the path. Rounding a spinney, they saw a small house across a field, surrounded by a posse of farmers. The men were mum, yet they seemed to thrum with anticipation, gazing intently at a man slumped on a horse, rope attaching his neck to an outstretched branch of a single tree.

"Wonder if he'd wished upon a yellow star?" Jonas motioned to the man's coat, the identifying patch sewn on his sleeve.

"Like my mother always said at Purim, 'They used to want to kill us. They still do, but they used to, also,'" Motl said. "We must save him. As the saying goes, 'No noose is good noose.'"

The delirious overreaching humour of tragedy.

Standing to the side of the horse with the condemned man on it, a man with an eye patch held a gun.

"Save him how? There's a dozen of them," Jonas said. "And the pirate has a gun."

"How can a cowpoke sleep under yeller stars if his heart is yeller too?" Motl said. "We used a gun once today. We can use it again."

"First rule of being a hero: Do no harm. To us. We need to get out of here before they see us."

"Not this cowboy."

"What are you going to do—shoot the rope?"

"A gunslinger moves like a coyote in shadows. I'll figure it out as I go. Today, we pistoleros shot Hitler."

"These aren't pretend Nazis. We need to go." Jonas shook the reins. "Haw," he said quietly. "Haw."

Jonas's horse exhaled dejectedly, considering if it would move again, a horse's life apparently a never-ending procession between brief respites of grass.

The horse's nickering was enough to attract the posse. The men turned.

"Hombres," Motl announced. "We have travelled far and find ourselves mighty parched. We could use a gut-warming snort of revivifying lamp oil if available."

And up he stood.

Just then, Jonas's horse decided that it would, after all, haw.

What it did not consider was that its turn would unsteady Motl and he would fall, the men would run toward him, and in the confusion the horse beneath the noosed Jew would spook, buck and then gallop to freedom, leaving the man dancing a frenzied klezmer Tyburn jig until the branch broke and he too fell to the ground.

Motl was on his back beneath the historical sky, only he and the clouds to witness the one-eyed leader of the posse training his gun on the exact convergence between Motl's continued life and his death.

Jonas called, halting the existential cavalcade of horse and wagon. "Whoa," he said.

"If'n I were to pull this trigger, you'd be no longer thirsty," the one-eyed man said to Motl.

"Or I'd be parched forever, since Heaven is dry."

"Colandered with holes, reckon it'd be hard for you to keep the drink in."

The noose-necked Yid, apparently not captivated by the sparkle of this repartee, staggered to his feet, raised the branch he remained attached to and swung it at the gathering of men. Those who were not toppled were lassoed between rope and branch and so, too, fell. An artful trick by the near-hanged man though it choked him indigo.

The thwack of wood startled the leader, who pulled the trigger, and Jonas's poor old horse was shot dead as a nail in a Litvak's grave, free now to graze the Elysian Fields.

Not sure who else might have a gun, Esther leapt from the wagon and wrestled the leader's gun away from him. In the land of the one-eyed, the one-armed is queen, even if she winces in pain. Pointing the gun at him, she ordered him to remove the noose from the neck of the gasping Litvak. Jonas, meanwhile, had retrieved Esther's pistol and was sheepdogging the other men with the promise of bullets.

Motl remained down, his head resting against the hard sod, as the story unfolded above him.

"Who are these men?" he thought. "Not *Einsatzgruppen*, not regular Germans, not seraphic man-farmers radiating hay-gold beams of angelic light and luminous beneficence to person, beast, Slav and Jew. Rather, these agriculturalists seek to reap the sorrow sewn by the National Socialists, threshing both life and possessions as the opportunity arises. Farmers turned rustlers. The Nazis think themselves bratwurst braves with muscles like gopher mounds—but they are actually cowboys clearing out Cherokees. Which makes me more Indianer than cowboy, or else hundred percent Hebrew."

He heard shouting, the sound of running, and closed his eyes.

"Perhaps my story is the story of the cowpunch who lay upon the red earth outside the Mein Kampfsite on the range and never rose again, though the yellow sun climbed and fell, men were hung, homesteads were burned, men drank, fought on empty main streets, shot each other through the back or between the buttons, spared each other, helped each other, found love then lost it, while others sought a Hebrew God who thought it no longer possible to write His poetry in these times and gazed instead silently into His corned beef in some transubstantial cosmic cookhouse. This broncobuster who had inadvertently parted the red curtains and led a delusional Yid into the backstage darkness, the sound and the Führer of his Hitler act now over."

A horsefly settled on the scrubland of Motl's unshaven chin and, batting it away, he recalled his shaveless revelation in Shnipishok, his resolution to stand and to retrieve.

His mother was in the belly of the Nazi whale, but, he decided, she had to have survived. Surely she remained alive from sheer bullheaded perversity and a conviction that the Almighty needed only the firm guidance of her maternal Midrash. What man, whether tailor, furrier or Godhead, really understood what was going on in the world? Didn't HaShem misjudge and spill divine light from the vessels and shmutz up the universe? Who was left to clean up, as always?

And his sister, too, and her daughter. Alive. Ready to clean up.

And he had his own vessels to salvage from distant Switzerland. There were Jews to be created during this time of death and *Rassenkampf*.

So he must rise, although perhaps it was wise to strategically play dead until the crisis passed. It had worked for Jesus, and surely it couldn't be long until the end of the world. The signs were strewn everywhere.

Before he could decide, he got kicked in the head. Darkness.

17

"Motl," said Esther. "Motl."

He was on a bed and beneath blankets. Esther leaned over him, granting him her warm breath and energizing scent. "I made soup."

A spoon hovered near and as he opened his mouth to speak, Esther inserted it. The liquid was a hot comfort moving through his insides. His temples throbbed.

"You are lucky," Esther said. "The farmers thought you were dead. The others weren't so lucky."

"Others?"

"Jonas and Isaak—the man they tried to hang. The Lithuanians too. I was able to hide."

"Jonas, a good man—a righteous Gentile—may we survive to remember him."

"Let's not speak of it. At least, not now." And she inserted more soup into Motl.

Later, she climbed into bed beside him. They slept.

Sun through the curtains. Esther waking, her arms around Motl.

"I'm holding on," she said, "so the wind can't blow me away

like one of your tumbleweeds. In case I roll through the doors of the Reichstag or out to sea where seagulls will eat my eyes."

Motl was half-asleep, dreaming of fire.

"Or maybe we'll both be carried into a purple valley, covered in sage," she said, and kissed him. "I don't believe in hope, but I don't believe in hopelessness either—"

"Can you think of something worse than being scalped?" Motl murmured.

"Not off the top of my head," Esther said. "Now wake up. I want to kiss you properly. Before I'm dead, I don't want to be dead."

Here in history, a latitude and longitude, a mark on some kind of celestial day planner. How we find ourselves in a particular moment, a triangulation between tragedy, absurdity and beauty, space-time bent by emotion, and it feels like we've stumbled on something built into the fabric of the universe.

"Esther—" Motl began.

"Shh," she said.

"I have this injury . . ."

She ran her fingers across his mouth. "If it isn't your lips"—she tugged her scarf away and her hair tented about them—"smooching is possible."

They smooched.

Later: "We can't stay here. We need to leave."

"I didn't want to ask—where is here?"

"In the farmhouse. We're alone. For now. We need to leave."

"Let's eat first," Motl said. "Bacon, coffee, flapjacks. Maybe beans. Range fuel." He opened cupboard doors but found only tea, sugar, a sack of kasha, a bottle of vodka and a dented tin of condensed milk. "This recalls what every seasoned cowboy knows," he said. "It's important to be flexible."

They had tea loaded with milk and sugar and bowls of kasha, then they gathered their things—they had no things—and walked out the door.

A rattletrap of an old car was parked in the weeds behind the house. Esther tried a door, which opened with a buzzard-like rasp, and she climbed inside. She pressed the button to start it and, after hacking like an ancient asthmatic sheep, it did. Motl cleared the rocks, old farm implements and a broken chair from the weeds in front, then scrabbled in beside Esther.

"Back to the main road," she said.

"Not an aficionado of the posse and the fatal necktie for which these byways are known?"

The road was empty except for the usual mud and ruts. The car, some medieval variety of Russian-made GAZ with its distinctive silver deer logo, sputtered and convulsed but kept going. Light rain began to fall and Motl had to lean out the window and manually move the broken wipers. Both of them scrutinized the fields and the road ahead—Nazis, armed Lithuanians, major potholes and the unexpected. Too late they discovered a seemingly innocuous puddle to be a small pond of surprising depth and the car violently lurched as a wheel struggled to clear it.

"Ugh." A grunt from behind.

They turned to find a young man emerging from under a blanket in the back seat, pointing a pistol at them. "What's happening? Tell me or I'll caviar the windshield with your brains."

"It's likely, then, that we'll crash and at least one other of us will get hurt," Motl said.

"At least you'll know who's boss," the young man gasped, then fell over, the wound in his chest leaking more blood, already having saturated the seat.

Motl seized the gun. "Seems I'm running this outfit now."

The man said nothing.

"Are you deceased?" Motl asked.

"If he says yes, we're in trouble," Esther said. "I'd better pull over."

He wasn't. He was Lithuanian—but he would cease to belong to any earthly place if they didn't find him a doctor. Esther tied her scarf around his chest and they set off.

"Semeliškės—the next town—do you know it?" Esther asked. "Is there a doctor there?"

The man said nothing for a long time, but then, eventually, "They've put the Jews in a ghetto there."

He said his name was Kazimierz—they'd been at his father's farm. It was his father's car. He wanted nothing to do with either the Nazis or the Lithuanians and the war. When the other farmers had gathered in a posse, shouting, gathering rope to hang the Jew, he'd tried to pull his father back inside the house, but his father—the man with the eye patch—had broken free of him and taken the lead. Kazimierz had been shot in the melee after the branch had snapped and he'd staggered to the car to hide, then passed out. The other men had been killed or wounded and the wounded had run away.

When they drew close to Semeliškės, Esther nested the car behind stacked hay bales in a field on the edge of town. Motl dressed the man in his coat, and since he was unable even to stagger, they slung his arms over their shoulders and walked him, his head lolling.

And ran into Germans with German guns posted on the road as they walked into town.

"*Ach, ein anderer* drunken Lithuanian," they said. "Can't hold their schnapps for *Scheisse*."

"A doctor?" Esther asked.

"Won't help. He'll have to sleep it off."

Two Jews and a Lithuanian walk into a town. Past Nazis. How?

The Lithuanian was drunk.

They came to a shlumpy yellow one-storey, its paint peeling and several windows boarded up. Outside, an old man roosted in a sclerotic chair, smoke rising from the woolly sagebrush of his beard, his visible skin the ancestor of a century-old raisin.

"Drunk?" he inquired.

"Wounded."

"Dead?"

"Not yet."

"Inside." He indicated the door with his pipe.

In the inside dimness, an old woman formed of knackered satchels, knotted scarves and paleolithic prunes sat on a chair. Her voice, a husky gust. "I help," she said, and got up and began shuffling toward a shelf of cloudy bottles. "Lie him by fire." The majority of her gnarled finger pointed at the ceiling, but they knew she aimed for the defeated bed sagging near the hearth.

They stripped the man down to the hole in his chest, and the old woman poured a slurry from one of the bottles over it. Steam hissed and rose as the young man shuddered.

"Kazimierz, Kazimierz," the old woman crooned, and poured green fluid into the steam. "I know your baba." Kazimierz only moaned. The woman stuck her oblique finger into the wound and stirred.

Kazimierz shouted, *"Plek ne, plekshne!* Blundering clod woman. Dog doctor. *Shundaktaris!"* And then appeared to pass out as the woman pushed her finger in up to the last conker of a knuckle. Her cockle-shell lips pursed and, with tilted head, she seemed to be listening to the heavens.

"Ah," she said, and jerked away as if having snatched a fish. Her finger was covered in blood and some beef-like chum.

"This little boy," she said, displaying the bullet she'd retrieved, "makes big trouble." Then she uncorked another bottle and tipped it over the wound. A kaleidoscopic purple-and-blue swirl drained into Kazimierz. Next, she crumbled broken green leaves over the hole, pressed a larger leaf over it, and retrieved a needle and a thread spool.

"Hold," she said, and Motl and Esther held Kazimierz's shoulders. The woman stitched a circle of thread and then a red cross-hatching, eventually pulling the skin taut. Surgery by an expert in sock repair.

Kazimierz remained unconscious, blessedly.

"A gunslinger punched through the hide needs bunk time to heal," Motl said as the woman tucked a blanket over Kazimierz.

"Laima," the woman responded. Her name.

Then she ladled soup into bowls and placed them beside dark bread on the table. The old man, drawn by the scent of food, wobbled in the door.

"Tadas," he said. His name.

They spoke little until Esther asked about children.

Children? Without children they'd be just dust with withered legs waiting for a puff of wind to scatter them over the fields, no reason not to return to where they were once but seed. They had sons and a daughter.

Where were they?

Lina, she had moved to Trakai, the nearest large town, to marry a Karaite sales clerk and have a boy, beautiful little Gvidas, who—is it really possible?—they'd seen only a few times last year, how is that right when Trakai is so close? Their eldest son, Simonis, had been killed fifteen years earlier, fighting the *coup d'état* against the democratically elected government, and still they ache with loss, such a good boy, so handsome and brave.

The other son, a policeman, had been living in Trakai before he joined the 11th Battalion of the Schuma, the Lithuanian Auxiliary Police, which became the PPT, a security battalion forced to work with the Nazis. What could he do? They were sure he wouldn't kill Jews or Poles or Russians, they knew their Jurgis. No matter how much they hated the Russians, surely he could never become like the murdering Nazis or their Lithuanian collaborators. Also, they'd heard that he'd deserted and was hiding, maybe with the Karaites in Trakai. He'd be able to blend in because his skin was dark for a Lithuanian, dark as a Karaite, and his hair was brown, as if he'd been born Romani.

The couple knew Motl and Esther were Jews, though they weren't wearing stars. So how did they recognize their Jewishness? How do you know it's raining? In your bones, you just know.

Kazimierz could stay, but the Jews could not. Old man and old woman as they were, it was no longer time for excitement and their house was small, no place to hide. Also, there were better places to go. Trakai, for instance. They knew there were Jews who had been able to get papers saying they were Karaites. And maybe they could look for Jurgis, their hidden son, while they were there. They could ask the Karaites.

Karaites. Who were they? Motl and Esther wanted to know.

Depends who you ask. They were Jews, or at least they had been Jews. Maybe. Like chickens had once been pterodactyls. Or a car had been a horse. Or, more exactly, as an ox is a cow. The Karaites had spoken Hebrew and prayed from the Torah. It was the seventh century or the fourteenth. A long time ago. Were they descendants of the Khazars? Either way, they'd ended up in Crimea and eastern Europe, and for a variety of arcane reasons, both strategic and religious, the Czar had exempted them from Jewishness—it was like being granted a pardon—and thus from the rich panoply of persecutions available to the modern Jew. And so later, the Nazis had exempted them too, because of the Czar, but also because the Nazis had asked some Ashkenazi rabbis and scholars.

"Are these people Jews like you? Should we kill them also?" the Nazis had asked, and the rabbis and scholars said no. It would take a particularly bitter variety of misanthrope to condemn others to die with you when you could say a single word and save them.

"On the other hand," the old couple said, "if our Jurgis wasn't able to escape the Auxiliary Police and is still with the 11th Battalion, he'll be in Ponary killing Jews. Maybe you'd know some of them?"

18

The golden hour. The barley light of the sinking sun makes you aware you're moving through the slow honey of your story. Motl could have been riding, half-asleep, drifting west through the warm winds and sagebrush, holding on to the pommel as his horse's hooves drummed quietly and steadily through the gauze of his reverie. But he was in the car with Esther as she drove to Trakai, riding shotgun or, more exactly, handgun, as he still had Kazimierz's loaded pistol and was on the lookout for danger. It was madness to be on the road, but it was madness to be anywhere, except perhaps in a cellar beneath a trap door, on the moon, or in Switzerland, on a mountain, safe as a testicle.

The old couple had given them the Trakai address of their daughter, Lina, on Karaimu Gatve—Karaite Street—near the old castle. They were to ask her if maybe she could tell them where to find a Karaite, since their *kenesa*—their synagogue—would be closed for the night.

Then tell her to bring their grandson, beautiful little Gvidas, to see them maybe once in a while.

———

A Karaite house has three windows: one for God, one for family and one for good ol' Grand Duke Vytautas, who centuries earlier had invited the Karaites to Lithuania to form his personal guard. Also, one supposes, the windows were for the view: looking out of, or gazing into, observing activities either illicit or quotidian. And to put the Father, the Son and the Holy Ghost off the scent.

Lina's house was painted yellow and the luminous rawhide moon glinted blond in each of its three windows. Esther rapped on the blotchy door.

A face appeared in one of the reflected moons as if surrounded by a lasso of holy light. Motl and Esther stood docile and un-German as two full-grown Jewish babies left on a doorstep.

The door opened a crack.

"Lina," Esther said. "Your parents—"

"My parents!" Lina said. "They can't have died, don't tell me this—age has cured them into jerky. They can no more die than a saddle can."

"No, it's—"

"And I cannot tell them where my brother is because I do not know . . ."

"No, we'd just—"

"And I cannot bring them the child." She inhaled sharply and held her breath.

They were all silent. Wind in the pines. A blues-harp dog keening from a distant yard.

Then Esther said, "We too have lost our family."

More silence.

Finally, Lina opened the door, sat them at her table, brought cups of tea from a tarnished samovar and some *kybynlar*, half-moon pastries stuffed with mutton.

"There's much my parents don't know," she said, sitting down too. "They're old. They may be too leathered to die, but not to be hurt.

"My husband was a Karaite, yet he was shot by Germans when I was at the market. Perhaps his being a near Jew was good enough for them. Then they shot my baby, my Gvidas, my little moon, for no reason at all.

"I would not wish this death on their Nazi children, nor on them for their children's sake. May they carry like a heavy stone always the gasp of Gvidas as he died, the convulsion of my heart when I was told. May it fill their nights and days so they do not become old with time but maimed with these thoughts and seek a high place from which to leap. There is no high place here and so I keep on. I help those I can. For example, I give you more tea." And she filled both their teacups. "Being Jews, you understand."

"How do you know we're Jews?" Motl asked.

"As my mother says, 'How do you know you're drinking tea? You just know.'"

"I do know. And I know this is Christian tea. In a Christian cup . . . But the sugar, the sugar is Jewish. How do I know? Because it's hiding. Your parents thought you could help us parlay with a Karaite who might permit us to bed down for the night. We're travelling to Ponary to find family."

"You travel toward hell itself."

"That's why we're going. They could use some help there."

"You can sleep here. One night only. I have loved a near Jew and his child and so I will help you," Lina said. "Tomorrow, I take you to the Ḥakhan, the Karaite leader, at the *kenesa*. Until then, you must hide in the cellar. I've learned that the Nazis suspect even the unsuspected."

"And inspect even the uninspected," Motl said.

"We thank you for your kindness," said Esther.

They dragged the table to the side of the room and rolled back the carpet to reveal a trap door.

Lina hauled it open. A square of darkness exhaled a chill.

"I have no more oil for the lamp, but here's a candlestick and some matches. I will get blankets. Also, some of my husband's clothes."

Thick with clothes and woollen toques, they gingerly descended the ladder. Lina dropped blankets after them. There was scuttling.

"Prairie dogs," Motl said.

"Or underground sheep."

"They're shy."

The cellar wasn't anything more than a narrow burrow with a louring ceiling, malodorous and unsettling.

"Imagine we're squeezed together in a stagecoach," Motl said. "Travelling the Oregon Trail on a winter night."

Esther unfurled a blanket and wrapped them together. More scuttle of prairie dogs. A sack wheezed dust as they lay down. They did not wheeze, but they did sigh. A summation of the last weeks. Fear. Grief. Tenderness. Contentment. A few moments of rest.

Motl blew out the candle.

They woke to footfalls like the pinched rapping of hammers. The raspy consonants and smirking umlaut singsong of German voices above. Chairs scraping and falling against the floor. The scuff of the pushed table.

"Give me the gun," Esther hissed just before they were blinded by a square sun. Motl scrabbling the floor around them for the pistol as the black ghoul of a Nazi silhouette loomed.

"*Ungeziefer.* Jewish vermin."

"Here." Motl pressed the gun against Esther's hand. Pointing up, she squeezed the trigger. A shout of *Ach*, the shadow falling like a crow tossed from the sky, a body dropping beside them with a disquieting oomph.

More shouting. Another black ghost. Esther fired again. A shout of "*Scheisse*," and the wraith descended, slamming against his colleague in grim parody of a wrestling move. The trap door crashed shut. Further furniture rearrangement and then quiet. Only the quick breaths of Motl and Esther, the pounding of blood in their temples.

Then a Germanic moan. Then silence. They waited. And listened.

Nothing. A quiet pure as Aryans.

If any neighbours heard the shots, they stayed away.

Motl and Esther held hands beside the two Nazis, dead, somewhere in the dark.

"The only good Nazi is a dead Nazi," Motl joked, but neither of them laughed.

After many hours, they felt a change in the air, then heard Lina whispering through the barely raised trap door, "You must go."

Before them, the bodies of the Nazis darker than the cellar save for the uncanny glint of insignia and a gun still in the second soldier's hand. Esther uncurled the fingers and pulled it away. She rolled the body over and it toppled onto the stone floor with a thud. She frisked the other. Nothing but cigarettes in a silver case, a handful of loose gold teeth rolled in a handkerchief, an expensive-looking watch and a roll of shabby bills.

"Render unto Esther the things that were probably Jews'," she said.

19

The *kenesa* was being watched closely for fugitive Jews and so wasn't safe, Lina explained. They were to go instead to Trakai Castle, a brick-towered pile on its own island in a lake, which looked like it was home to squat and ruddy fairy-tale dukes. After five hundred years, renovation was needed. Workers ferried boat-loads of stones, bags of tools, homemade vodka and their almost complete lack of ambition for anything but that vodka, adding a few more stays to the old girl's aging corsets.

The single raised boardwalk to the island castle would have a couple of sentries posted, so Lina led them to an overturned rowboat, oars stashed beneath. It was early morning and the lake was still.

"Thank you," they whispered to Lina, the simple phrase filled with all their complex stories, then they turned the boat over and slid it into the water.

The lapping of the oar blades as Motl pulled them across. They heaved the boat onto the narrow shoreline and stowed it between trees.

They straddled a broken-toothed window low in the castle wall, trying not to be floss between the shards. Waiting for them inside, they found a stoop-backed older man named Yefet, a Karaite, his scraggly hair the unkempt white of chicken feathers. He led them through dim passageways to an obscure brick-vaulted room lit by lager-coloured light. He removed a stone from high in the wall and produced some papers.

"These will make you Karaite," he said with a smile. "Now, here's how to pass. Don't act like a Jew because, as they say, if you look like a Jew, shrug like a Jew and tend toward an ironic yet earnest engagement with the inscrutable, numinous, ineffable mystery best approached through speculation in the context of tradition, intellectual community and daily ritual, then they'll probably say you're a Jew.

"Also, I'm going to give you new names. Motl, you're Yochanan Firrouz, and Esther, you're now Sima Babovich. And wear this traditional Karaite headgear." He rummaged in a trunk and produced for Motl a round black hat with a white top like a lid, more hat box than hat. Esther: a lace shawl flowing from a domed black headpiece, with a fringe of coins.

"Any more tips?" Motl asked.

"Don't be seen by Nazis."

Yefet stared at them, then reached again into his trunk and pulled out new clothes for them both. It wasn't that their old clothes were particularly Jewish, but rather that they looked as though a rag-and-bones cart had run over them several times before they were trampled by a goat. And not the cleanest goat.

With their new names and costumes and papers, they'd be able to leave Trakai and travel wherever they needed to go in relative safety. There was still a war going on, after all; not only Katzes and Greenbergs but cats and dogs as well were sometimes casualties. Yet first, Yefet insisted, they must have an audience with the Ḥakhan, the Karaite leader, the self-styled "His Excellency Hajji Seraya Khan Shapshal."

And so Esther and Motl followed Yefet out of Trakai Castle, this time by the front door, and strode over the boardwalk planks. The sentries did not salute but nodded.

Who goes there?

If only they knew.

The *kenesa* gate reminded Motl of the iron his father and grandfather once hammered and twisted into ornate shapes.

"We make gates to keep the rich people out," his father would say. "Except when they come to pay for them."

A Magen David—a Jewish star—was braided into the gates' slender bars.

"The Ḥakhan ordered it removed," Yefet said. "But we couldn't remove it without removing the whole gate. There was a star on the *kenesa* tower also, and the Ḥakhan had it taken down. Too Jewish. It was replaced with a rising sun."

"How do you know it's rising and not setting?" Motl whispered to Esther.

"Ask the Nazis. It's up to them."

They passed through the gate and entered the *kenesa* by way of large brown doors.

"Your shoes. Take them off," Yefet said. "It's a *kenesa*, Yochanan, not a field."

"Right. Of course."

Inside, there were no pews, only carpets in the manner of a mosque. Gold-painted beams of light shone from the twin bread slices of the Ten Commandments high up between the columns of the elaborate altar. Below the tablets: the Ark.

"It's not like a synagogue," Yefet said. "There's only one Torah inside. What's good enough for Moses is good enough for us. We don't require a sequel. And if we want to know what it means, we just read it. We have God to tell us what to do. Why would we need rabbis?"

The Ḥakhan, Seraya Shapshal, entered from a side door. He wore a long, sleek silk jacket with a large, bright star brooch over an ornate embroidered shirt and matching glossy skirt. On his head, a two-coloured *shashia*, a short fez with no tassel.

"Our new Karaites," the Ḥakhan said, spreading his arms in ostentatious welcome.

To Motl he looked more Arabian Nights conjuror than religious leader. Do we bow? he wondered.

"We are Karaites," the Ḥakhan said. "Not cucumber farmers from the East, but a nation of warriors. Hitler and the Patriarch, like the Czars of yore, know that, before the betrayal of Jesus, we had travelled from Judas and Judea and so, unlike Jews, we bear no blame for his crucified demise. We hold both Jesus and Muhammad to be prophets who speak the wisdom of Moses and his Pentateuch. Though our numbers are not abundant, we are strong as the sacred oaks that take root in our burial places and in whose branches sing the plentiful birds of Heaven."

He motioned to the Persian flowers of the carpet. "Please. Sit." Shapshal slid to the floor, the susurration of his silks like a breeze shimmering through leaves. Motl and Esther lowered themselves slowly, Motl's knees crackling like footfalls on those leaves, now fallen and dry.

"We have made you Karaites, and so have preserved your lives," the Ḥakhan said. "We have been asked to produce a list of true Karaites for the National Socialists, and your names—your new names—have been inscribed there."

"We are very grateful," Esther said.

"Yes," Motl said. "You saved our hides."

"And, I hope, the flesh and souls inside. I ask two things: That you leave the country immediately. And that you transport documents that contain, along with money to aid your journey, and some other papers which must remain hidden, the list that was requested." An infinitesimal inhalation, a micro-sniff, a signal. A man emerged silently from the shadows, carrying a satchel. He opened it and removed a leather portfolio closed with a wax seal, which he held out to Motl.

It hovered there, waiting. Clearly, Motl would have to take it—to accept possession.

What could he do?

"A kind of Pony Express?" he asked.

"Hmm," Shapshal said. "You will carry these documents to Berlin. I have provided the details."

"Berlin?"

"To Himmler."

"You ask the ant to travel up the anteater's nose?"

"As Karaites, you'll be safe, and you'll be Karaites as long as you take these documents to Himmler. If you fail to deliver— Well, perhaps you know our traditional food, *kibinai*. So delicious, ground mutton and onion in a beautiful pastry. You, my little lambs, may find yourselves so minced and shrouded."

They didn't know exactly what this meant, but it didn't sound good.

It sounded like they had no choice but to deliver these documents.

"There's a man heading west who can take you part of the way," Yefet said as they left the *kenesa*. "He's going to Warsaw carrying papers like you. He'll be waiting behind the second blue Karaite house on Trakų Street."

Simhah Lutski was hairy and small, more wiry coyote than man, and he greeted them from the back seat of the dingy black car they found parked, as expected, behind the blue Karaite house.

"Welcome! Yochanan Firrouz and Sima Babovich. Already I know your names. They told me! Who will drive? I suppose it'll be Yochanan. I don't drive, but I am a skilled passenger. I can sit, I can sing, I can tell stories, and I sleep. And though I have no meat or cheese, I do have some bread."

Esther and Motl had a brief exchange. Though a woman at the wheel would attract more attention, it was better that Esther drove, as Motl's success in refraining from contact with trees, soldiers or ordinary citizens was not assured as he did not know how to drive.

Motl, wearing the satchel, walked around and climbed aboard the passenger side. "I ride shotgun," he said to Esther. "Though you hold the weapon."

Esther started up the car and they headed out of Trakai, and Simhah Lutski began demonstrating his exemplary abilities as a passenger.

"I was thinking of way back when everything was wild frontier, except for the Garden of Eden. You could hear a grunting and a snoring. It was Adam asleep on the ground. He was dreaming whatever there was for the first human to dream. He was lonesome by himself except for all the green things and fruits and animals. And then his rib became a woman. What seemed made of man became woman. She was there all along in the man's body. The Eve of Adam became her own Eve. And after, you could also make an Adam out of Eve. There was never two separate things, man and woman. They were always part of the one thing. One thing becoming another. A fleshy human thing in the middle of Eden that wanted an apple. I mean, this was before shoes.

"Also, belly buttons. When you look at the paintings, Adam and Eve both have them, right in the middle of their perfect hairless bellies, just above the leaves. If Adam and Eve weren't born but made, why did they have belly buttons? Was God just practising making belly buttons to make sure he knew how? Or was it where the snake bit them while pretending to be an umbilical cord, all part of its sneaky knowledgy convincing act?

"I want to ask about this, hear what the sages think, the ones who sit up late into the night, pull their long beards and argue in dusty libraries for hundreds of years. But the Karaites say that you don't get to ask these wise men, you just have to read the book. I'd like a guide. It's okay to walk around, but it's better to have a map if you want to get to where you're going.

"Still, it's as they say, better a live Karaite than a dead Jew."

"Right," Motl said. "Can't ride a horse if you're dead. Besides, in these times, being alive is the best revenge."

"Where are we going?" Lutski asked. "The fastest way to Warsaw is usually toward Warsaw."

"First, an errand," Esther said.

"The Ḥakhan gave you another mission?"

"Don't worry. You can wait in the car. Unless it's not safe. Then you hide."

"We're going to Ponary," Motl said. "Karaite vigilantes coming to take back what's ours. Then we'll mosey on west to Warsaw and Berlin. Where the sun sinks like the heart of an executed man over the rest of the Reich. Where our little job for the Ḥakhan will end and we can escape the Reich. And my original quest can begin. Like Adam, I intend to make a new life from a lost part of myself."

"But Ponary . . ." Lutski protested. "While I was away, my family was taken there. Afterwards, I saw villagers wearing their clothes. Heard them say, 'I bought this jacket for fifty kopeks but found five hundred sewn into the lining.' Maybe that was my family's five hundred kopeks."

"We're Karaites now," Motl said. "Outlaws dressed as tinkers and traders, pedlars and opportunists. We'll ride into town, say we're looking to buy watches, clothes, eyeglasses, gold teeth.

We'll be practically invisible among so many other people looking for deals. Nothing hides you like capitalism."

"What is it you need to take back?"

"My mother. My sister. If they're alive," Motl said. "They're like gold—except they complain more."

Close to Ponary, they saw Lithuanians walking in the opposite direction along the roadside as if on the Oregon Trail. Jews also, walking or packed like soon-not-to-be-livestock into trucks, herded by men with guns. Lithuanians. Germans.

An *Einsatzgruppen* checkpoint. Rifles pointed through the windows.

Who are you? Where are you going?

"Vilnius. It's not safe here. We're Karaites. We go to our community," Esther said.

"Karaites? You mean Jews?"

"No, no. Do we look Jewish? Here are our papers."

A soldier held the documents by their corners, turning them over, regarding them as if holding a dead rat by its tail, looking for plague.

"Karaites?"

"Yes—we go to our Ḥakhan, our leader, at the *kenesa*, our church. And maybe, on the way, get a deal on a suit or a dress or some new shoes."

The soldier grinned knowingly. "*Ja. Sehr gut.* Many have been vacated by their former occupants." He waved them on. "Also, watches and gold teeth," he called as they drove away.

"It's true?" Lutski asked. "We could buy these things? I have only little money. I could use something to trade. If I'm to end up in Warsaw, I don't want to starve. When I was a boy, I had to steal bread from those who stole bread. And often it came with a side of fist. But you feel less hungry when you're hurt. Or unconscious."

Some minutes later, they saw a cart piled with clothes and a variety of baskets stopped at the side of the road. "Let me out," Lutski said. "Wait while I buy."

Esther hit the brakes and Lutski ran like a mustang through a gate toward the plunder.

"I leave him to his stolen teeth," Esther said. "May they help him smile." And she drove away.

Ponary had been designed as a Soviet fuel depot deep in the forest south of Vilnius, but never completed. Now the pits excavated for oil storage tanks were a place to execute Jews. Esther negotiated the car down a gravel track and parked in a space between trees. They disguised the car with branches, leaves and dirt and decided to wait until nightfall to creep close to the pits.

The moon was full and luminous as they wove through the trees to the edge of the woods, making a shadow forest of the dark pines' columns on the clearing. Near them, a boy, about eleven, slept against a large accordion in the black lee of a shack, an arm slung over the instrument as if they were two siblings sharing a bed, or a boy and his hound snoozing. A star was sewn onto his jacket, its yellow turned night grey.

"If we succeed, this is a quest. If not, it's a pilgrimage," Motl said to Esther.

The boy sat up, looked quickly round. "Who is it?" he whispered.

"Come with us," Esther whispered back. "We'll help you."

"I can't. They'll find me and kill me. Or my family," he said. "I'm only here because at the end of the day, they want music." He looked fondly, regretfully, at the accordion. "Polkas. And waltzes, mostly."

Motl passed him one of Simhah's loaves. "Eat."

The boy scanned them suspiciously, then took the bread and ate it with desperate enthusiasm. When it was gone, he turned his gaze on Motl and Esther. His eyes: the world was nothing but sorrow and longing.

Motl passed him more bread. As the boy ate, he and Esther surveyed the field beyond him, filled with uneven grass, small hillocks and ditches. They tried to understand, and gradually they came to see the incomprehensible. The ditches were filled with bodies.

"Some crawl away," the boy said after he'd finished a second small loaf. "Wounded but not killed. They wait under the other bodies until night, when they can escape. They run or creep into the forest. I don't know what happens then."

Motl and Esther imagined the bodies, ghosts awoken from the nightmare ditches, disappearing like mist between the trees. Alive, but their lives scarcely more certain or solid than will-o'-the-wisps. Desperation, sorrow and will an uncertain current, fluttering them forward.

Why had he returned Esther to this Boot Hill of horror and desolation? It was weeks since his sister had slipped into line behind his mother and enabled Esther's escape into these woods.

"How could I have dreamed they were alive?" Motl said. "I imagined my mother escaping, if only to keep cooking in the face of history. I could hear her saying, 'What is history compared with my soup? What did history ever do for me?' Even if they are alive, they're long gone. How could we find them? They've disappeared into war. It is like soup, everything boiled beyond recognition."

"Of course, it's terrifying and probably futile," Esther said. "But we must try to learn the stories of those that are living as well as those that are dead."

They sat beside the boy, who eventually drifted to sleep as the moon set.

Esther—once again in the place where her death had been certain and where she'd been saved—remained silent, her arms wrapped around Motl.

A bird call from in the forest and a flutter of motion, the scurry of an animal.

"Come with us," Esther said just before dawn, shaking the boy. "Your parents want you to escape. Maybe the soldiers don't know it yet, but eventually they will kill you. And your family."

The boy gazed at her, considering, but before he had decided, they all heard footfalls. Two Nazi sentries, rifles rested on their hips, striding across the grass. The boy stood suddenly and dashed toward the woods.

Gunfire resounded against the trees, the boy's back filling with patches of blood, dark grey in the pre-dawn light. The boy kept running as if untouched. Then he fell forward, his reaching fingers resting on the soft loam of the forest floor.

"*Ja*," said one of the sentries. "*Ja*."

Motl and Esther pressed themselves against the shack's wall, shimmying around the far side, the few feet between their hiding place and the forest a second of naked vulnerability.

"Now," Motl whispered, and keeping the shack between themselves and the soldiers, they made three ridiculously exaggerated

What Time Is It, Mr. Wolf? strides into the trees, then crouched down and waddled deeper into the woods.

They said nothing about the boy.

What was there to say about the boy?

What waltzes did he play? Who taught him accordion? What was his name?

The stars above them a thousand knives. They found the car deep in the woods, still buried in its sarcophagus of branches, dirt and leaves. Thankfully, it hadn't been discovered. They cleared it off and drove it back to the road leading away from Ponary. They couldn't risk being on the road, yet they couldn't risk being near Ponary. They crept along, taking side roads, until finally they chose a small path, ropy and rutted, that snaked into a grove of trees. They rumbled the car slowly into the woods, not certain where the path would lead and what they'd discover at its end. A witch's cottage, a bear's den, or *Einsatzgruppen* and their Lithuanian collaborators dancing around a fire, picking their teeth with the bones of children and roasting Rumpelstiltskin on a spit. "Admit it. It's really Rabbi Stilt*stein*, isn't it?" they'd say.

"This road couldn't be German," Esther said. "The infrastructure of evil is well paved."

They parked, then lay down together in the back seat of the car.

"Okay, cowboy," Esther said, kissing Motl. "We'll use each other as blankets, see what dawn brings."

Motl lying in the dark, listening to the twitching around him, rodents, Esther, trees, restlessness. Outside, the defeated exhalation of the wind. What could it do? If it lifted the killers up, it'd have to put them down somewhere.

A creak, likely one branch rubbing against another. The sound, vivid as scent, twitched in his mind. The scrape of a violin. A memory.

He was a small boy and someone—was it Hershel, the neighbour?—had brought a fiddle into the kitchen. Its voice was like his grandmother's, raspy and indomitable. But it rocked and swayed, whereas old Faigel's jowls were the only thing that moved unless she was cheek-pinching or sighing the pains of her ancient bones.

They'd pushed the chairs aside, along with the Shabbos table with its white cloth and braided loaves. The silver-bright candlesticks burning low.

His father began to croak his own song along with the fiddle. Ay yi yi.

Oy yoi yoi, he sang, and rocked back and forth.

He was short and squat, with thick blacksmith arms and a white, trimmed beard below his round spectacles, which glinted in candlelight. He had cleaned the soot and ash and grime of the forge from his hands and arms and face and wore a fresh new apron as if he would spend his day of rest ostentatiously demonstrating his worklessness.

Lili lili lili li, he sang with the fiddler, who sawed a roiling *nigun*, a wordless song, or rather one to be sung with only lilting syllables, each sound meaningless individually but, taken together, able to carry whatever burden of joy or sorrow the singer wished.

Then his father reached out for his mother, sitting stolidly at the table beside her own mother. "Gitl," he said. "It's Shabbos. We must dance."

"I look like a girl? A *maideleh* with a figure like a sapling, maybe?"

"You do to me. At least when there's music."

Ay yi yi yi. And he took her hand in his and pulled her toward him. Nijinsky and Pavlova they were not. More like Wild Bill Hickok and Oliver Hardy, Stan Laurel and Calamity Jane.

For one moment, as they torqued around the kitchen, Motl saw what might be a smile wrestling with his mother's pursed lips.

Then—oy yoi yoi—his father reached for him and he was dancing between his parents as if between two bears.

He was giggling and his father kissed the crown of his head and his mother said, "One day you'll have a family of your own."

And Faigel, his grandmother, sighed. And the fiddler began another tune. Lili lili li, his father sang, and Motl joined in, almost inaudibly, his thin voice cracking, a small bird being born from an egg.

⊰ PART TWO ⊱

When the woodsman first carried his axe into
the forest, the trees whispered to each other,
"At least the handle is one of us!"

—TURKISH PROVERB

I

ON THE ROAD TO
THE VILNIUS GHETTO

Light beams filter through the trees and into the car window. Esther and Motl awake together in the back seat.

"The ghetto," Motl said. "We'll find them in the ghetto."

"Which one?"

"Vilnius. It's closer."

"No, I meant which family member?"

"Very funny. There's an old saying—maybe you know it? It takes a hero to avoid a wisecrack."

"Like that one."

"Glad you understand," Motl said.

"I do. And Motl—Motl—I'll go with you, but you do know that there's little chance that . . ."

"I know. I still have to look."

"And after the ghetto, we'll take the Karaite papers west?"

"Yes," he said, though he didn't sound entirely sure. "Whatever they turn out to be—I don't dare break the seal."

"My grandfather used to tell this story," Esther said. "You're in a train travelling from Pinsk to Minsk. A man across from you says, 'Oy, am I thoisty.' Then again, 'Oy, am I thoisty.' For hours, 'Oy, am I thoisty. Oy, am I thoisty.' And again, 'Oy, am I thoisty.' You can't take it anymore. When the train stops, you jump up, burst out of the compartment, slide open the train-car door, run out onto the platform, return with a tall glass of water. 'Here,' you say, as if you had found Yahshua's Grail itself filled to the golden brim with sacred water from a tap in the train station and would extinguish this man's holy excoriating fire. 'Slake your thirst, my friend. You say it is great and unrelenting. You say you suffer much. You say you suffer long. Not even when we were slaves in Egypt did Jews suffer so. And as for me, I suffer just hearing about it.'

"The man raises the glass in both hands like the victory cup of a great Viking then drinks the water in one long gulp. He smiles, his body opening like a river fanning wide into the sea. Before long, the train begins to move and you both settle—blessedly relieved, content, sated—back into your seats. Through the window, the land in its infinite variation passes by. Farms. Trees. Villages. Cows. Villages. Trees. Farms. More cows. Time passes. Five minutes. Ten. Then the man begins, an expression of exquisite sorrow on his face, a look of harrowing, soul-grieving memory in his eyes. 'Oy, was I thoisty. Oy, was I thoisty.' He claps his hand against his brow, holds his other out into the unforgiving air before him. 'Oy, was I thoisty.'

"'And what does this story mean?' my grandfather would ask. 'Cossacks may dance and kill, but Jews can kvetch. Also, life is suffering. It's either now or soon or is just about to happen. And what can you do? Don't travel from Pinsk to Minsk. Go somewhere else. The world is stuffed full of other places. You'd think it would *plotz*.'

"So we'll not go to Pinsk or to Minsk. We'll go to Vilnius," Esther said.

"Also," Motl said, "these days, it's best to avoid trains."

Back on the main road, northeast to Vilnius, they travelled through territory that was Lithuanian, Polish, Russian, then Lithuanian, then Polish, then Soviet, then German. And everywhere stuffed full of Litvaks. Those who kvetched, who sang, who studied, who danced, who braided bread and welcomed each Sabbath with resigned yet vital fortitude. Those who were bitter but did it anyway. Those who were Jewish only to others. Or to Nazis. Those who weren't Jewish until they were. Those whose mothers wished they were more Jewish. The I'm-only-staying-alive-to-see-your-bar-mitzvah grandfathers. The secular Jews. The I-don't-believe-in-God-but-I've-got-this-joke-about-Him-anyway Jews. Those who read and read and read and argued. Two Jews but three opinions. Or one Jew but three opinions anyway. And all of them wrong, even to the Jew himself. What's a life without argument? Oh yes. Death. Except in these times. We'd be fine to take life in almost any form since it seems there's so little of it going around. And what's left is marched, starved, rounded up and extinguished the way yellow stars are doused by the black milk of day.

After a while, "So we're really going to the ghetto?"

"Yes," Motl said.

"But we are no longer Jews. We're Karaites."

Then a gunshot. Through the passenger-side window, a single hole; through Motl's Karaite hat, two holes, on entry and exit; through the scarf Esther wore around her head, many holes as the bullet found its way through multiple folds, then through the driver's side window, and flew free into the air, the air itself one vast and all-encompassing hole, an absence.

"We're lucky," Esther said.

"Or the shooter is."

"Is it a warning?"

"What's it saying?"

"Don't have a big head? Life is random in beautiful, precise and surprising ways, but also horrifying and arbitrary?"

"I think it is saying, 'Drive faster.'"

Esther stepped hard on the accelerator, and the engine nickered as it strained to comply.

"Do you think they were shooting at us?"

"Maybe. Or at someone across the road."

"Or just into the air. Practising. Trying out the gun."

"Or just needing to shoot."

"At the world?"

"Maybe."

"And we got in the way."

"The way America got in Columbus's way?"

"It's one thing to aim. It's another to pull the trigger."

"I've shot a gun and I've seen them fall," Esther said. "What's inside me then? 'Oh, please, get up, get up. Let me help you up.'"

Train tracks crossed the road and, ahead to one side, they saw a railroad station on an oasis of bare red soil.

"Sure fancy some vittles," Motl said.

"Vittles?"

"Breakfast."

Esther pulled onto the shoulder near the station. An old Jewish couple, stooped, defeated, hopeful, holding a suitcase that couldn't even imagine having had better days, stood on the dirt outside the station since Jews were forbidden public transport, couldn't use the sidewalks, had to walk in single file near the gutter. In front of them stood an abbreviated man like an oil slick, the twin beetles of his moustache twitching as he grifted them.

"For only fifty rubles, I can send money, or letters or parcels filled with any necessaries, to your family in the work camp. In Ponary. Or the other work camps. The Seventh Fort or the Fifth."

"Do you know where our grandson is, our Johnny? Where he has been taken? To which work camp?" the old man said.

If he'd been taken to Ponary or either of the Forts, the only work he was doing was keeping the other corpses company. Maybe the last glow of his cells gave consolation or companionship to his neighbours.

"I know people. Fifty rubles and I can take a message, another fifty I can bring one back. I could do this for free, but in these difficult times a man has to eat, as I'm sure you understand. My children. I have many and they are thin."

The old man pulled out a wallet, more dim and worn than he was, and extracted some bills. The grifter winced a rodent smile, pocketed the money before the couple could hesitate and reconsider.

"The message. What is the message for your boy?" He now had in his hand a grim-looking little notebook and a greasy pencil stump.

The man wrote down the missive wheezed by the old grandfather and amended by the doleful emendations of the old woman, pulling on her husband's sleeve.

"Soon. Soon he'll receive the message, and soon you'll receive news back. You have my word." Then the man slid back into the train station, a slurry of deception.

"Good. Good. Soon we'll hear from our boy, our Johnny," the old man was saying as Esther and Motl passed him, hoping their Karaite disguise held.

Inside, there was neither fry bread, biscuits, succotash, beans nor chuckwagon stew, only a ticket agent standing behind the bars of his wicket, drinking tea. Those nearby and on the platform gave only a quick, wary glance at Motl and Esther—Yochanan Firrouz and Sima Babovich. In such times, divergence was dangerous. Best to be part of the forest rather than be seen as one of the trees. Neither Christian nor Jew, Karaites were exotic anxiety.

"I know this tale," Motl said. "We're strangers come to town. We ride in, and there's a chorus on the verandah, men leaning on the back legs of chairs, guns ready. Their women, curious, spying us through the break in the curtains, troubled by the anticipation of story and what comes from outside."

An intense young man in a large coat and slanted hat approached, tipped his head to a corner of the room. "Over there. Let's speak." He was a stew of Roy Rogers and Groucho Marx—round glasses, black moustache, smooth face, earnest smile.

"I've been watching you," he said. "Sure you've got that headgear, but I don't believe you're Karaite—you don't move like Karaites. But you'll be useful." He smiled, earnestly but slyly also. "We're all outlaws. Part of the resistance. And you're on your way . . . where? To the ghetto?"

Something in one of their faces must have confirmed it.

"Good. Then we can help each other. If you want to get into the ghetto without too many questions, you need me.

"A few days ago, I stood before a minefield. I watched as a black bird circled then landed. An explosion and soon its wings were smoke. 'Only smoke, smoke, hovering smoke.' I had to cross. To stay where I was would be death. To walk would be death. Where to step, to place my feet? So I imagined a song. I imagined a song and I stepped to its rhythm. Li-li-li-li. Li-li-li-li. I stepped into the field. I walked a mile and here I am and only part of me is smoke. Not more than before. And what was the song? Maybe help remember me what it was, because after that walk, I don't recall.

"But I remember other things. On Yom Kippur, the very Day of Atonement, I witnessed the 'cleansing' of the Small Ghetto and its people. Proving that our God is a poet, a good poet, but a *mamzer*, and a shmuck. Now only the Large Ghetto remains. How did I survive? I hid in a coffin. It wasn't difficult. As I said, part of me was already dead. And while I was in there, I wrote a poem. I said the coffin was a boat, an ark, my cradle, a badly made suit. Unfortunately, not an escape pod. But here I am. A partisan. And you're going to help."

"What do you need—an editor?" Esther said.

"Some would say, but being edited is the very thing we're trying to avoid. We need to smuggle goods into the ghetto."

"I'm looking for my mother and sister," Motl said. "Gitl and Chaya."

"Chaya saved my life," Esther said. "So you'll help us also."

The man—he went by Avram—said, "You must wear this to be allowed in."

An iron badge pressed with a star and an ID number.

"Now I'm Indian," Motl said. "Or Inuit. This year, there's a law. They must wear number tags in Canada too. I read this."

They would be Jews disguised as Karaites disguised as Jews.

"But wait until we're at the gates. It doesn't pay to be Jewish too soon."

They retrieved Avram's suitcases from a locker and then walked back to the car. Once inside, the man pulled some cheese from his pocket and fragments of what were once crackers and ate distractedly.

They parked the car amidst the dust and empty oil cans in the garage of an abandoned house near the ghetto. Avram took out the suitcases and they tucked the contents under their clothes. Motl slung the satchel over his shoulder and they began walking to the ghetto.

"My house is down there," Motl said, pointing to Visų Šventųjų Street. "I don't want to see what's happened to it, or who's moved in."

A tall wooden barricade blocked Rudnicki Street, the entrance to the ghetto, along with a sentry box and a sign that forbade the transport of food and wood inside. Also, *Achtung! Seuchengefahr.* A warning about the danger of contagion. Two Jewish Ghetto Police armed with German rifles stood guard.

Motl imagined the guns pointed interrogatingly at his face. "Smugglers? Contraband? You've got us all wrong?" he'd say.

But instead, Avram walked nonchalantly up to the guards and offered a wry smile. "Soon it is Shabbos," he said to them. "I brought something for the kiddush." He opened his jacket and revealed a bottle of vodka.

He told Esther and Motl to maintain a discreet distance while he did what needed to be done. They watched as one of the guards strolled around the corner and squirrelled the bottle beneath some rubble then returned to his post.

"So," Avram told the guards, "yesterday after prayers, I told God a funny story about the ghetto, but He didn't laugh. 'Guess you had to be there,' I told Him."

Grim whinnying from the three of them as Motl retrieved the bottle. Avram said, "So long," and slipped through the gates without being searched, as the guards continued to chortle.

As Esther and Motl drew near, they picked up the scent of rotgut skull varnish on the guards' breaths, noticed their red, rheumy eyes. Avram had not been the first to offer them drink.

Esther pulled back her collar, revealing her iron badge. Then Motl did the same, and also lifted the wing of his coat to expose the illicit hooch.

The other policeman took the bottle from him with a grin and went to nestle it beneath the rubble.

"What happened to the first donation?" he asked his colleague when he returned.

"I left it right there," he said. "For safekeeping."

"Hey," Esther said, interrupting their musing on the first bottle's current location. "I just heard this good joke. A professor had a mummy and worked for years to figure out what pharaoh it was. Eventually, the mummy was confiscated by the SS. The next day, the professor got a call. 'We know the mummy's name.' 'Herr Obergruppenführer, how did you find out so quickly?' the professor asked. 'It was easy,' the officer said. 'He confessed.'"

Drink spins even old gags into gold, particularly when fear is involved.

On another wave of the guards' laughter, Esther and Motl

walked past the barricade. They found Avram waiting for them in the doorway of what had been a tailor's shop.

"Come." They crept through the convolutions of Vilna's narrow alleys. Jewish rats attempting an arcane maze.

"Shh," Avram warned, scouting for watchful eyes as they ducked into a short lane. Then he shifted two dented garbage bins in an alcove and raised a maimed hatch. Down steep steps and into a basement gloaming green in the dim light. Three small windows covered in mould. "They open onto an inside air shaft, not to the outside," Avram said. "As Solomon said, 'For God will judge every deed, along with every secret, whether good or evil.' And in the meantime, it's best to keep your secrets hidden from the Germans. Now, for what you have concealed."

Guns, meat, books. The Holy Trinity of the Jewish resistance.

Esther had several salamis tucked around her stockinged thighs, a portfolio crammed with papers strapped to her back and bullets stuffed into her brassiere. And she'd weaponized her décolletage: between her breasts, her pistol.

Motl: the satchel; in his pants, a gun; around his waist, a leather journal, a book of poems in Yiddish; smoked meat in his socks. "Glad there were no dogs."

Avram had books corseted under his clothes, packages of smoked meat wrapped around his legs. Hunting knives in his socks.

"We hide books and papers down here, the weapons we keep elsewhere," Avram explained. "In walls, in mattresses, in the false bottoms of buckets. We carry forbidden papers mixed in with the documents the Nazis want us to collect. They want them for their Institute for the Study of the Jewish Question because, they say, there'll be no one to ask once they've erased us all."

"Like the Indianers. Maybe they'll dress like us too."

"This portfolio"—he removed it from beneath the straps holding it to Esther—"is filled with drawings by my friend Marc Chagall. And this journal"—he took a book from the waistband of his pants—"is Theodor Herzl's diary."

"And the book of poems?"

"Mine. If I'm risking my life, I need my own weapon against death."

Esther took the portfolio and extracted a page. Chagall's sketch of a dead Jesus in a Jewish prayer shawl, lifted down from the Cross and held tenderly by a chicken-headed man with curly Jewish hair. An angel with blue wings. A three-flamed menorah. It was a William Blake vision drawn by the earnest hand of a sad child.

"The least Nazi thing I can imagine," Avram said of the drawing. "Now the food. We give it to those who need it most—children, the old. Pregnant women. For them, we need to put meat on the bones of two skeletons."

"And the guns?"

"We want to be ready."

"For what?"

"Who knows? But that's even more reason to be ready."

Avram removed some brickwork, wrapped the books in cloth, placed them in the hollow then returned the bricks. A Nazi would observe only wall. "'Help us turn to You, and we shall return. Renew our lives as in days of old,'" Avram said. The synagogue prayer when returning the Torah to the Ark. "Now to find your sister. And your mother."

Motl managed to joke, "When I find her, I'll ask, like every waiter attending a tableful of Jews, 'Is anything okay?'"

———

They headed for a makeshift community centre in an unused Yiddish theatre. "A good place to begin," Avram said. "We'll ask if anyone's seen them."

Those in the ghetto were in the business of knowing who was there and who was gone.

There was a group of women kibitzing at a table in the lobby.

"Let me tell you, I know of one good Lithuanian," a woman called Chava said.

"Maybe one, but not two," another replied.

"All right, so maybe only one, but listen," Chava said. "You know that Pioneer Camp in Druskininkai where the kids go? On the first day of the war, the leader, some guy called Sviderskis, stuck them all on a train—he didn't ask for permission—and took them east into the Soviet Union, to Sarapul in Udmurtia, almost at the Urals. He saved them. See, a good man."

"Okay, so a good man. But one good apple doesn't change a bad barrel."

They continued into the theatre, Motl's heart beating a little faster.

"There are many people and little space," Avram said. "Someone's cheek will recognize your mother's jowl if she's here."

"How to live without my mother?" Motl said. "She's your head kicked by a mule. Sure your skull hurts, but you can't survive without it. 'It's not my time,' she'd say. 'I'm busy. I'm still raising a child. A Jewish mother's always raising a child.'"

"Right. A Jewish child doesn't become viable until it's a doctor or lawyer. And even then."

From a seat near the front, Motl heard a voice he recognized.

Lev. His aunt's neighbour, who had disappeared with Gitl from the farm cabin.

"You're here? You're safe? Where's my mother?"

"Motl," Lev said. "Can it really be you?"

"Depends who's asking."

"Let me embrace you, my Motl. I thought I'd never see you again."

"What happened to my mother?"

"Gitl . . ."

"Yes. I know her name."

"I had no choice. They came to the cabin at night. I was in the field making a pish on flowers. I called for help and your mother came out. They took us both away. Here. They clubbed me with the butt of a rifle." He touched a puffy scar running along the side of his face. "They beat me."

"And my mother?"

Lev looked down. "Also."

"You gave her to them."

Esther placed her hand on Motl's chest as he made to rush Lev. "Motl," she said.

"That's not how it was," Lev said.

"Then where is she? At Ponary? At a fort? In a ditch? Wherever she is, it's because of you. Where's the gun, Esther? I'm going to shoot this traitor right in his poison heart. Give me the gun."

"Motl," Lev said. "I was terrified and so I shouted. I didn't mean to call for her. I was calling for you, but you were too drunk to wake up."

"So where is she?"

"We were thrown in a wagon with others. They drove us somewhere, then locked us in a barn. There was a farmer who wanted us to strip naked, to steal our clothes and sell them, but also to shame us. When he said to your mother, 'Take off your dress. Take everything off,' I punched him. I knocked him down. Then I ran. They shot at me, but I escaped into the forest."

"But you didn't bring my mother with you?"

"What could I do? I had to run."

"But where is she now?"

"I don't know."

"And my sister?"

Lev was silent.

2

What family? Which town? What neighbourhood? Who the father? The mother? Triangulation on top of triangulation like a Jewish star. A taxonomy of Yids. It was *that* Chaya they were looking for. *That* Gitl. Motl the brother. An encyclopedia of story, the trail twisting across Lithuania from Kaunas to Ponary and—if the constellations of yellow stars allowed it and Gitl had crawled from the grim pit—perhaps now to Vilnius. Lev had left her in the barn and he had not seen her here, but he had not been in the ghetto for long, his path having taken him into forests, attics, cowsheds and swamps. And the ghetto was actually two ghettos, one beside the other, separated by Niemiecka Street, their single entrances on opposite sides so no one entering or leaving the two ghettos could see each other.

The large ghetto and the small one, the division created by the Nazis on the principle that one hand wouldn't know what the other was doing, or rather, neither would know what the Nazis had planned. Perhaps Chaya was in the Small Ghetto. Avram would send a message. He had ways. Though he'd said that ghetto had already been "cleansed."

Evening. Moon in the sky over the narrow streets and their

arches. Motl wasn't expecting it, but there it was, pale, docile, obtuse as a cow.

In the night, they were offered blankets and floor space in a house as crammed as a stable. Children, old men and women, parents and the unmarried roosted on the landings of stairs, in corridors, kitchens, attics and closets. Under tables, on couches, chairs, carpets and bare floor. First, though, they would share what food they had. Bread. Some cheese. Cabbage. Potatoes.

Esther: "If only we still had salami in our pants."

Motl: "You don't know the half of it."

Two brothers—Jakob and Abe—were chawing at some obscure foodstuff on the landing. They had a flask under their blankets, and took alternate swigs between bites, becoming louder with each snort.

"I'm older," Jakob said.

"No. It's me," Abe said.

"You're wrong. I was born first."

"That doesn't make you older!"

"It does!"

"Not necessarily. I'd ask Mom and Dad—but they're dead."

They each had another gulp, and then their bleary eyes came to rest on Motl.

"Wait. That guy down there."

"Who?"

"The new guy."

"Motl?"

"Yes."

"He's older than me."

"I know."

"I've something to tell him." Abe staggered to his feet, gripping the banister against the convulsing of the world around him, and lurched downstairs.

He bent close enough to Motl that Motl was able to definitively determine the young colt's age by a close yet involuntary examination of the occlusal surfaces of his lower incisors.

"Motl," the youth said. "Motl. I have something to say. I have something I must tell you."

In such circumstances, an appropriate response is both irrelevant and impossible.

"Your sister is Chaya?"

"Yes," Motl said, suppressing hope, expecting spittle.

"I saw her. Here. In Vilnius. It was when the Germans came and made Rabbi Kessler take his clothes off. They made everyone take their clothes off. They piled a heap of Torahs in the middle of Żydų Strasse and set them on fire. They made the rabbi dance in the flames until he died. They made your sister dance in the flames too. Then she died. Sorry."

The vodka-sloshed youth turned and staggered back toward the stairs, achieved the second step and toppled back, insensate and silent.

Motl said nothing, his insides a braid of impossible feelings. What to do now?

What was there to do? Motl and Esther turned to their bread and cabbage and those who had shared their meagre biscuit supply. Hershel, Ruth, Isaak, Viktor, Bela, Pinchas. A woman, Chava, passed them each a section of knobbly apple.

"My father was a teacher in the yeshiva," Chava said. "He had no sons, so he taught me. Torah and Talmud, everything the sages said, all their teachings, all their stories. But everything's different now. The only thing left, the only story, is this world."

Esther said, "Think I'd rather hear about Exodus. I'd rather be whipped, spend the rest of my life building pyramids, kowtowing on my knees and sticking my nose in the sand before pharaohs."

"If I got to choose, I'd rather this was Egypt too. A few boils, bugs, blood. And it was only their first-born," Hershel said. "They had others."

"Why's God doing this to us? Why can't He allow us peace?" said Isaak, the old man.

"Maybe He prefers us to suffer?" Chava said.

"What happened to Him that He takes it out on us?" Bela asked.

"And what kind of home," Motl asked, "could He have had without a mother?"

"It's not God, it's the Nazis," said Hershel. "God sucked back all the kiddush wine and scrammed off to His dacha outside of Heaven, far from head office with its secretaries, angels and all-powerful Holy red phone, which He left off its divine hook in case He heard it dinging on the other side of the clouds. He's not involved in this. He's gone."

"Not to mention He doesn't exist," Chava said.

"My father would say He created everything, including atheism," Bela said.

"And *my* father would say that atheism created Him," Pinchas said, "so we had something to not believe in."

"Why make more? There's more than enough of that already," Hershel said.

"When my mother was ill, her body knotted by pain, I was helping her shuffle from porch to table," Esther said. "And in the few feet between, she told me that once, as a girl, during the revolution, she'd watched soldiers take her neighbours to the end of the street. They shot them, then piled the bodies on a wagon with others who had starved to death. The wagon trundled by her front gate and it was then, she said, at sixteen, that she knew she no longer believed in God. She lived on to spite Him, in spite of Him, because she would not be bested by the world or, at least, its bitterness. Until she was."

"If you believe the world exists outside of you, then it does. If you don't, there's no way to prove it's actually there—no matter how many times someone punches you in the face," Chava said.

"I could make this war up?" Hershel said. "To create something like this—it takes a god or a monster."

"They say that little house painter Hitler—with his you-have-to-be-this-tall-to-ride salute and sputtering-copulation-of-tractors speeches—has only one ball."

"And that makes him a monster?"

"It doesn't make him a god."

"Well, at least he hasn't used the one he has."

"Good thing he had no children. 'Sorry, kids, I invaded your bedroom.'"

"'Sorry, sweetie, I didn't attend your dance recital. I had to deal with the Jews.'"

"And the kids' haircuts? 'Make it look like a dead crow's wing, *Bitte*.'"

"Think of the bedtime stories."

"And, 'Please, Dad, we'll wash. But no showers. Baths only.'"

How does a ghetto sound at night, gates closed, streets empty, lookouts in windows, a weary vibration worrying everyone inside? Who sleeps? Sighs, grinding snores, muttering, weeping, the small sounds of intimacy, prayer, words to children, those awake shifting, twisting in makeshift beds.

Esther and Motl on a blanket in an empty kitchen. Another blanket covering them both. Esther, head on Motl's shoulder. Motl on his back, looking up into the darkness.

"Motl," she whispers, kisses his cheek, then kisses his cheek again. Her hand on his chin, his face turns toward her. She kisses his lips. Then she kisses them again.

"We can be brave," she says.

"Yup," he says, soothed for just a minute.

Sleep.

Motl in a dream of a prairie night, crammed with stars, jingling like spurs.

And howling.

3

Morning. Plonked in the middle of history, the ghetto acted as if life were normal. For now. What else to do? There were schools. Theatre. A library. Musicians. Newspapers. Children.

"Not sure I want to find out for sure about my mother," Motl said as he and Esther woke. "At least not like I learned of my sister last night."

"But maybe Avram has heard something."

"What will we do then?"

"Depends what he heard."

Shouting from the streets. Gunfire. Banging. Screams.

"*Raus. Raus.*" Out. Out.

"Soldiers."

"Hide."

"This way," Esther said, and they barrelled out the back door, racing for Avram's cellar.

When they got there, they found the bins toppled and the hatch open. They didn't risk going inside, but went down another alley and up the stairs behind a butcher shop where they'd been told the resistance met. One knock then two then another single knock. The password.

The door opened: Avram.

"Come." An inside staircase to another cellar, where Esther and Motl, together with Viktor, Avram, Moshe and Chiena—heavily pregnant—clustered in the pearlescent dusk of cobwebs. A heap of stones beside a foul hole, a broken-open sewer, three feet wide.

"Where does it go?"

"Somewhere outside the ghetto. Hopefully not right into a Nazi latrine."

"We've guns. They'll be surprised."

"'Friend or enema?'" Motl said. No one laughed.

They squeezed through, feet slipping on the slick floor. To begin, they had to crouch or almost shimmy through the narrow way. It was a challenge for Viktor, who was large, and of course Chiena, the pregnant woman. Giving birth in a sewer was far from ideal, unless one were a rat. Only the Germans imagined them that.

And they had to be silent in order to remain undetected. It would not be difficult for a Nazi to lob a grenade into the tunnels and mash them like potatoes. Or else to open a valve and flood them. Or the soldiers could lower themselves into these dank passageways like Wehrmacht terriers hunting, except with lights, rifles and sociopathic anti-Semitism.

Escaping, they moved in the dark of their burrow. They reached out blindly, one hand resting on the person before them, one hand helping them balance against the sludgy sewer wall. Where there was water, or the sudden abyss of a downward pipe, they would pass a rope between them as if navigating a peak. Jewish exodus as charm bracelet. It was a fearful place, the city's colon, toxic with waste.

At a convergence of tunnels, they discovered a ledge. A moment for food, water and rest. A grunt from Chiena. She looked at them all: a contraction.

"Wait," Avram said. As if it were within her control. Of course, he should have spoken to the baby.

Above them, soldiers on patrol visible through the sewer grate. Their boots. The staccato sibilance of German.

They felt the temptation to shoot. But instead, they would be silent. Avram motioned for them to keep moving.

Another contraction and Chiena groaned.

Scuffing of the boots above. "There's someone down there," a soldier hissed. The barrel of a rifle pushed through the grate.

"The wall," Avram whispered, and they pressed themselves against it. The reverberation of gunfire. Muzzle flash. The tunnel lit as if by fireworks. Echoes. Not the ping ping of movie shootouts. Viktor managed not to cry out when a bullet hit him, just grabbed his thigh, blood leaking between his fingers.

Chiena suppressing another groan. Esther tore a strip of cloth from her skirt and wrapped Viktor's leg.

They moved down the tunnel.

"Seems they now know we're here," Esther said to Motl.

"There are a few indications."

"What about his leg? He's limping."

"And Chiena . . ."

"Do we get out of the sewer?"

"It's not safe. Outside the ghetto we'll be certain to be killed. Inside, also," Motl said.

"Then we stay here."

———

Western tales of mine shafts ended in collapse and death. Fumes and explosions or shootouts with bandits trapped in darkness. Nothing glittering, nothing gold. Everything turned smoke and ghosts.

But then the good man, the middle-aged last-chance sheriff, a wizened tumbleweed, rolled in against the odds and changed a town's luck to sun-over-the-mountains brightness. Maybe he gets the girl, finally after all these years, becoming a mensch. Fills his drawers with new-found goolies.

What does a hero look like when the West—or the East or the borderlands—is a building in flames, a library, the roof collapsing, the books on fire. He remembers what he was reading and runs. He grabs armfuls of books and runs. He scoops children in his arms and runs. He goes down with his people then turns to story. He leaps onto the back of his horse and rides and the people see him riding for a hundred miles, a hundred years, across the vast chimerical plains and know that they too can go on, despite the burning, the killing, the tragedies and thirst. When a story falls on you, just make sure to be in the middle, like an actor in a silent film saved by the doorway.

The tunnel began to slope down. They held on, careful not to lose their footing and slide as if in a chute, falling into further darkness and what else?

They reached a cavern and a large cesspool, which caused them to grimace in its reek. Scuttling. Cold vapours. Viktor clutching his leg, grimacing. Chiena, labouring, sobbing with each pain.

On a brick shore, they took off their jackets and laid down the bags to make a place for her to labour. A delivery room in the underworld, necessity being the midwife of invention. Necessity making Esther a midwife, also.

"I have the parts," she said. "I myself was born, but other than that, I know nothing about it."

Chiena gasped out, "I also want to know nothing about birth. Just give me morphine and twilight sleep." She laid her head on Esther's lap, biting her hand in an attempt to keep quiet, but her agony was still clear. Esther stroked her head and spoke softly. Perhaps labour was unfamiliar to her, but pain and consolation were not.

The contractions accelerated, waves rushing in, a tide quickly pulled by moon.

Avram clambered toward the tunnel. "I'm getting help. I know where we are—I think. There's a Polish couple—allies and doctors."

She'd had to endure most of the labour while they were on the move, but the actual birth was a series of mercifully brief earthquakes, shaking and twisting through Chiena's body. Then Esther caught the child, soon placing it to feed, wet and bloody, covered in a food sack, on Chiena's breast. A boy.

She'd tied a rag around the umbilical cord, then cut it with a knife. "Welcome to the world, baby."

"Hershel, after my father," Chiena said.

"Hershel," Esther said.

Another contraction and Chiena delivered the placenta.

The baby began to suck feebly, then to wail, his tiny lungs huge with discontent, made larger by the chamber, like the long shadow of voices thrown against mountainsides.

"Shh, shh," Chiena hushed, trying to keep him at her breast. Wailing infants had been silenced when their cries threatened to reveal those hiding, suffocated in the arms that were their only world. What was one life, even one newly born and soft as oyster flesh, compared with many? Chiena softly sang to Hershel, *Makh tsi di eyglekh*, a lullaby from Łódź she had learned from a ghetto newspaper.

> *Close your little eyes,*
> *Little birds are coming,*
> *Circling around*
> *The head of your cradle.*
> *Suitcase in hand*
> *Our home in ashes*
> *We are setting out, my child,*
> *In search of luck.*

Esther embraced both mother and child, calming them both. Motl covered all three with a couple more sacks and offered food. Cheese. Pickles. Bread. Instead, mother and child slept, Esther now the one singing a quiet song. She motioned to Motl: Chiena was still bleeding. Nothing could be done but wait for Avram to return with help. Motl remained near, keeping watch while the others slept too.

They did not know if the unchanging half-light was half day or half night, nor how many hours had passed by the time Avram returned with the Polish doctor.

"I'm Dr. Chaimovitch—Tania. I don't often make house calls to such locations." She smiled at them all.

The baby was resting on Chiena, hardly moving. Chiena remained still. Esther lifted the sack so the doctor could examine both mother and child. The doctor came close, gently touching her palm to Hershel's palm-sized back. She turned her head, listening, then placed fingers on Chiena's neck. After a moment she removed her fingers, then leaned to kiss the brown swirl of Hershel's damp hair.

The doctor moved quickly, but in silence. If she were to be discovered, she would be shot with as little hesitation as with a Jew. She swaddled the baby in sacking and picked him up, cradling him against her. "I'll keep him safe," she said, and crawled toward the opening of the tunnel. "I know the way," she said, and Avram nodded.

He turned to Chiena, lying still in a pool of her own blood.

"Yitgadal v'yitkadash sh'mei raba," he said, and moved a sack to cover her face. "Now we must move on," he said. "It's not safe to stay. May she forgive us for leaving."

What do miners know of mines—the tommyknocking rumbling and cold drafts, the otherworldly slurps of water and slurry? Like everything in the western, they keep going until they can't.

And so Esther, Motl and the others pushed forward, trying—like Lot's wife—not to think of what they were leaving. Avram went first.

"'Despair is the most intense enjoyment, especially when one thinks about the hopelessness of one's position.' How apt to quote from *Notes from the Underground* when underground," Avram said.

"The most intense enjoyment isn't your own despair, it's other people's. It's hard not to appreciate what you don't have," Motl said.

"That also Dostoevsky?"

"No, Gitl. My mother."

———

The striped and jaundiced moon was visible through the street grate where the tunnel divided into three. They decided they would all take different routes to minimize the chance of discovery. If one group was caught, the others might still survive. They separated without more than a look or a nod. It wasn't the time for spoken farewells. Once they started saying goodbye to those they might never see again, when would they end?

Motl and Esther crawled into the leftmost tunnel. Above them they heard children's voices, coughing, metallic clinking, rushing water and then quiet. Light through a grate, leaves intertwined in the bars, turned their tunnel as green as if they were in pond water.

"Born again," Motl said as he lifted up the grate and pulled himself up into a small fenced yard behind a stone building. "Stay low," he said as Esther climbed out. He replaced the grate. "What gunslinging bandits roam the skirts of this stockade, I can't rightly conjecture, but they'd be pleased to use our heads for target practice."

Ducking down, they splashed themselves with water from a trough, then extracted their Karaite headwear and identity papers from Motl's satchel. Break open in case of Jewish persecution.

"Like Buffalo Bill riding for the Pony Express, we still have post to deliver." Motl indicated the Ḥakhan's portfolio.

"Berlin?"

"We'll be hiding in plain sight. They won't look for us if we're right in front of them."

"Also, if they unseal the portfolio, whatever the Ḥakhan's other papers are, the list only makes us more Karaite."

"And after that, we go to Switzerland."

"To safety."

"And new life."

Through the slats in the fence, the street looked empty. They needed to be ready to explain who they were if they were encountered, to not surprise anyone. Never startle a bear, especially a bear with a semi-automatic.

"My mother," Motl said. "She could be anywhere. And alive."

Esther waited.

"'You can't chew with someone else's teeth,' my mother would say. Also, 'Make sure it's your own tuchus you're wiping when your tuchus needs wiping.'"

"Wise words."

"I mean, when it's not possible to save those you love, you have to at least save yourself. As it says in the Torah, There's a time to plant, and a time to pluck that which is planted, a time for war and a time to plonk your keister in the saddle and ride the holy Hebrew hell out of the fire."

They slipped out the gate and into the street. "In the ghetto, we were Jews pretending to be Karaites pretending to be Jews," Motl said. "I hope they see us as Karaites and not Jews pretending to be Karaites pretending to be Jews pretending to be Karaites."

"We'll explain it to them," Esther said. "Remember when we were driving out of Trakai, Lutski taught me this Karaite blessing: *Gomitkum khadrah.*"

"'Don't shoot'?"

"In Arabic, it means 'May your week be green.'"

"Good, if you're a tree."

"Or a greenhorn."

4

It was time to round up their car, furtively grazing inside a garage near the ghetto. Two steps toward freedom, one back, though in this case freedom meant travelling like Dante down through Hell and then up toward the bright trail of Heaven's stars, namely, the cold and testicle-studded Milky Way of Motl's Swiss glacier.

They kept close to walls, feeling the need for protection, secure from gunfire, observation or storm. They came unexpectedly to the wide expanse of Didžioji Street, near the city hall.

Two soldiers raised their rifles and stepped forward as one, in their jackboots. "*Halt.*"

Motl and Esther raised their hands, then offered ID.

The first Fritz squinted at Motl's papers, then passed them to the second Fritz. He turned them over, apparently unable to decode the German symbols.

"Karaites? This means *Juden*—Jews, correct?"

As if anyone would proffer their own death warrant to armed men.

"No—*nein*—officer, sir," Esther said. "We are Karaites." She touched the silk flowing from her headdress. "Not Jews, but from Crimea. We have permission from the Reich."

Permission: To live. To survive.

The second Fritz cocked his rifle. "But you were Jews? You use Hebrew. You are—what is *das Wort?*—scroll-kissers?"

"We left Judea before the Crucifixion. Our forefathers had no part in it. Not like Jews. More like Christians."

"The Czar and the Reich allow us . . ." Motl stuttered. "The Reich Institute for Genealogical Research . . . the Deutsche Volksliste . . ."

"And we recognize Jesus as . . ."

"What is in the satchel?" The first Fritz motioned with his rifle.

Motl opened it and gave it to the second Fritz, who stirred around the contents then extracted the portfolio. He untied it to reveal the documents. Each was sealed with an antiquated red wax seal.

"Documents we are bringing to Berlin. From our Ḥakhan. Our spiritual leader. For Reichsführer Himmler."

The two men regarded the sealed documents. They looked from the papers to Motl and Esther then back to the papers, then back to Motl and Esther, likely considering ideal Platonic forms as represented by the written word versus material reality as embodied by the corporeal presence of Motl and Esther. As corporals, they had not yet received advanced training.

"*Ja,*" they said, with some trepidation. "You may go."

"*Gomitkum khadrah,*" Esther said. "As we Karaites say, 'May your week be green.'"

Except for a twilight filigree of spiders, the car appeared untouched. After they climbed in, they relaxed against the seats and sighed, an exhalation specific to neither the Karaite nor the

Jewish tradition, but rather partaking of the more general human genius for expressing relief—*ahh*—though it is possible an "oy" and a "yesiree bob" was represented in their various utterances.

5

ON THE ROAD
TO POLAND

"So, we're just going to keep barrelling west until we arrive at Himmler?"

"Take a left at Göring, second right after Goebbels. If we get to Rommel, we've gone too far."

"You know there's a war on?"

"Those heading from Fort Laramie to Montana didn't give the battle against the Indians no mind. Or those on the gold rush to California. But I do have a contact. An American Pole. Mordecai with the partisans gave me the name after I told him I was headed to Switzerland. Piotr—Peter—with the Związek Walki Zbrojnej, the ZWZ, the Union of Armed Struggle. They're publishing bogus newspapers and pamphlets horn-swoggling people into believing there's more opposition to the Nazis than is real. Nothing makes a varmint braver than other varmints."

"And nothing makes them more cowardly too."

"My mother would say that if there's one bandit at the table and ten other people talking to him, that's eleven bandits at the table."

"Or one bandit and ten scared diners. You're a regular Sancho Panza with all these proverbs."

"In the absence of wisdom, there's always my mother. Besides, our ancestors wandering in the desert didn't have time for proper jokes, so they invented one-liners."

"More portable, too."

"Sometimes it's better to just let history be a heap of fragments. Better not to connect dots, instead let it be one damn thing after another, a tragic picaresque."

"One damned person after another."

"I'm hoping, Esther, that that won't be us."

"Motl," she said, taking a hand off the wheel and touching his shoulder.

They continued west. Though many people tramped the road, they saw no Germans, neither schnitzel-fond nor *Schutzstaffel*ing, no partisans, neither arm-banded nor plain, no *Hilfspolizeitrupp*ing Lithuanians nor collaborating Poles, indeed no one *Einsatzgruppen*ing nor ersatz, not even a single anti-Semitic dog wishing to hump only Aryan strays.

Until they came to a roadblock outside the beet sugar factory at Marijampolė.

When they stopped, a townsman with a ratty moustache, a rifle and poor personal hygiene asked them to step out of the car. They stood together while he considered their haberdashery and the satchel slung over Motl's shoulder. The man was clearly not thinking very quickly.

"Stand over there," he said eventually, and they moved to the shoulder.

He climbed in the car and drove away.

"How's that for a one-liner?" Esther said.

As they walked toward the train station, they encountered an old woman who sat at a rattletrap stall selling beets. She possessed two teeth, both stained purple, enough to anchor her knobbly pipe between them. With her black babushka, her wrinkled face like an ancient creek bed and the cloud of smoke she sat within, she appeared both earthly and preternatural. An oracle. She told them that thousands of people had been killed in Marijampolė, the great majority of them Jews. "I was there," she said. Young men had been made to dig trenches then told to strip naked, climb in and lie down. Then they were shot. Next came the women and children, who didn't comply and instead rioted. The gunfire was chaos. Many were buried alive.

"The earth over the trenches moved for hours," the woman said. "Until moonrise. Many of the shooters were students from the high school and university here. They'd volunteered. They celebrated all night."

She raised her single eyebrow and asked, "Thirsty?" They nodded and she held out a bottle of home-brew vodka made from beets.

"A slug of this isn't so much belly fire as electric shock," Motl said to Esther.

"But in a good way," she replied.

Outside a factory, Motl spotted their car. "One quick quip deserves another."

They crossed the road and hid behind a pine. "If the key's there, we'll steal it back from that rustler." Motl ran beside the car and ducked down, squinting over the door. The key was on the dash along with some leather gloves.

"Lithuania was Polish was Russian was Lithuanian was Russian was German and will be Lithuanian again," Esther said. "One day it'll be repatriated, just like this car." She climbed into the driver's seat and they pulled out onto the road and drove away. Esther began to sing the last verse—the only happy one—of a song that had won a ghetto songwriting contest:

> *Like the Viliya River—liberated,*
> *The trees renewed in green,*
> *Freedom's light will soon shine*
> *Upon your face,*
> *Upon your face.*

A shout from the road behind them. As he ran out of the factory and onto the street, it wasn't exactly a light shining on the face of the man who had confiscated the car, it was more of an inner red glow. He flailed and spluttered in an idiom rich in plosives, fricatives and gutturals ripe with local colour. He shook his fist like a silent movie bad guy. "I'll get you for this, you scoundrels!"

It got dark. It got dark every night. They didn't need night to remind them of how dark things were, though it's true, endless light would have seemed a galling, unrelenting examination of what was unforgiving and cold.

Earlier, Motl had fallen asleep against the door, the sun shining through the window, bright and dark clouds floating across his closed lids. Tiny illuminated rivers red with blood. Snakes like tendrils of fire.

He climbed from a stallion, hand against its russet side, about to join Esther, who waited with a picnic basket under the cottonwoods. High overhead, a black bird with outstretched wings, lazily riding a gyre of rising air.

She had spread a blanket and laid out bread, meat slices and cheese on plates. An apple. The shake and jingle of his spurs as he walked, pushing back his hat, wiping a sleeve against his forehead's dampness.

Something sudden in the brush.

"Motl . . ." Esther called.

He leapt forward, and his fist closed around its neck. It writhed, held away from the body, tail whipping his thigh. A diamondback, its tongue flicking in and out like a guttering flame. The heel of a boot on its neck and a quick bullet to the head, the shot reverberating from the distant hills.

The fangs had sunk into Esther's leg, two red marks above her knee. A quick X with his knife and his mouth on the wound, sucking out venom. Her thigh salty and muscular, her fingers in his hair.

"Motl," Esther said, waking him. She'd parked beside a small, grim tavern. "Some food, maybe a place to stay."

A small town. A saloon. Motl knew how this worked.

They walked in.

"Karaites," Motl said, indicating themselves and their hats. They were on a mission, he said, travelling to Berlin with important documents from His Excellency Hajji Seraya Khan Shapshal, the leader of their faith. "We'd be mighty grateful for some vittles, some lodging."

"You Karaites eat cabbage rolls?" the barkeep said.

"*Pork* cabbage rolls?"

"Yes, sir."

"Then definitely, *yes*."

"And beer?"

"Certainly."

Behind the bar, the bartender lifted two formidable steins from the shelf, then pulled two enormous porcelain tap levers toward him, filling both mugs with draft. The curtain of his large moustache was something from squirrel burlesque.

Bursting through the kitchen's saloon doors, the barkeep's wife bustled toward them carrying two large plates. Butte-high stacks of cabbage rolls, perogies and a mesa of sauerkraut.

"Eat," she said. "You Karaites must be hungry. This is a time for hunger." She herself was bountiful ground meat squeezed into a dirndl. "We have beautiful bed upstairs. Feather bed to make the mattress soft. Eiderdown to keep you warm."

She fetched the steins and set them on the table, the froth sloshing onto the cloth. "You can read your future in the bubbles," she said. "Look close."

It was the first cooked meal they'd had in a long time. They ate and drank with the rapture of wolves, no time for words.

Finally, Motl indicated what was left of the foam and asked Esther, "What do you see? Ocean foam? A glacier? Spit? The future?"

"The soft bed upstairs. The feathers, the eiderdown. I'm exhausted."

Three men entered the tavern just then, japing and kibitzing. They settled at a corner table and one drew a deck of cards from his coat and slapped it down. They looked to the bartender with expectant hangdog, beer-ready faces. What a world, the least there can be is drink.

"I'm ready for shut-eye in our foamy bed," Esther said. "Let's not wait for the future. It's just upstairs." She laid her hand on Motl's, but Motl was a small boy beguiled by the corner table. One of the men ostentatiously accordioned the cards into the air and let them drop back into a pile. Another then took the deck, split the cards and shuffled them with a single hand. The third lifted the tall mug that the barkeep's wife had set on the table and, tipping his head toward the beamed ceiling, finished the beer in one glorious gulp. He exhaled with triumphant satisfaction and the three laughed together.

"Go," Esther said. "Just don't gamble both your livers. Because one's mine."

As she climbed the stairs, Motl rose and, transfixed, floated toward the men. "*Czerwony król,*" they said, indicating the open playing field of the table. "Red King."

He took a chair. The barkeep's wife, whose name he learned was Grażyna, brought him a beer, and the game began. He held his hand tightly fanned, close before his eyes, peering appraisingly at the other three over the cards. This was Slavic hold'em and Motl was ready to pony up what was required, ready to "steal the blinds" or "suck out on the river" as seasoned poker players did. The only ace in his sleeve was a cool hand. He was a Litvak stranger come into this burg, ready for soft townsfolk, a night of gambling, and then, come what may, he'd stride out of town on his own two feet, fists like Talmudic hams, and into the future.

One of his new friends, Mikolaj, deals them each two cards face down.

Frančišek puts down the small blind: two coins. Aleksander, on his left, places the big blind: four coins.

Motl, who has only a few remaining coins from the Ḥakhan, calls the big blind. Frančišek raises. Aleksander calls.

Mikolaj burns a card, flops three cards.

Motl sucks a gulp of suds. Frančišek raises the left corner of his soft mouth, the left of his eyebrow.

"Hmm," Mikolaj says.

Motl swigs another brew.

Call. Raise. Call.

Button burns a card. Reveals a turn card.

Call. Check. Raise.

Dealer burns a card. Adds the river to the community.

Call. Call. Call.

Showdown. Reveal.

Last raiser shows first. Aleksander.

Motl's shirt is lost. Tall glasses of Pilsner.

Again.

Two coins down on the first hand.

Frančišek on his left meets. Aleksander raises. Mikolaj folds.

Further suds into Motl. Where's his hoss? Right. Tied outside. Esther asleep. Another round.

Beer. Cards. The Poles click coins on the table. Again.

Motl empties another stein. He's plastered. Fully shickered.

He calls. Raises. Is on the button. Now the big blind. No more coins. What to put into the pot? What does he have of value? He gulps more malt. Mikolaj has a watch. "A farm goose," Aleksander says. "I can be trusted, ask my friends, not my wife." Frančišek has a gold chain. Motl?

"I can't stop now—not with this hand—but I have nothing left."

"Nothing? What's in that satchel?" Aleksander asks. "You keep it so close, it must be something valuable."

"The most valuable."

"So use it."

"It's too important. And what would you want with papers, anyway?"

"We're gambling here. If they're valuable to you, we'll accept them. Frančišek? Mikolaj?"

"We agree," Frančišek says, and Mikolaj nods to confirm. "Put them into the pot."

His Karaite papers? He's definitely going to win. Besides, they're of no use to them, he thinks. They won't actually keep them.

So into the pot.

Call. Raise. Check. Fold. Frančišek wins Motl's papers. Also a goose.

"For what can I sell these? How many kopeks when I go into market?" Frančišek asks. "Ach. I'll figure it out tomorrow. When I'm sober . . . Another round!"

Motl drains another stein, sings with the Poles.

I'm old and fat
I'll die soon, I fear
But Jesus, send me
where saints drink beer.

He woke on the floor beside the bed where Esther was sleeping. He'd staggered into the correct room, the only one upstairs, considered that act of orienteering a feat of extraordinary wayfinding, and, having achieved that success, pulled a yard of floor up beneath him, made a bed of nothing and so discovered sleep.

You wake and find you have no teeth. It was a night of splendid gnashing and unrecallable gnawing. Who did you bite? And where? Have they slung a leg over, ridden a pony to the next town, your teeth in their haunches? Despite his mouth tasting like a goulash of rats, Motl did have his pearly whites when he woke, but he was not the Karaite he once was, nor with the ability to prove it. What now?

"Frančišek, Frančišek," he roared. "I am sober now. Without papers, I'm not Karaite but a dead man. Save me and we'll find you some cash. Or we'll try your back window and repatriate what we need."

Esther turned and, half-awake, murmured, "Motl?"

Hard to maintain an illusion of aplomb when one is speaking from the floor.

"Esther," he said. "I lost something last evening that I must get back."

"Your dignity?"

"I reckon that was left in the Alps, years ago."

"Surely you didn't wager the car?"

"If only they'd thought of it. Or I had."

He confessed the whole sorry story, and between them they decided they had no choice but to find Frančišek's farmhouse and retrieve Motl's papers.

"And," Motl said, "take a gander . . ."

"I know," Esther said. "For the goose."

Breakfast was eggs, bacon, buttered bread.

"What's the Karaite *bracha* for bacon?" Esther whispered.

"I just cross myself: Nose. Toes. Rump and snout."

They settled with Karol, the barkeep—"Go, go, you owe me nothing. I don't know your story, but I know you are escaping. This is a small thing we can do to help. Besides, after last night, I know you have nothing."

They asked the whereabouts of Frančišek. The barn over the bridge, just before the forest. There was a painted blue chest at the end of the drive. Frančišek sold eggs from its drawers.

They found the place, just where Karol said it would be, but when they got there, the house and the barn were both on fire and the animals set loose. A pig in the road, shot through the side. Red wound on pink skin. The family, too, gunned down.

A retelling of these years too often unfolds like a *Wunderkammer* of tragedies, each set on a mahogany shelf behind glass, something to marvel at, to observe with prurient fascination, but not to grieve. The past: it's always here, just distributed unevenly, like pox on a chicken, or money. Inside some of us the past is radiant like the sacred heart, inside others it's a tumour lurking in hidden dark. But still, we tell the tale, backwards and forwards, waves pulling toward shore, or away.

They turned, drove quickly back to the tavern. Grażyna was at the door, red face wet with tears. "Aleksander just left. He told me the Nazis came before the sun was up. They thought Frančišek was hiding a family of Jews. It wasn't true. He would not take such a chance. He had family." She covered her face in a handkerchief, weeping. She handed Motl some papers. "For you."

His Karaite identification.

"Frančišek left these before he went home last night. He said he knew most of the Germans in Poland don't bother with papers. They shoot and, because they've shot, you must be someone who deserves to be shot. It's logic. He says even if you are Karaites, you're not safe. But, still better to have the papers . . . you need every chance you can get. As they say, 'If you're running from a bear, best to have both shoes.'

"Last night, Frančišek told me one more thing: you could have the papers, but you cannot have goose."

6

"Frančišek, may his memory be a blessing," Esther said as they drove quickly away.

"It is for us," Motl said, placing a finger on the papers in his jacket.

"And the memory of his family."

"I thought him simple as a plough, guileless as ducks. I did not expect such kindness."

"But, just in case, maybe next time gamble your liver instead. Or at least don't drown it, then you won't undertake such wagers."

Piertanie was only a few shanties at a crossroads, so close together if a dog in one house licked its scroggs, a dog in another would taste them. It was the woods around the town they were headed for. They hoped to find the American Pole that the partisan Mordecai had told them about.

He was in hiding in a shack hidden deep in the trees, the ZWZ—the Union of Armed Struggle—publications hidden with him, likely providing effective insulation against cold and bullets.

Motl slipped out of the car and rolled away a large boulder

blocking a path that led into the woods. Esther manoeuvred past while Motl tipped the stone back into place. He kicked up the pine needles to make the road seem less travelled—a path less trodden makes all the difference when Nazis are sniffing about—and joined Esther as she emerged from covering the car in pine branches.

Together they would seek the hideout of this outlaw. They had no plan but walked along a stream until they arrived at churning rapids, then headed west.

Mid-morning, the forest was still, few birds called, there was no wind.

Grażyna had packed them some apples and when Motl bit into one, the chomp reverberated through the silent trees.

A human disturbing our intimate quiet. A settler eating our compatriot.

There was a rustling. "Shh," Esther whispered, pointing to a gap in the trees. Something moved. There were structures there, tents of some kind, the honey-mustard colour of hide.

"Teepees?" Motl said. Then stopped. "Teepees."

What is the word for when what is inside definitively aligns with what is outside? For Motl it was a mixture of hope, sadness and disbelief.

Three Indianers strode toward them, their bows drawn but pointed at the ground. One was warrior tall, a red broom-brush of hair arcing over his pale shaven head. Another was older, a chief in a splendid headdress of red-tipped white feathers, the impressive rays of an avian sun. Both were shirtless, their chests the colour of perogies. The third man sported striking coal-black braids that hung down over a tan jacket decorated with fringe and bone.

They stopped in front of Esther and Motl, and the chief raised his hand, palm toward them.

"Howgh!"

Motl hesitated, then raised his own hand. "Howgh. *Dzień dobry.* Good morning."

"*Dzień dobry.* Good morning," the three Indianers said. They could speak Polish.

Should they trust these Indianers? Himmler had designated many groups as *Ehrenarier*—honorary Aryans—and was considering turning Indianers into Aryans too. Hitler had said that he would give them their land back when the Reich came to North America. But surely the Indianers would stand with Jews and others who had been persecuted and dispossessed. It was an ethical syllogism war would put to the test:

True strength is to fight for the weak.

Sometimes survival means siding with the strong.

Therefore the solution is . . . to hide.

"We welcome you onto our land," the Indianer with the braids said. "I am Raven Wing."

What would Motl's Indianer name be? Schnitzel Owl? Wrinklepurse? Son without Mother? Stoneless One?

"We are Karaites," Esther said. "Yochanan Firrouz and Sima Babovich."

"Lakota," Raven Wing said, indicating himself and his Indianer brothers. "This forest is our home. We live here with our wives and children, with our old men and women, our animals and our traditional knowledge."

He and his companions led them toward many teepees that circled a central fire, around which several women and men sat cross-legged, scraping hides, eating, smoking pipes. Their voices were a soothing susurration mixed with the crackling of flames and quiet laughter.

When one is on the land, one should speak the language of
the land, the language of those who live with and know the land,
its green words, the words of its wind, its trees, its animals and
spirits, the green language born when the green land itself was
born, the language learned from the land.

And if one hasn't learned this language, then one should speak
Polish. It's what all these Indianers were doing. They were speaking Polish. Their actual indigenous language.

Raven Wing motioned to Esther and Motl, indicating they
should take a seat in the circle. They were offered wooden plates
heaped with bannock and a pemmican-like jerky of dried fruit
and suet. And ham on a kaiser. And beer.

A rattling behind one of the teepees. A man in a vigorous green
robe covered in bright metal discs emerged, shaking and wailing,
gyrating in the direction of the fire. Several men pounded sticks
on a tipped-over marching band drum covered in deer hide and
ululated intently. The man continued his trembling and tintinnabulation as he entered the circle, his feet performing an obscure
scuttling, a clog dance with moccasins.

"Some countries—Czechoslovakia, for example—do not allow
men to dance this way for it is tradition that the jingle dress dance
is only permitted to women," Raven Wing explained. "But this
warrior consulted an elder and was told to dance what was in his
heart. I suppose he is jingly inside and so this is how he dances."

The older man in the feathered headdress stood up. "Chief
Eagle Feather will now tell how he killed a bear with his bare
hands and a gun," he announced.

"I was a young man then and my chest was broad as an eagle's.
It was night and the owls with their eyes like moons swept their
wings over the grasses. I was alone—my father had been shot and

my brothers taken to school far away. I was determined to be brave as I stayed in the forest, with only my gun and memories of Karl May stories of Winnetou and Old Shatterhand for company.

"What sound does a bear make padding through the forest searching for midnight blueberries and gathering salmon from the river? I fired at the branches, at leaves, at mice, at the hooting of owls, at the wind, the dark, the beating of my heart and my own fear. By the time the moon began to rise, I had only a few bullets left. I remembered the words of Intschu-tschuna, Winnetou's father, when he said that without fear an Apache knight cannot be brave."

"For me it's more 'without a gun I cannot be brave,'" Motl whispered to Esther.

Chief Eagle Feather continued. "I waited by the river until the bloom of dawn began to suffuse the sky. Then I heard a sound across the water—a deer between trees, questioning me. Could I be a man? I stood and raised my gun. The deer was in my sights, then from behind me a bear stuck its snoot into my bag of food. I turned and fired. The bear fell. I wrapped my hands around its stump-thick neck. I looked into its eyes. There was understanding between us. As you see, I still wear its claws as a sign of this around my neck."

The other Indianers nodded and clapped, so Esther and Motl nodded and clapped also. The man in the fringed coat moved to sit beside them.

"Hitler doesn't know we're on this land," he said. "If he knew, he'd march us out. Put us in a camp. Starve us. Shoot us. He only says he'd give America back to the Indianers, he doesn't mean it. But we're ready for a Little Bighorn/Battle of the Greasy Grass rather than Wounded Knee—a war we'd win. 'Honorary Aryan'? I don't want to belong to a club that wouldn't have me as a member.

"But where are you from? What are you doing here? You didn't just climb in a boat and bump into our land accidentally. We'll only believe that story once."

"We are Karaites," Motl said. "People originally from Judea and then Crimea, but we ourselves, Sima and I, have travelled far. From Trakai. From Vilnius. We're looking for a man named Piotr who lives among these trees."

"Piotr? We do not know this Piotr. However, lately a North American named Mike has come to live among us. Today he is not with us, as he lies sick in his cabin."

"Mike? Perhaps he is our Piotr by another name," Esther said to Motl. "How many can be living in these woods?"

"Besides, what would an American be doing here—hiding in Plains' site?"

A pig roasted on a spit. Further dances, speeches, stories and songs until night fell. Then, Raven Wing led Motl and Esther to Mike's cabin on the edge of the encampment. He had been laid out sick all day.

"Perhaps it was my kielbasa," Raven Wing said. "My father made it. Months ago."

"An anthropologist eats everything," Mike explained when he opened the door. "You can't learn without eating." He closed the door, vivid blue eyes sparkling as he smiled. "I told them I was too sick to attend the circle today," he said. "Sometimes my subjects' hospitality is overwhelming. Tea?" He made a place for them around the barrow of books filling his table.

A researcher from the University of Toronto, he'd been stranded in Poland because of the war. "I'm an Oneida of the Haudenosaunee Confederacy," Mike said. "Doing a dissertation on Polish Indianers. Why? Back home they prefer white people to write about the Indigenous. You know—experts. I mean, what would we Oneida know? Besides, it makes for more palatable results. Here, they don't know I'm Native," he said. "Blue eyes, blue jeans, white shirt. No feathers or fringes."

Esther and Motl peered discreetly around the cabin. It was filled with books and papers, but there were no signs of newspapers or pamphlets. How do you ask an undercover resistance fighter if they're undercover? "Excuse me, is your true identity concealed . . . and if the answer is no, how do we know if we should believe you? Also, we see your hidden publications aren't visible, so do they really not exist?"

The water boiled and Mike set a pot and some cups down. On the table in front of Esther was a ragged-eared, annotated bibliography. A partisan might fake a bibliography, but to annotate one takes an authentic egghead.

Mike provided excellent biscuits, which they opted to immerse in tea.

Then came shouting outside. Engine noise. German voices. Gunshots. The furious red of a fire burning large. Screaming. It was becoming familiar, but was no less horrifying. Before they could leave the cabin, the butt of a rifle bashed against the door. They stood up, hands in the air.

"We are taking the Indians. They will go to the camp. Who are you?"

"They're not real Indians," Mike protested. "They're—"

"Feathers, arrows, teepees. They look like Indians."

"We have papers," Esther said. "Motl, show them the papers."

"I don't look at papers," the soldier said. "Papers can be made to lie. I look at faces and then I know."

"We're Karaites," Esther said.

"Don't know what that is," the soldier said. "But from what you're wearing, you don't look like Jews or Poles. And you?" The soldier pointed his rifle at Mike, who had remained with his hands in the air, motionless. "Well, I don't know who you are, but with blue eyes you're not Gypsy, Jew or Indian. Unless you're a Communist or faggot or both?"

"*Nein*," Mike said. "Of course not. *Heil, Hitler!*" He stretched his arm out, slowly making the Nazi salute. No sudden movement when the other guy has a gun.

"*Heil, Hitler*," the soldier responded instinctually as Motl and Esther saluted also.

"Fritz!" A shout outside and the soldier turned to investigate what further Nazi-ing was required of him.

Mike grabbed some papers off one end of the table and crammed them into his briefcase. Standing on the bed, they slung themselves out the back window and into the shadows between trees. They'd creep farther into the woods while they had the chance.

"We've heard there's a cabin nearby, and a man who lives there," Motl said.

"Piotr," Mike said.

"Yes, but we must be careful. Since it wasn't you the Nazis were looking for, it's likely that Piotr was actually the one the Nazis were trying to find."

They walked some way in a stream.

"The only footprints you can track in water are Jesus's."

7

Naturally, Mike knew about Piotr. He'd sometimes taken long walks to get away from the counterfeit Indianers. Sometimes he took a copy of a Karl May novel with him so he could recognize this European Wild West.

Sometimes he couldn't see the West for the trees.

The two had not actually spoken, but Mike had seen Piotr's cabin, seen people leaving late on mostly moonless nights, plodding away with heavy rucksacks, heard them say, quiet and wistful as they departed, "Be safe, Piotr."

The cabin sat on uneven ground in a small glade. It was a kind of counterfeit, made to look as if it were abandoned, its windows covered with down-on-its-luck sacking to show no light.

"If we don't surprise him," Mike said, "we won't be surprised. By bullets, for example." And he began to sing in an elastic and nasal Western twang:

The cowboy's a-prowlin'
after cows and their cowlin's

his spurs are a jinglin'
and the ol' ki-otes call.
This cowboy's misery's
adding Injuns to injuries
shooting at everything
he knows nothing at all.

And then he yodelled, some variety of coyote tooth extraction or ontological woe. "Just so he knows we're not German," Mike said after—praise Roy Rogers—he stopped.

A small triangle of light as the sacking was lifted from the corner of a window.

"Two Jews and an Oneida," Mike announced as they came to halt twenty feet from the cabin.

"Karaites," Motl said.

"What?"

"We're Karaites."

"Right, you said that. What's a Karaite?" Mike asked.

The door opened, and a short, grisly-bearded man peered out, a combination of hobbit and rabbi.

"Quickly. Inside." Piotr scanned the surrounding forest with squirrelly vigilance.

They entered the cabin of a hoarder. Boxes covered the walls. A small space remained: a table with a mattress underneath, a chair and a printing press. Bread and cheese on the table amongst paper reams. Candlelight.

"They call me Piotr. Who are you?" he asked.

Now that they had found him, it wasn't clear to Motl and Esther what exactly they were to do since his peril seemed greater than their own. It don't pay for an outlaw to hide on the gallows of another.

"Mordecai—a partisan we stayed with in the woods back in Lithuania—told us to look for a man named Piotr, and so here we are," Esther said.

"I'm not really Piotr, but since the first Piotr is gone, I am now Piotr," the man said. "Cheese? Bread? Pamphlets, which outline the wide opposition and the conspiracy against Hitler in the Wehrmacht, including generals and officers?"

"Is that true?"

"Convince one fact to change, then maybe the rest will too."

They sat on boxes of unsupported truth and shared the bread and cheese. The meagre segments, stale and dry, required prolonged and committed engagement with the jaw. In between they spoke of Mordecai, the partisans and Lithuania.

Eventually, Piotr said, "It's probably safe for you to return to the Indianers' camp. Now that it's almost dark, the Germans will have left. There's likely food left behind and shelter where you can sleep."

He led them through the dim shapes of the forest, showed them the stepping stones to cross the river, the deer paths through the thickest woods, until they returned to the Indianers' camp.

Bodies around the remains of the fire. Blood on the naked backs of those who tried to run, headdresses like killed birds. Teepees toppled, everything strewn about, pushed over, kicked in, set on fire.

"It's just like the Wild West to the Nazis," Mike said. "They think they're better than the people here and the land is for the taking, no one from the outside world watching or caring what they do. Hitler wrote, 'When we eat a piece of bread, why worry the soil that produced it was won by the sword. When we eat wheat from Canada, we don't think about decimated Indians.'

Hitler said, 'The Volga is our Mississippi,' so the Germans can act as innocently as the Americans did."

A moaning from under a fallen teepee.

"Motl," Esther called. Together they pulled the skins and the long wooden beams away. Underneath, a man, his face wet with blood, one leg twisted, his black wig askew, the braids tangled. A small blond girl beside him, silent, also covered in blood.

"My wife . . . my daughter . . ." he implored.

Motl lifted the girl, placed her down on one of the teepee skins. Esther, her arm around the man's shoulder, helped him sit up. He wept.

"They tried to pull our daughter, Anna, away from me and Maja—her mother. They said they were taking her to a Lebensborn home to make a good German of her. She's only four. Maja held on so tight, and they shot them both right in front of me. I tried to help, but they got me too. They thought they'd killed me."

Esther put an arm around his shoulders. "It's okay, it's okay," she said.

Sometimes words are an oasis, a salve when there's nothing else.

Motl signalled to Mike, and he knelt beside Motl and the girl, leaning close, listening for breath, feeling for a pulse. The child was dead. Motl covered her with the skin. A painted image of a red bear pawing at the sky.

"The others?" Motl asked.

"Taken to a labour camp," Piotr said. "If they're lucky. Or at least, less unlucky." He looked at the man in Esther's arms. "He, at least, still could use your help. I must go back to my cabin—I can't risk discovery. I've work to do."

———

They decided the safest place for the man to sleep overnight was in Mike's bed. After they laid him down, Esther wrapped a blanket around him and had him drink a cup of water. Mike pulled over a chair and a book. He would read out loud until the man slept, and then watch over him. Sobbing, the man finally did, exhausted by shock and loss.

"What happened to them is hideous," Mike said quietly to the others, "and yet here I am, an Indigenous person."

"It's a grim fable. They chose to be someone else—until they couldn't," Esther said.

"Who gets to choose?"

"Not sure who I am at this point. I'm just trying to hang on before it all shatters," Esther replied. "Because of what I see. What I've seen. You know the joke: 'Why don't Jews drink? Because it dulls the pain.' But at least it's my pain. If I'm shards, I'm shards. A smashed window is still a window."

Motl suggested that someone should keep a lookout. He'd sit outside the cabin in case the Germans returned. It was a grim fable of its own. Sitting in the dark in a destroyed village, bodies on the ground beside an extinguished fire.

When the sun rose, they were able to see well enough to retrieve food from around the camp. They couldn't risk a fire, and so they ate cold bannock and pork sausage with pemmican as they sat around the ashes in the central clearing. They'd bury the dead afterwards. Customs change in such times.

"I wonder if it is safest to stay here or to go somewhere else?" Mike said.

"How likely is lightning to strike the same place twice?" Motl said.

"Depends if it's Nazi lightning."

"Makes me think of the two bolts in the SS insignia."

"We've had one strike. They might come back to look for Piotr," Esther said.

"I should go with you two," Mike said. "Maybe I could find a way home, or at least to where it's safer."

The injured man, Krzysztof he'd said his name was, had asked to be helped outside when he woke so he could lie on a blanket in a sunlit patch near the cabin. He was sleeping again.

Esther glanced his way. "What about him?"

"Leave him like a newborn on the steps of a church," Motl suggested.

"Or at the tavern. I'm sure Karol and Grażyna would know what to do."

"Before we leave, we should at least cover them," Mike said of the dead. "And some kind of ceremony—maybe what I remember of what we'd do back home. I think they'd have liked that. As my mother would say, 'Misfortune cannot touch another without piercing us too.'"

They cut the teepees into shrouds. They dug trenches. They laid the wrapped bodies in the earth. Esther pulled a chair close to Krzysztof, and they watched together, Krzysztof weeping and Esther wiping the tears from his cheeks.

Mike broke apart a cigarette and burned its tobacco over a small fire.

"*Yisgadal v'yiskadash sh'mei rabbaw*," Motl said.

"I don't know much of my language, but what I know is important," Mike said, and stood before the trenches chanting prayers in Oneida.

Then they packed what few things they could fit in rucksacks—eggs, bannock, an assortment of Mike's papers, a few books, blankets, a knife. They'd hike to the pine-shielded car, leave Krzysztof at the pub, then once again head west toward Berlin.

As they were about to set out, they heard footsteps in the woods, and then a voice singing a new verse to the tune of the "Colonel Bogey March":

This Jew, he's taking great big risks
printing pamphlets 'bout National Socialists
it's alphabetical, my last will and testicle
but how else could my balls raise their fists

Piotr had arrived.

"I figure that even as Karaites you might need some contacts, especially if you get into trouble," he said, and he gave them names of people who could help in Warsaw and Berlin. "And take these with you." He handed Esther a bundle of leaflets tied with string.

"What if we're caught?"

"If they search you, you're already dead."

"I've been sitting here thinking," Krzysztof said. "Now that it's all gone, I know I should ask, 'What do I want from life?' But I can't. Maybe I should ask what a cow asks at the abattoir door: 'What does life want from me?' We camped here because the world lost its mind and became unrecognizable. It was better here in the trees, together around the fire. We hoped for courage and connection, for something to make sense. Let me join you, Piotr. Let me help."

"Recover first," Piotr said. "Then come find me."

He disappeared into the trees.

"As my mother used to say, 'Man can get used to anything. Even feeling better,'" Krzysztof said. "Can you help get me to the car?" Without the black wig and kohl, he wouldn't be noticed, except for the broken leg. And being Polish. Schnitzel and lederhosen were safer than pemmican and braids. Or kielbasa and a *krakuska*.

Arms around Mike and Motl, he limped to where the car was still undiscovered in its bower of pine branches and shadow.

They left Krzysztof at the tavern—a surprise for when Karol and Grażyna opened up—and once more took the road west. It led past farmers' fields, trees and bushes, geese, sheep and white-painted cottages, and while it was only a trick of the sun, the world was morning light.

A country church.

"Stop here," Motl said.

"You forgot to get baptized?" Esther said.

"No, we need water."

"So, you do need to get baptized."

Esther parked the car.

"I'll stay here," Mike said. "My people don't go into churches. We're not always allowed to leave."

So he waited in the car with Esther while Motl heaved open the large front door and stepped in. A priest was at the far end, ministering to something on the altar.

"Howdy," Motl said.

The priest turned. He didn't look friendly.

The two men regarded each other, gazing warily over the length of the nave. The priest took a few deliberate steps toward Motl. Motl stepped farther into the church.

"I'm looking for water," he said.

"I know what you need," the priest said.

For several minutes, there was silence, Motl standing inside the sanctuary, the priest at the chancel. Incense from the thurible rose to the vault. Both men unyielding, resolute.

In the aisles, the light of votive candles was steady.

Then the priest put a hand in the pocket of his cassock. "Don't move," he said.

Motl remained still. Vigilant.

Ready.

There was a sudden flash as the priest whipped something large and bright from his pocket.

Motl's hands flew up.

"The key," the priest said. "To the rectory."

Motl followed him out a side door and down a cobblestone path into the kitchen of the stone cottage where the priest lived. He filled several bottles with water then gave them to Motl to put in his satchel. He also found some bread.

"Where, my Karaite brother, are you travelling?" the priest asked.

"Łódź," Motl said, explaining that a relative, a Karaite priest, had fallen ill and he was on his way to tend to him and his cattle.

Motl returned to the car.

"In stories," he said, "some things occur to surprise or build character. But sometimes, it's just about bread and water."

8

Twilight like smoke through the trees. They skulked down a lane into the woods to hide for the night. Shut-eye is best when one believes such sawing will end in dawn and not the business end of a gun.

Mike shouldered his rucksack and walked a short distance from the car, where he made a shelter by slinging a piece of scavenged teepee tarp over a low bough. Esther and Motl climbed into the wide back seat and huddled under a blanket, talking quietly.

Stars visible above the pines in the black night like countless gunshots that had missed their mark, instead piercing the sky, the dead looking down through pinholes of light.

"Maybe my mother's up there," Motl said, pointing. "Which is the 'Don't worry about me' constellation? Soon she'll figure how to make the clouds pour soup, though there'll be a chance of matzo balls."

Esther pressed close to him. He carried the scent of smoke. They both did. Washing was only a romantic's ideal as they tumbled forward, a braid of ashes and fire, body and word, trying to remain in the cracks of history. Her lips against his temple, her fingers intertwined with his.

"Esther." His hand inching through the curls at her nape, his lips this time at her temple, then from her neck down to the soft ridge of her shoulder.

Legs. Essential if one chooses pants or walking. Good also as a setting for loins.

Her fingers proceeding along his thigh, a combination of lightning and a fall into an abyss.

"I'm not . . . I mean, I want . . . I wish . . ."

Esther lifted his hand onto her breast. "My heart. My breathing. The ghost of who I am inside. Where it's dark. Safe. Can you feel?"

A scream in the woods. Then many.

"Kiotes."

"Ghosts," Esther said.

"Wolves."

"Hold me."

The howling surrounded them as if wraiths moved in the dark. They locked the car in case wolves could lever the handles with their jaws.

"What about Mike?"

"Do his people not know what to do with wolves?"

"Maybe. But he's unarmed."

"Then I hope he is good at climbing."

They lay close, shadowed by blanket, listening, eventually sleeping. What were wolves or kiotes when there were Nazis about?

Morning. Mike's shelter was abandoned, but they found him nested in a tree, hardcover books like fallen fruit scattered on the forest floor around it. Copies of *Winnetou: The Apache Knight, Old*

Surehand and even the original German *Winnetou der Rote Gentleman* tumbled open, on the ground.

"I threw them at the wolves," Mike said. "They ran. The next best thing to a fearless warrior is a book about one."

He lowered himself to the ground, put down his rucksack, then yawned and stretched the kinks from his spine. "Trees are okay, but it's more comfortable to chop them into beds *before* you try to sleep in them." He gathered the westerns, slipped them back in the bag with his other papers. "Breakfast," he said. "Motl, can you trap us a gopher?"

Eggs. They had eggs. Also the rest of the bannock. They built a small fire beside a stream and cooked. Motl cut some pine twigs and made tea from the needles. "I read about this, but you have to be careful—some, like the flat-needled yew, will cause your guts to writhe like a rattler."

"I know," Mike said. "I was sent to Boy Scouts in Toronto. After I was taken from my reserve. But I also remember this tea from my father when we went fishing. And coffee with lots of milk and sugar, the way my dad liked it."

"I'd kill a *Schutzstaffel* for some coffee right now. Of course, I'd kill one anyway, but the coffee'd be nice."

9

The road toward Warsaw. Esther driving. Mike shotgun.

Motl, half-asleep on the back seat. Reverie rather than reveille, a fenceless roaming. Muttering, mostly to himself.

"It's German-speaking cowpokes who ride the pages of the westerns I've read. Rheinstein cowboys *schnell*ing their appaloosas with Bavarian spurs, squeezing Sudetenland horse ribs with knobbly blond Austrian knees, the backs of their brains tickled by half-remembered Schiller from gymnasium schooldays, 'Ode to Joy' Ludwiging their lips while they *sprachen 'achtung kleine doggies'* at the steers in Deutsch and eyeball the twinkling *Reichsternen* up above. But to be a Jewish cowboy is to be more Apache than those Eurosavage bratwurst-coloured Österreich rustlers, stealing across the plains like the herd of plagues they drive.

"What are we if we're not leather-faced steer punchers— chopped liver? We're more than Karl May cowpokes or costume-party Indianers, blood brothers because our quantified blood is judged less human. We wake on our bedrolls after a shut-eye of only the usual dreams and find ourselves transformed into vermin.

"And then the 'blintz'-krieg. We're crammed into ghettos, starved, unable to leave, our houses appropriated, our gelt and our goods stolen. A betrayal of tears, learned from Americans.

"Mike," Motl said, sitting up and leaning over the front seat. "You're the first real Indian I've met."

"And you're the first Jewish cowboy."

"'Wrangler of the sorrowful countenance,'" Esther said.

"More an agnostic buckaroo. Lapsed or at least Reform," Motl said. "Not so sure Moses rode down the black Sinai hills, two stone-cold westerns in his saddlebags. Least if he did, someone first had manifested the helluva *untermenschen* destiny out of his Hebrew hiney and exiled his furry prophet face for the as-long-as-green-grass-grows-and-water-runs duration."

"We're not so much trying to get out of Egypt as get it back," Mike said. "Or at least, as my mother says, 'to be well treatied.'"

That morning they drove past fields of rye and potatoes. Pig farms. Pastures pocked with cows and their ripe or crusted patties, the audible cluck and crow of poultry. Barns both tumbledown and recently painted. Fallow lands where the cultivation of scrub, subjugation, abandonment, weeds, farm implements and rust clearly flourished. Farms where hope was not a viable crop. Fields green only because it took an unseasonable resistance to do anything but just keep going, hoping for the German outbreak to pass.

And then they arrived at a corral beside a stable, barn-red with white trim as if from a child's drawing or Motl's softcover brain. Esther stopped the car.

Palominos, gold, brilliant white and yellow, cream and champagne. Muzzles mottled and skewbald. Amber eyes.

Green, hazel, brown. White manes rippling as they ran, tails foamy as waves.

The golden steeds of myth, heroes and gunfighters, honeyed by amber light.

Billy the Kid, the Clantons, the Earp brothers.

Winnetou's father and sister, Intschu-tschuna and Nscho-tschi.

Old Shatterhand and Winnetou riding bareback on Iltschi—Wind—and Hatatitla—Lightning, their hooves touching neither sage nor brush, scrub nor ground fouled by Nazis nor cavalry.

"Swack my jingo," Motl said. "This cowboy longs for the feel of leather beneath him, the sudden undulation of the gallop."

"So now you want to get lucky?" Esther said. "Had your chance last night."

"I'm afraid that's as different as whiskey and soap. I'm saying I could cotton to riding one of those broncs."

"Let's not attract attention," Esther said.

"But they think I'm Aryan and you're both Karaites." Mike was out the door and at the gate. A stocky Pole in a frowzy suit jacket and a battered straw hat, held together by a tawdry fabric band, was leaning on the top rail. Mike spoke to him. They laughed, nodded and pointed at a few of the horses. The Pole made some cryptic yet philosophical hand gestures—perhaps "Why not?" "How can it hurt?" "As if we're all not going to die soon anyway?" And "If that man still in the car is an idiot with limited understanding and suffering a terminal illness, surely I could grant him this one wish?"

Mike arrived at the car window. "These horses are used for 'therapeutic horseback riding' at the Göring Institute—that's Ernst Göring, Hermann's nephew—but I explained that you Karaites are from an ancient horse-riding tradition. You pray to them as you ride."

"We are?"

"Motl does," Esther said. "A lapsed buckaroo still hankers for horse sweat."

"Are you trying to seduce me?" Motl said.

"Maybe."

"So, Motl, he says he'll allow you to ride."

"I only ever harnessed Theodor Herzl to a wagon. I never climbed on. But, Mike, you can teach me."

"What do I know? I grew up in Toronto. We had a car."

"I'll show you," Esther said. "It's like riding a bicycle, but wider. And the bicycle might choose to kill you."

"Won't he notice?"

"Karaites ride Karaite horses. And they use Karaite commands. Also, I told him that you're both sick and simple."

The Pole in the haystack hat examined Motl and Esther as they walked toward him. In their Karaite headgear, they seemed like a vision from the Arabian Nights. Exotic Orientals wise in the way of stallions. Silk would flow as they floated over the minaret-shadowed sand. And Motl was the terminally ill simpleton out for one last ride.

Since the Nazis usually euthanized "life-unworthy-of-life" like him, the Pole figured he must be a prince whose father sent magic carpets laden with open-sesame spoils to fill their coffers.

"I am Tadeusz," the Pole said, opening the gate to let them in. Then he called, "Shusha," to a glimmering palomino. "Here." And the horse brought its white-striped nose snorting over the gate. "Good boy." Tadeusz bridled the horse, then passed the reins to Motl. "Hold."

He whistled, and a boy ran out from the stable carrying a saddle, slipped through the rails of the corral and strapped it to the horse.

"Stefa, Bialy," Tadeusz said, calling a champagne mare and a stallion the colour of a gold coin. The boy saddled them too, and handed Mike and Esther the reins.

"So now, you ride," Tadeusz said. The boy opened the gate and they led the three horses into the open field.

Mike and Esther both took hold of the pommels, stepped into the stirrups, kicked out at the horizon and scissored their legs over the saddles, settling themselves on their horses.

What was a cowboy to do when there'd been an incident with his prairie oysters at the crossroads of his legs and now he must grand-jeté up onto his hoss as if it were nothing but a pony-headed broomstick and he a rodeo clown? Take the bit in his mouth, wince like the sun had juiced lemon in his eyes and get the job done. One foot in the stirrup, a lifted leg, and Motl fell, his back on the damp grass, Karaite hat rolling like a fallen coin.

The sky. A bell jar over the earth, beyond it the endless and irresponsible universe. Clouds: doltish billows juddering the blue. Then Tadeusz's sardonic face looking down.

"They make it more difficult when they stand still," he said, passing Motl his hat. "Maybe Karaite horses are different. But I know you are not well. Let me help."

He held out his hand. Motl untangled his foot from the stirrup and stood.

"Not so easy being a cowpoke," Motl said. Then, "Or a Karaite rider."

Tadeusz helped him up onto the horse, patting the long knolls of its golden neck. "Easy now, Shusha. Easy."

And then Motl was a cowboy. High upon a golden horse, you could see farther, know what brewed over the horizon. The wind spoke directly to you, whispering as it brushed past your face.

"Shusha," Motl said, and the horse knew what to do, cantering toward Esther and Mike, who had already trotted their horses to the end of the field and were waiting, looking back.

Esther said, "Now I'll teach you both how to ride."

"I actually know quite a lot about horses," Mike said. "Just didn't want to be Motl's 'Little Red Riding Instructor.'" He turned both palms up and shrugged.

"Then, Motl, I'll just tell you what my father taught me: Keep your hands down. Relax your legs. Don't clothespin. Look where you're going, not at the horse. And breathe. Remember to breathe, else you'll fall off and become hoof mash."

She showed him a few tricks with the reins, and he walked the horse in a few figure eights and then trotted out the letters of his name. They were now ready to ride the road between fields. Motl took the lead, beginning slowly then spurring the horse forward, exhilaration filling his chest with a hive-like buzzing. The horse broke into a gallop, and Motl, like Kafka's Red Indian, instantly alert, leaned against the wind as they quivered over the moving ground. Spurs? Were there spurs? He didn't need them, maybe he had shed his spurs then thrown away the reins—he needed no reins—he hardly saw that the land before him was smoothly shorn scrub, and together they were one thing—the horse and Motl, the air and ground, future and past, they were neither cowboy nor Indianer, Jew nor man, grief nor fear, history nor its angel, wind nor storm, or were all of them at once.

Then he was clutching the horse's neck as he realized he was unable to slow her, panting, electric with fearful joy and the present.

Mike was beside him, "Shusha, whoa, Shusha, whoa," and the horse began to slow, and then Esther was on his other side, "Whoa.

Whoa." Soon they were walking slowly, and Motl steered the horse into a field of long grass. Shusha stopped beside a rock, flat as flagstone, nosing it. Sniffing.

A fringed red scarf half-visible underneath. Esther climbed from the saddle, pulled on the scarf. The stone lifted, revealing a mouth lined with moss-covered stones. A stone-lined cavern. A hole to store potatoes. But what about the scarf? Daylight fell on blankets, coats, the shadowy shapes of people huddled at the cellar bottom. A whimpering. A girl whimpered until a hand covered her mouth. "Shh."

"Don't worry," Esther said. "We weren't looking for you. You're safe."

A family hiding in the dank. The girl crawled up to them as Motl looked over the fields, over the horizon, ensuring no one was watching.

The girl reached to touch the horse's nose, petting it. The horse sighing, its long-lashed eyes steady on the girl. "We've been underground for so long," she said.

A man's voice. "Raisel, you must come back. It's not safe."

Esther embraced the girl. "It'll be all right. The war will end." Wrapping the girl in the red scarf.

"Ask Tadeusz to bring more food if he can," the girl said. "We're so hungry."

She crawled back underground.

Motl got down from his horse. "I want to see," he said. "Esther, you and Mike can ride while I do." And he crouched then slid into the darkness of the entrance. A rope to lower himself down the sloping, slippery surface. The cellar was surprisingly deep; perhaps it had been an abandoned well, further excavated to become this crypt for potatoes.

"So, you're joining us?" An old man, bent and knobbly as his own knees, greeted him in the dark. His tumbleweed beard twisted over his chest. "Were we expecting you? We expect many things, mostly Nazis. And death. Is it a holiday you're hoping for?"

He and his three daughters had been living like moles in the low tunnel for many months. His wife had been shot as she left the synagogue, his synagogue, for he had been the rabbi there.

He lit a small lantern and guided Motl farther into the cave.

"She died in my arms," he said. "I ran from the bimah, from the open Ark, from the unfurled Torah, I had been teaching a boy to chant—and I found her on the threshold, fallen. I held her and prayed. I, a rabbi, could not remember the psalm's words, nor their proper order.

"The sun will not harm you by day, nor the moon by night.
The Lord will guard your going and your coming from now and
for all time.
I lift my eyes to the mountains—from where will my help come?"

His daughters, sitting on ledges in the cave, wept as he recounted the story. Motl thought of old folk tales where maidens turned into lakes of silver tears.

From his jacket pocket, the rabbi produced a small prayer book. "My wife's. I keep what she held close with me. Near my heart. But we have been safe here. Thanks to Tadeusz and his family. They have risked their lives for us." From another pocket, he took out a revolver. "Can you fix this?"

"Papa," the girl with the red scarf said.

"I keep it for protection, but I don't know how to make it work," the rabbi said, and passed the weapon to Motl. Motl had read about Sharps. Henrys. Derringers. Peacemakers. Colts. He could smell their gunpowder, the click of their hammers, their flash and crack. He could see an outlaw topple to dust on Main Street, a Lakota from his horse, or buffalo sink to its knees. He could imagine a gun's feel in his hands, its handshake of power and promise. How holstered six-shooters on each hip would charge his walk with grace and swagger. But he had never pushed a cylinder to the side, placed ammo in its chambers, spun it with satisfaction, glee or steady resolve, pulled back a hammer and aimed, squinting into the future with fortitude and the certainty of fate. As a young man in Zimmerwald, he had been handed a loaded gun, but he'd immediately given it to a comrade, as if it had burned him to hold even for a moment.

Motl turned the rabbi's gun over. He imagined it would be the weight of a sparrow or fish, but it had the heft of a book or a small chicken.

"I can't help," he said. "I've read so many things, but I know nothing." And he turned to leave.

10

"You hit your head," the rabbi said, leaning over him. "You were out cold." He dabbed at Motl with the girl's red scarf. "Have some water."

Motl lay on the ground, his head on the knee of one of the daughters. She put a cup to his lips. He drank.

"Use the rope, if you can," the rabbi said. And Motl got up and pulled himself unsteadily on his hands and knees up the mossy stones and into the blaring light of the field.

"I was knocked out for hours," Motl said, touching his temple. "They showed me a gun. They gave me water. His wife's heart was in his pocket."

Esther said, "I know not to believe everything you say. You were only there for five minutes. But I was worried."

"Any longer and we might have left you," Mike said. "Figured you were never coming back."

Esther helped him hoist himself back onto the horse. She pulled the stone across the entrance, smoothing the earth around it. She climbed back on her own palomino. They returned to the path. They rode.

They said nothing to Tadeusz about his underground cache of

sentient potatoes, only nodded and smiled with quiet respect as they trotted into the corral.

He raised an eyebrow at the cut on Motl's temple.

"It's been so long since I've been on a horse," Motl said. "I fell. The wind. The fields. The horse. Like I was flying from the war."

"'If I had wings like a goose, I'd fly away . . .'" Tadeusz began singing, the tune itself having mostly already gone south. He sent for the boy—his son—to get a bandage. They corralled the horses, then Tadeusz offered them food.

"I also have homemade beer. Do Karaites drink?" he asked. "I know we Europeans do," he said to Mike.

Was it better to be unsafe with a drink or unsafe without one? They decided they'd stay for Tadeusz's bread, cheese, onions and Pilsner. And a plate of perogies.

"*Jezusku!* My mother knew perogies. I am lucky she taught our Marianna to make them because I listened. But that was before the war, and before Marianna . . ."

And he filled their mugs with Pilsner.

After a plate of perogies and fried onions, Motl said, "So delicious. My mother made such kreplach . . . such—"

A look from Esther.

"Such dumplings. Our Karaite virtiniai . . ."

It was delicious comfort to eat and drink around a table in the shade, the whinnying and whickering of horses, the tail flicks, bees and flies, a fine intermittent breeze riffling the fields.

They had some more cheese. Then more beer.

Then they thanked Tadeusz, patted a few muzzles while the horses exhaled their hay-scented hot breaths, and all three climbed into the car and set off for the lone Polish prairie.

II

Mike was in the back seat now. He leaned forward. "So," he asked, "what's with all the cowboying?"

"I'd give my pony and saddle to return to a stubby painted cottage on the range rather than roam these wild Sinai plains, exodusing the East in hopes of a new life," Motl said. "But I'm a wandering cowboy, an ingenious knight, a Litvak rambling from the Pale, aiming to outride the sorrows of the world. The cowboy has no land but takes fate by the horns, wrestles it to the ground."

"You're quick on the draw with the tongue-gunning," Mike said. "I understand wanting to be something else. Me? I want to be myself again. Oneida. As I said, I don't have my language, though I've learned some from elders. Maybe that's why I chose to study these Indianers: at least I know more than them. Better to be an Indian who doesn't Indian than to Indian without being Indian, if you know what I mean."

"I know where I'm from," Motl said. "Just don't believe in it these days."

"Well, your world is ending. Ours already did, but it's not entirely gone. We're beginning again. They can starve us, move us, kidnap us, separate us, ban our language and ceremonies. But

200

no matter how many times you wash and wring a squirrel, it's still a squirrel."

"Seems an unnecessarily difficult way to get nuts."

They spotted a checkpoint several fields ahead at the edge of a town. Esther slowed and reversed the car, intending to turn onto a side road they'd just passed.

"Don't think you'll get by on looks alone," she said to Mike.

"My mother told me that," Motl said.

The car shuddered. She'd backed into a rock. When she drove forward, the car was askew, a tire flat, and they veered into a ditch.

"Jesus, Joseph and Shmuel Leibovitch!" she cried. "We'll have to get out and push." But like kicking a hive of wasps, their antics had aroused the Fritzes at the checkpoint, and they started running toward them.

"Out," Mike said, and the three of them climbed out of the car and into the trees. The food and blankets were in the trunk, so they left with nothing except Motl's satchel and gun.

They ran out of the forest and across a field, crouching low, using cows for cover, and then back into another stand of trees. It seemed the Germans had not followed.

"There were train tracks crossing the road a few miles before we got to the checkpoint," Mike said. "We could follow them back to the station—maybe we can hop a train when the coast is clear."

And that's what they did. When they reached their destination, they waited until the sun was low in the sky before they slipped out of hiding in the woods and crept alongside a freight train parked at the station. The boxcars' shadows were blunt-toothed as they went from car to car searching for an unlocked door. Finally, Esther found one and heaved it open. They retreated to shelter behind a shack in view of the car. Best to wait to board until the train began moving in case the cars were checked. Once things got rolling, they couldn't be stopped.

Just ask Sisyphus.

A ricochet down the couplings as the engine was started and the brake released. A shudder. As Motl, Esther and Mike crouched, ready to run, soldiers, shouldering rifles, strode out of the station and along the train, inspecting cars. One closed the door that Esther had opened.

Motl tied a handkerchief around his face and took the gun out of his satchel. "I'll move in like a bandit, stick my Colt in his kuchenhole and spätzle a few mine shafts into his brain. Then we do what we want."

"So we colander a Nazi then take a seat and ride to the next town? Maybe we could sit in the club car and have tea and scones too," Esther said.

"Let's just open the door and jump in as the train moves. Not great for our train robber CV, but safer," Mike said.

A metal screel as the train began to move. The soldiers had reached the front end of the train and so they had a chance to scrabble aboard. First Esther, then Mike. Motl tripped and the train car went by. He clutched at the next one as he ran, heaved open the door—which luckily was unlocked—and scrambled in. Mike stuck his head out the door. Motl also. They looked at each other.

"Yours has a better view," Motl said.

"At least while that bandana covers your face."

"Can you climb over to me?"

"Both of us? You come here."

"Don't think I can. We'll just jump out together when it's time."

Motl gathered up straw, cardboard and sacks from the floor of the boxcar to fashion something between a fainting couch and a nest. The motion of the train made it impossible to close the door. He lay out of sight, yet still tree shadows brindled over him as he attempted to sleep.

On his own, he reckoned his losses. Had his family survived? His mother? What had happened to them? Did they suffer?

Esther in the boxcar ahead of him, a single room into the future. Esther sleeping in the dark. Did she smile as she thought of him? Did she think of him? He imagined her hands on his shoulders, his forehead, his leg, her breath as she slept, her shudders and snorts as she turned, remembering in her sleep, muttering or crying in dreams. His darlin'. They crossed a sea of sage grass, russet hills in night shadow, the moon shining through their separate doors as they journeyed west together yet apart. There was war and death, but above Zimmerwald there was life and potential, his frozen ranchers that could rustle possibility. Esther and Motl, mother and father of what was conceivable. Of what could be hoped for.

He hoped they could hope together. Perhaps they already did.

They could father and mother, could pet and smooch, give and receive, could lover and lover. He'd be a new kind of cowboy, a new man in an old world, an old man in the new. Together they would travel to Zimmerwald, would make a new life.

He was woken by hammering from the end of the boxcar. Something different than the ambient clanging and rattling of moving trains. Something urgent. Dire. A wolf's howl amid a homestead's lowing and bleating.

Danger.

The history of Jews and Indigenous people, a cowboy shoot-'em-up, an adventure tale. One narrow escape after another. One damn unbelievable thing after another. Apparently, this would be another.

Two wolves and a sheep vote on what to have for supper. This, also, was the woolly history of Jews and the Indigenous.

Except the sheep has a gun.

But so do the wolves.

More banging. Mike leaning out of the car, shouting back at Motl. "We're slowing down in the middle of nowhere. That means we're coming to a checkpoint. It means we have to get off. Now. We have to jump."

As Motl stuck his head out to survey the situation, Mike and then Esther jumped for an embankment filled with weeds. They landed and then rolled through the weeds into a mucky trench at the bottom.

"Motl," Mike shouted as his car went past.

So Motl jumped.

He felt suspended, the train rushing past with an urgent hiss, the ground silent, patient, motionless. He was the single still point in the eye of an eagle. A bullet before it entered the body. Then he hit the embankment with a sudden bloom of pain, and rolled several hundred feet farther along the trench than Esther and Mike. He'd bit his tongue, and his mouth was filled with the bitter iron of his own blood.

They'd been seen. A pack of soldiers came running toward them along the side of the track. They had sniffer dogs and hand-saws. If they caught you, they sawed you apart. The sweet sadistic irony of not shooting you, but killing you slow. Of turning their horror and fears into this external misery. If the worst thing was outside you, then it wasn't inside.

Motl ran straight into the woods, then angled toward where Esther and Mike were headed. All of them stung by nettles, almost tripped by vines, holding their forearms up against the sharp of branches and needles.

What is the sound of a Jew running in the forest? Same as that of an Oneida.

The only difference, the choice of expletives.

As Motl finally caught up with Mike and Esther, they heard dogs and so they kept running—along a small gulley, then down one side and up the other. Breeze from a swamp like the tender touch of the dead.

"We'll show them our Karaite identification," Motl panted.

"Don't think they're interested in paperwork at the moment," Mike replied.

Motl came to a climbable tree and climbed it. He hung his satchel high in the canopy, where it was hidden by leaves. "In the West, they do this to keep their food—and themselves—safe from bears."

He climbed down again, and then they all crawled into the swamp so that the dogs wouldn't detect their scent. They sank into the fetid water between tall rushes, only their eyes, noses, the tops of their heads exposed. Escape is ninety percent waiting, ten percent leech bites.

They could hear the dogs and the soldiers coming closer, then moving around the edges of the swamp until they faded back into the forest.

"When they don't find us, they'll return," Mike said. "We must wait."

And so they remained immersed through the night in the slurry, the quick beating of their hearts in the hot nests of their chests, their breaths in clouds as they exhaled. The cold was painful, knives cutting their bodies everywhere, but they didn't dare move.

Motl woke stuck against the earth, but realized that overnight a thin sheet of ice had formed around him as if he were trapped in glass, an outlaw in aspic. He thrashed—quietly, carefully—to break the ice, felt his feet nearly frozen in his shoes. Esther found fragments of water-saturated cheese and meat in her pocket, which she shared. It hurt to stay still. It hurt to move.

The three of them crawled from the swamp on their hands and knees, tetrapods leaving the sea and smelling as bad. They lay in the morning sun on the side of a hillock, eyes closed.

"Wonder what the poor people are doing today?" Mike said.

"They don't even have clothes to get slimy and cold."

"Or leeches."

A dog bark. Then more. The dogs were barking in German. It was worse than wolves. These were German dogs, thoughtlessly following their masters. The soldiers were returning.

Motl and Mike slid down the bank and lowered themselves silently into the cold swamp.

"Where's Esther?" Motl asked, looking frantically around them.

He couldn't see her in the water or on the bank.

"We have to find her," he said.

"Yes," said Mike. "But when the dogs are gone. We're no use if they catch us."

Motl hesitated. "Yes," he said finally. "We'll wait."

They waited for hours, crouched behind reeds, swamp water up to their chins. Hours. The Germans kept circling. Then eventually the barking and the voices receded.

"I'm going now," Motl said. "It's too late, but I'm going."

He found no trace of Esther. Nothing but the stillness of the forest. A few birds hesitantly began to call again, as if the dogs had been tracking them too. Sub-avians. Gay, Jewish or Romani, disabled, Communist, Indigenous, or mentally ill birds, hiding in the trees, unable to fly away.

Motl called for Esther, his voice muted by the forest. Mike called too.

No answer.

They slumped down against a tree. What had happened to her? What had she done?

Can't see the forest for the grief, the trees ignorantly stolid, refusing to fall, each a middle finger pointing at the sky.

Motl stared at a rock by his feet. Farther away, a hollow tree, its empty trunk a prayer shawl draped around missing heartwood. He picked up the rock and hammered it against the hollow. A living drum. He hammered then hammered again. Then the stone shattered, fracturing in his hand. Motl fracturing, breaking apart, falling to his knees, forehead against the ground. Not in prayer but a bitter curse at the earth, at the sky, those in between.

Then there was a cracking of branches, and a shuffling, half-naked figure, blood rivering its skin, staggered toward them, branches and leaves in its thickety hair, leeches and insects attached to its dripping clothes, a spectre, a haunted creature, arms grappling the air as if it were blind and lost and falling.

"I went to find my ring. My mother's wedding ring. The ring my father gave her. It's the only thing I still had. I've become so thin that it fell from my finger while we were on the embankment, and I went back and then I was lost and the Germans came and I hid and . . ."

She tipped forward as Motl ran to catch her in his out-stretched arms.

"Esther," he said.

"I heard the drum. I knew it was you."

Motl held her close.

"I thought it would bring me luck. My ring. I thought it was important. But everyone is gone. It's all gone. And my father. I left him."

Motl said nothing but carefully lowered her to the ground, where she leaned against him, sobbing. He held her ringless hand.

Then the three of them, Motl, Esther and Mike, staggered to their feet and wandered farther into the forest until they found a grassy glade, where they laid themselves down. They slept like dogs, one eye open, meaning they listened for dogs and Germans as they rested, their bodies saturated with swamp water, fear, exhaustion and relief.

It began to rain, a precipitation of cold fingers. Goosebumps from on high. When one has bivouacked in swamp water, such full-body baptism approaches holiness, fire not the first and greatest human achievement, but personal hygiene.

Esther let the deluge wash away the mud and leaves and branches and smooth her tumbleweed hair. The three of them now skinny kittens bathed in a bucket, the poltergeist pong of the swamp no longer a noxious haze around them.

Motl took off his wet jacket and gave it to Esther to cover her torn clothes. "I have to go back to climb the tree and get my satchel," he said.

Did they hear barking? Were there shouts? Motl and Esther climbed up together into the branches of a large tree. Mike climbed up another nearby. They disappeared behind the cover of the leaves.

They waited, but the dogs and Germans, incorporeal or earth-wurst, did not arrive. Motl climbed down and surveyed the scene. "We should go," he said.

"Where? The train?"

"Why continue to Berlin?" Mike asked.

"The documents."

"But why not Sweden or straight to Switzerland, where we'll be safe? Why risk your life for this?"

"The Ḥakhan threatened that if we don't deliver, there'll be problems."

"Worse than Nazis? When someone's shooting you, why worry about cholesterol?"

"Maybe the Ḥakhan will punish us by punishing others. As long as we're Karaite, everything will be fine."

"As long as everyone else got that memo."

"They're Nazis. They all got the memo. And you'll be safe if you can just get papers that give you citizenship."

"Tell me about it. And while you're at it, tell the Canadian government too."

"The train is still the best way out of here. It may not be safer, but it's faster," Motl said.

"Like pulling a bandage off in one go."

"Exactly. Though it might leave nothing but bones, at least it'll be quick."

12

They searched until they found the tree where Motl had hidden the satchel. Once he'd climbed up and retrieved it, they crept to the edge of the forest. The checkpoint was just around the curve of track. They'd wait for the next train to be stopped, then, as it started to roll again, accelerating slowly, they'd climb aboard on the other side of the checkpoint, the Little Engine That Could Avoid Them Being Snuffed Out puffing as it chugged along, "I-think-I-can, I-think-I-can help them escape being shot or sawed up by sadistic Nazis and instead ride across Poland, their only possession vagabond hope and cross-cultural chutzpah." Brave little train.

They waited for several hours, then at last heard the soughing of an engine coming, the clanking as it slowed and was halted. Soldiers shouting.

The train wheezed into motion.

"Ready?" Esther said. "Now!" And they ran from between the trees and leapt up and grabbed the sides of the cars. They were cattle cars, the doors locked, openings covered in barbed wire. They stank.

They scrabbled up the sides, grabbing on handles, nails and broken wood until they lay flat on the sloped cattle car roof. No leather-fisted Nazis ran down the track chasing them. The acrid fog of train smoke blanketed the tops of the cars like snowcaps on mountain peaks. Esther thought of her father's beard hanging like a cloud on his not-seen-since-boyhood chin. His stratocumulus eyebrows.

They closed their eyes. Their breath would return, their hearts would slow.

Beneath them: voices.

"Buy my boots. Buy my boots," a man called out in German. Some bitter, debilitated laughter greeted him.

"He doesn't know he's already dead," someone said. "Though I'd take even the illusion of new boots."

Children's voices. Adults'. The elderly. Crying. Wailing. Moaning. Weeping. Sobbing. Snivelling. Listening from the roof, they became connoisseurs of these expressions of sorrow, of hopelessness, of pain. Their boxcar chests filled with such feelings also.

They held on as the train rumbled forward, not yet sure what would happen next. What happened next was that midges and mosquitoes found them in the dusk. They sat up, flailing.

"They say you can tell a Jew by the terror in his eyes, so maybe you're all Jews," a voice said.

A young guy in a military uniform that looked as if it had maybe been in several previous wars leaned against a small chimney on the roof of the boxcar ahead of them.

Imagine you reach to scratch yourself and find another body in bed beside you. Or you're in the half dark clutching the roof of a *Sonderzüge* special train transporting Jews to a ghetto in Poland and there's a stranger on the roof of the boxcar ahead of you, sitting up and talking to you.

"Come here often?" the man said. "I ride mostly for the convenience, but also for the scenery. The club car service is second-rate, though."

Nothing like a wise guy to pass the hours before possible death.

He was speaking Polish, which they all could understand, but his accent twigged something for Mike. To him, the other boxcar rider sounded Indigenous.

Of course. Two Indigenous men meet on the roof of a train in Poland during the war. Sounds like the set-up for a joke. Except the train is full of Jews. Okay, so that's another kind of joke.

But one Indigenous guy says to the other—

It turned out that the man, Gerry, was Lakota—an American soldier behind enemy lines. A communications expert, his mission had been to parachute into occupied Denmark and communicate with the Allies from there. In the Baltic night, his plane had been intercepted by the Luftwaffe and chased into Poland and shot down. He parachuted through flames and landed on a cow in the dark.

Besides surprise and displeasure, he didn't know what the cow thought of an American dropping in from on high. He couldn't tell if it was a Nazi cow.

And so the second Indigenous guy says, "You enlisted?"

"Good way to get off the reservation, get paid and learn something. Also, a general told my father I had to. My father was working in a restaurant near the base when the general came in, puffing away on a cigar. My father comes home and says, 'Gerry, the general wants to see you. So go get a haircut, take a shower and put on clean clothes. When you get there, don't stand closer than two feet from him, make sure to salute, and give your full name.'

"'What did I do?' I asked. 'Am I in trouble?'

"'Don't know. What *did* you do?'

"So my father and I go to the base and we're taken into the general's office. We both keep our distance and salute.

"'Your father tells me you speak Indian.'

"'Yes, General, sir.'

"'And you write it too.'

"'Yes, General, sir. Lakota Sioux.'

"'Like the warriors in the movies I watched as a boy.'

"The general opened a drawer and took out three tumblers and a bottle of bourbon, poured us each a couple fingers and slid the glasses in front of us.

"'That's enough with the "Yes, sir" and the "General, sir." I want to talk man to man. Are you brave?'

"'Brave enough to drink bourbon. Though I'm only seventeen.'

"'Good. Brave enough to help your country? The Krauts are intercepting American communications. We're going to make their heads spin and send messages in an Indian language. In Lakota Sioux. I need you to enlist.'

"'Yes, sir. I mean, just yes.'

"'You okay with that?' the general asked my father.

"'Yes, sir,' my father said.

"'Never met an Indian before,' the general said. 'You guys were first in this country.'

"'Yes, before Columbus. Before he was even born. Before his grandmother too,' I said.

"'I like your spunk, son,' the general said. 'We need spunk. Know anyone else who knows Lakota?'

"So I told him about my friend Roy White Bear, and he enlisted too, and we learned all about communications. Military radios and how to make code out of our language. I worked for a bit in

England and France. Then they stuck me on that plane to Denmark, and now here I am holding on to the roof of a train like I'm trying to ride a steer. What about you?"

Mike explained they were heading for Berlin.

"Because Poland isn't close enough to certain death?" Gerry asked.

"Always better to go to the source," Mike said.

"You do know that the train is going the other direction?"

Esther and Motl looked at each other, on the precipice of surprised laughter rather than trouble. With the world upside down, why shouldn't they be going in the wrong direction also? But what to do when you find out you're escaping into the fire?

Gerry was heading for a rendezvous in the countryside near Gdansk. A midnight plane in a potato field, or else a small boat in a cove on the coast. No point planning to avoid bears if you're going to end up eaten by wolves. He'd find out the details when he was closer.

"Come with me. You don't have to stick with those two," he said, indicating Motl and Esther. "Maybe it's as dangerous as Berlin, but at least it's sooner."

13

The track curved through dark woods. The train clattered on past the Dopplering of owls and the dark saraband of bats. Over a bridge, through towns and over another bridge, then the train began to slow and finally shuddered to a stop. They waited— Esther, Motl, Mike, Gerry and perhaps others more invisible than them—trying to breathe silently, trying to blend with the train.

Then they saw flashlight beams scanning the sides and roofs of the cars, searching for an infestation of Jews, stowaways, undesirables. The lights were coming closer to their cars.

"Climb down," Gerry hissed. They waited until the light swept the side of their car, and after the surveillance moved away along the train, they climbed down onto the gravel. Gerry motioned at them to follow him. Ahead, a boxcar was open. "Inside!" There were crates stacked against the walls of the car, and they squeezed behind them.

They waited.

Light beams turned the car into a shadow play, then it became dark again. After some time, the train moved again. Inside the crates, the rattle of glass. Clinking.

Bottles.

Gerry pried one open and raised a bottle by the neck. "Vodka." He pulled the cork and swigged, then passed the bottle to Esther, who also took a swig. And so to Mike.

Motl, sporadic aficionado of the bottle, infrequent enthusiast of Bacchus schnapps and kiddush hooch, did also hose his insides with firewater, and so caused his tender liver to buck like a stallion. He staggered to his feet, unsure how his legs were attached to the floor beneath him. Then he realized he'd left his mouth ajar and decided to use the fortuitous occasion to deliver some extemporaneous oratory.

"The moon shines bright as a sheriff's badge in the leather sky, and I have had a vision. I know the future.

"The world is broken. Black hats have come in storm trooper boots and brown shirts reckoning to destroy everything. But I see a world without the hankering to *Anschluss*, to Siberiate or to Big any Little Horn."

Motl threw a hand up above him and was almost thrown by the force.

"Now see this invisible six-gun held high in the Ashkenazi air where it glints and shines and tells us we can keep riding through death and shadows blacker than night."

Motl shakily waved the imaginary Smith & Wesson of his hand past the faces of those before him.

"We take this God-sized six-gun and we spin its cylinder"— here he spun his cylinder fingers—"we spin it like Dame Fortuna's Wheel and one of the bullets finds a way out. It bursts into the tunnel of the possible and into the world of light.

"And now you ask me, what happens next?

"And I stand here on my own two feet and tell you that this beautiful silver bullet shoots the world right between the eyes.

It shoots the evil that's got in there. Between Nazi and Jew. Cowboy and ten-gallon. Between the Indigenous and their land. It kills it dead. All that's left is the body and, outside of it, the big frontier, not of America, but of what we hope for, a place for new life. We blow everything apart so it will grow back as something good, a second chance from everything wounded.

"With this. With this here gun." And Motl waved his hand yippee-ki-yay style and toppled headfirst into the pile of crates. Esther and Mike steered him to a tarp on the floor, where he remained insensible until dawn, abrading their ears with the cacophonous juddering of his lax and copious nose flesh.

Daybreak was birds knocking into wind chimes as the vodka bottles shook. The vodka shook inside them, too. It had been a brief escape from their greater escape. They lay on the floor, their heads and guts in various states of hanging over.

"I was thinking," Motl said. "If someone ever asked for my story—and they weren't prattling to my grave or to the wind because they didn't know where I'd ended up ending—what could I say? Nothing'd be quite right—like having gas during High Holidays: your one end's prayer, the other's *plotz*ing. We're middle fingers, but also raised fists and a hand on the shoulder."

"Me," Esther said. "I have only one thing to say that matters. 'I'm here. The bastards didn't get me yet.' Unless, of course, they did."

"No horse, no hat, no saddle, no cows. The only part of the cowboy that's left for me is the riding," Motl said.

"What does that mean?" Esther said.

"Saddle sores and a place to go. And, hopefully, survival."

"And maybe a story?"

"Like tits on Jesus—nice for decoration, but useless."

"That a Jewish proverb?" Mike asked.

"No, just something my mother would say."

"Well, if stories don't change anything except stories, then stories change things," Mike said.

"That an Oneida proverb?" Motl asked.

"No, just something an old high school teacher would say."

"You think the world's asking us something?" Esther said.

"You mean like 'help'?" Gerry said.

14

They felt the train slowing again. It wasn't clear where they were, but out the open boxcar door they could see a large tent across a field, some variety of red-striped big top as if a circus had set up its wonder, horses, lions and little cars in the middle of war-consumed Poland. Maybe this was the best time for a circus. What is the opposite of a Nazi invasion? A circus.

"The circus," Gerry said. "It's the classic place to hide. Let's head there until we figure out where we are and what's next. The thing I didn't tell you was, I was on the wrong train too."

They leapt off the train and into the grass. Rolling was not high on the list of enthusiasms of the post-inebriated belly, but still they rolled until they all lay at the bottom of the ditch. They waited until the train had passed and the vodka ceased whisking their insides like omelettes.

"Do we just walk up and say we have a master's in Circus?" Esther joked as she sat up.

"Yeah, I'll tell them my thesis was a critical study of the Marxist ontology of big cat dung," Mike said. "You can't imagine how many clowns I fit in one footnote."

"You know, at my Catholic university we never mentioned the elephant in the room," Gerry said.

"So you majored in advanced big shoe studies?" Mike said.

"Maybe they need a western act," Gerry said. "Mike and I will play Indians, both originally from Drohobycz. Motl, you'll be the cowboy, originally from Białystok. And Esther, you're Miss Annie Oakleyevitch from Bratislava. We're a Wild West troupe and we got stuck in Minsk when the war broke out. Our circus was labelled a *Jüdenzirkus* because it was run by Jews, and so shut down. Since then we've been travelling, looking for work.

"'Yes, sir,'" Gerry hammed. "'The Oklahoma Spurs and Stripes Wild West Show and Nature Circus was where we was raised and schooled in the western arts by actual true live Indians and cowboys. Me and my compadres would be right grateful if you could help us out a spell. We're powerful worried about what to do but also, I could rightly say, powerful splendid. We dazzle and amaze the common man, charm the dimes from his pants.'"

They crossed the field and walked into an array of scattered pup tents, carriages, horses and a variety of circus people gathered around cooking fires, doing circus people things. Large, thick, tiny, piebald muscle-bound men and women, loud, laughing, melancholy and in between, young and old, ate, sewed, drank, joked, repaired and napped. The motley encampment of a small brigade on a campaign of conviviality and ragtag marvels.

Circus train cars were parked on the rail spur, which branched from the main track where the train they rode in on was now stopped in the distance.

No one from the circus either noticed them or seemed to be responsible for anything other than themselves, and so they walked on to the big tent, parted the canvas flap and went in.

A beefy, red-faced man, arrayed in a bright-green tailcoat and a stovepipe hat, stood in the centre of a sawdust-floored ring, his impressive brass-buttoned gut as streamlined as the rotund belly of a rowboat. He boasted the Spanish moss beard of an Orthodox priest and repeatedly cracked a whip, not encouraging any animals but seemingly directing the air itself, each crack like a lightning bolt. His eyes, too, held the sudden and unsettling energy of lightning. High above him, spangle-suited acrobats flipped about ropes and swung lithe arcs while hanging from trapezes. They heard roaring and growls from outside the tent—ill-maintained and nearly feral animals or engines. A clown staggered out of a door, seemingly both lame and intoxicated, his two legs feral also and certainly ill-maintained. Then he fell, a blur of red spots and gaudy tartan, somersaulted several times over the sawdust floor and suddenly telescoped to stand upright before the ringmaster.

"Guests," the clown said. "We have guests."

They thought they had not been noticed.

"It is hours before showtime," the ringmaster said. "Send them packing. Packing. Send them packing."

"There they are." The clown pointed across the ring at them as two more clowns, huge as dancing bears, came in through the entrance flap, possessed the ground and blocked their exit. Though they sported white greasepaint, exaggerated smiles and large red noses, their expressions were threatening.

"Come," the ringmaster said. "Come here. Let me see you."

The quartet of interlopers hesitated, but the hoarse, sweet breaths of the clowns behind them were like spurs and so they moved into the centre of the ring. Above them, the trapeze was still, the acrobats hovering like waiting vultures.

Gerry crossed his arms over his puffed-out chest and frowned with *gravitas*.

"I am Chief Black Heart, Lakota from the Sioux Nation. This my blood brother I name Steadyhand." He indicated Motl. "This German killed a buffalo with his bare hands. And a gun."

Motl grinned and shrugged as if he didn't even remember.

Gerry laid his arm on Esther's shoulder. "Miss Annie, most sure shot in all Oklahoma. And my friend Fire Tongue, a Dakota. He ride like arrow."

Mike nodded solemnly, keeping his eponymous tongue to himself.

Gerry opened his arms, inviting the ringmaster to behold: "The most excellent Wild West show in the Reich."

Impressive pause.

Then he said, "We would like to join your circus.

"Imagine Winnetou and Old Shatterhand in your ring. Imagine the horses—Wind, and his brother Lightning—as they blast past the audience at a gallop, riders balanced, standing on their saddles, lassos like snakes flying through the air, bullets piercing the edges of playing cards. The wisdom of the Sioux, sharp as arrowheads or a tomahawk blade."

"Take them to a train car," the ringmaster said. "Take them."

And the trio of clowns placed their gloved hands on each of their shoulders. "This way."

The clowns led them out the other side of the tent and up the steps and into a bright painted car.

"You will wait," one of the clowns ordered.

The car was like a hotel room. Red velvet couch, leather chairs, beds, clothes scattered over dressers and bundling out of drawers. A side table with bottles and a plate of bread and cheese.

The clowns closed the door, and they heard a click as the lock was drawn.

First thing: bread and cheese.

Next: mugs of Pilsner.

"*Chief* Black Heart?" Mike said to Gerry. "Why do you get to be the chief?"

Gerry crossed his arms. "Ancient Sioux wisdom: power comes to those who tell the story."

They clinked glasses, and settled in to wait.

An hour later, the lock was drawn back and a woman entered. She had the same red face as the ringmaster, the same lightning eyes and the same stovepipe hat, which she placed on the floor beside where she sat.

"I am prettier without the beard. And without a belly," she said. "Many of us here are in disguise. In disguise."

She held out her hand and waited. Was she miming a one-handed strangling?

They weren't sure what to do. Then Esther poured a mug of Pilsner and set it in the curve of the ringmaster's palm. She nodded.

"Circus folk know performers. Unlike dogs, we don't need to sniff, but we know. We know. And we know you're not. It's how you use the air. How you move through it. How you stand in it. How you use time."

She raised the glass to them. "*Za nas!* To us!" And drank the beer in a single draft, wiped her lip on the brocade of her sleeve and again held her hand out, motioning to Esther. As soon as the mug was topped with foam, she began again. "But circus folk are nomads. Some spend lives moving through the air, hardly touching the ground. Wandering Jews. Bucket Riders. Cowboys. Travellers. Rovers.

"So though I doubt you can shoot gnats or fleas, stars or wise-cracks from the air or dance on the spine of a filly, you can stay with us. Hide with us. Jew or Romani. Homosexual or Communist. There's always a broom and a cage or a bucket and comb. Or shoes to polish. Big shoes.

"We don't need to know who you are. Perhaps it's better not to know. Unless you're Gestapo. We allow our lions to crunch Gestapo skulls then suck their brains. Like eating Fascist snails. A delicacy. Though the next day, there's digestive problems. You're not Gestapo, are you? Are you?"

"If we were, we wouldn't tell you," Mike said. "But by saying this, perhaps you will believe us more."

"You're not Gestapo. This I know. Gestapo use the air, move through time differently also. Especially when in a lion's jaws.

"Nazis steal who you are, turn you to what their Zyklon eyes desire so their balls shudder with righteous loathing, their tongues coil in intoxicated revulsion. Most of their victims become wraiths haunted by memories of what was, if they can remember, and what could have been.

"But in the circus, it is us who tell Nazis who they are. Our enchantments twist and orchestrate, capture and con."

She downed her beer again in a single action, then wiped the foam from her mouth.

"But alas, this magic is for moments only, for the times they watch and cheer, turned into little boys in knickerbockers. And when it is done, they return to the poisoned world."

Esther refilled her mug before she asked, and then everyone else's. Together they lifted them.

When it is difficult to toast the future, then one raises a glass and drinks to the amber moment itself, to those who cannot drink. "*Za tych co nie mogą.*"

They drank.

"Tonight," the ringmaster said, "the Führer's bootlicking side-kick Heinrich Reichsführer Himmler himself will be in the audience as he has come to Poland to do some *Schutzstaffel*ing. And so, we will have the honour of providing him a rejuvenating distraction from the demands of his work. And Heinie loves Wild West shows. So you will, after all, perform in buckskin and loin-cloth. I'll send in someone to get you fitted."

And she left to attend to circus affairs.

"I am Gretl," a young woman dressed in a dark and too-large greatcoat announced to them all soon afterwards, and escorted the would-be Wild West troupe to the costume boxcar. She outfitted Motl in a ten-gallon hat, a leather vest, and a scarf of a striking Polish folk design of red, blue and black flowers, which would serve as a bandana. When tied around his face, its heritage wasn't apparent. His wasn't either.

Gretl helped him strap on an elaborately tooled gun belt and double holster around the waist of a pair of boot-cut blue jeans, images of swirling birds and flowers embossed into the brown leather. She gave him two brightly polished nickel-plated six-guns, mismatched but resembling Smith & Wessons. He held them up and spun the cylinders, listening for the sound of possibility.

Gretl retrieved two cowboy boots from a pile of mismatched and improbable footwear that were approximately his size, and decoratively stitched with what looked like the spiky leaves of weeds.

Spurs with golden rowels that resembled two bright suns with jingo bobs attached, so Motl made a pleasing tintinnabulation as he jangled around the boxcar.

Motl. Dressed for the first time as a Litvak cowboy, rider of the fabled Pale-of-Settlement range. Its open air, its fenceless opportunity, its wide-skied freedom. Its hard-won, leathery optimism.

Motl, who was not just a middle-aged Jew, mad with terror, forced to stampede by the crush of history, but instead a tough hombre woven into its tapestry. There he is, squinting into the hot sun and dry wind, teeth clamped around a cigarillo, facing life with resolve and determination. What heartbreak he carried would be only what he chose to ride toward, or away from.

But so often things come after their time.

The cure for the fatal disease arrives at your wake.

You tote your saddle to the corral, but White Flash is gone, wearing another's saddle.

You jump from the window, but the ground doesn't show up and, when it does, you're unprepared.

And now Motl was to be this cowpunch.

Gretl handed Gerry and Mike what appeared to be the wilted scalps of smeary geezers to use as their loincloths. They lobbied and were instead provided leather chaps and smocks. Black Pippi Longstocking wigs surmounted with chicken feathers dipped in paint completed their transformation into fearsome Indigenous warriors.

A farmer's straw hat, a floral skirt, a blouse and bright neckerchief served as Esther's sharpshooting cowgirl outfit. She was also given an almost comically large revolver with pearl handles by a rangy props man who resembled beef pizzle left too long in hot sun.

"It's our most feminine weapon," he said with the certain knowledge of a scholar.

The green room, an area at the back of the tent where performers gathered before going onstage, was a bustling market square of preparations. Clowns strode around, adjusting wigs, noses, tent-like costumes and suspenders, preparing trick flowers and step-ladders. Greasepainted soldiers in striped and spotted costumes prepared for a comic war.

Acrobats in spangles stretched their impossible spines, casually contorting as they chatted. Beyond the canvas, trainers purred intimately to their animals.

The sound of fervent anticipation filled the tent as the audience gathered, the singsong of vendors offering peanuts and beer and the enthusiastic patter of jugglers and magicians. Motl and the other members of his not-very-wild Wild West show had been led through their routines by the ringmaster only moments before and now they waited for the show to begin.

15

The ringmaster, clad in her tumbleweed beard and impressively rotund midriff, green tails and towering stovepipe hat, silently stepped into the middle of the ring.

A click and she was revealed to the audience in a moon-sized pool, brass buttons and silver whip handle sparkling. A dramatic pause and she spread her arms like a prophet and proclaimed: "Ladies and Gentlemen, boys and girls, Officers, Soldiers, Aryans, *Herrenvolk*, citizens of this our Third Reich and especially Reichsführer Himmler. Welcome. It is our honour to entertain you."

Cheering.

"And if you happen to be a Jew, please identify yourself so we can pay special attention to you on this, the last night of your life."

Laughter.

"Prepare yourself to be blitzed by marvels, invaded by thrills. Get ready to collaborate with clowns and surrender to joy. If it feels like the Reich has gone on for a thousand years already, relax, sit back and enjoy the delights we have in store. Tonight we are especially happy to feature a Wild West show. Real Winnetou

Indians and an Old Shatterhand Cowboy. A chief, a brave, an outlaw and a lady sharpshooter from Oklahoma.

"Why are these Americans in the Fatherland? They feel the same way about their government as we do."

More laughter and huge applause.

A flash of light and a blast of pink smoke. A tiny clown, fired from a tiny howitzer, lands, then somersaults into several goose-stepping clowns. They jump so they're not bowled over like pins.

A miniature Beetle careens in, honking.

A clown falls from the window.

"How many clowns can you fit in a Volkswagen?" the ringmaster shouts. "*Ach*, don't worry, if you need more room, just take your neighbours' car."

More clowns leap from the windows. An inconceivable number. Now they're soldiers in line. A self-important clown in an enormous feathered hat is Gruppenführer. He begins the inspection. First clown Hitler-salutes and knocks off Gruppenführer's hat. Gruppenführer retrieves it and examines the second clown who salutes and knocks off Gruppenführer's hat. Gruppenführer retrieves it and examines third clown. *Sieg Heil* and the hat is knocked off Gruppenführer. Fourth clown. *Sieg Heil* and the hat falls. And so on, a clown salutes and the hat is knocked off. Until the last clown, who sports a prodigious flower in his lapel.

"Soldier, that's not dress code!" Gruppenführer barks. He leans in and—just as the audience expects—water shoots, first in Gruppenführer's eye then at Gruppenführer's hat, which falls to the ground.

Exeunt Nazi clowns, Gruppenführer, shaking his hat, in pursuit.

Enter a battalion of poodles, feet and heads like meringue. Skinny chests half-immersed in hair like bubble-bath suds.

Enter the trainer in jackboots. *"Achtung, Pudelhunde,"* he barks, and the poodles run in circles, yipping and jumping miniature Arc de Triomphe hurdles. They're French poodles, after all.

The trainer whistles and more dogs rush in wearing Moulin Rouge skirts, turn tail to the audience and begin to cancan.

Again the trainer whistles and still more dogs appear, this time wearing berets. He pretends to pour wine into each dog's open mouth, and each dog falls down on its back, passed out drunk.

Then all the dogs sit before him.

"It is time, *mes chiens français*, to fight the Germans," the trainer says.

All thirty dogs fall down, playing dead.

Fade to black.

The sound of a banjo.

Spotlight on ringmaster.

Then spotlights on Gerry and Mike in full Indianer finery, holding bows and arrows.

"Though red as canyons, our warrior braves stand straight as pine trees, strong as *Reichsadler* eagles, their noses Roman, the six-packs of their bellies like Tuscan hills, or the bulging coils of bratwurst in a shopping bag. They gaze into the vast and unknown prairie night, last of a vanishing race, and know what courage is, what it is to fight without fear for their nation."

Spotlight on the other side of the ring: Motl and Esther, the light lustrous on their nickel-plated pistols.

"The outlaw and the sharpshooter. The front and the frontier. We make room for civilization, seek blood and soil for new settlement. And these valiant freedom fighters, range-riding putschists, soldiers of the future, dare to imagine a new world as our Führer did.

"Attend now to marvels, to these Paganinis of the trigger, virtuosi of the bullet and the bull's eye, as they perform feats even William Tell would tremble in the face of."

From the shadows, two women dressed like Indianer squaws. Pocahontasbergers. They balance bottles of Red Eye Whiskey on Gerry and Mike's heads. Gerry holds another bottle on his outstretched hand.

Motl stands steady, legs apart, arms akimbo, hands resting on his holstered guns. Esther holds her pistol at eye level, one hand supporting the other.

Two men, duded up as cowhands, blindfold them then spin them around several times. They do not end up where they began.

The audience: murmuring.

Drum roll.

"Are you ready, Billy? Ready, Emaline?" the cowhands say to Motl and Esther.

A quick nod from Motl. "Since I was weaned from Mama," he shouts.

He pulls the hammers on his guns.

Click.

Esther pulls the hammer on hers.

Click.

The ringmaster raises her whip.

It happens all at once. Esther squeezing the trigger. Motl's guns out of his holsters and smoking, the three bottles balanced on the heads of Mike and Gerry shattering. Glass jewelling their hair and faces.

The whip cracking in the air.

The audience: gasping.

The three circus clowns retracting their guns and slipping back through the curtains.

The ovation.

16

Intermission. *Der treue Heinrich*, the "half-starved shrew," Reichsführer-SS Himmler himself, requested to meet the Wild West troupe, the "cowboys" separately from the "Indians." Nazis maintain an interest in sorting by categories.

Esther and Motl waited outside the private lounge where Himmler was holding an efficient and ruthless reception.

"I can shoot a bottle blindfolded, but no matter the distance I'll never find his chin," Motl said.

"Or his heart."

"He's a bootlicker—trying to lick hard enough to please Hitler's stunted little toes."

"Still, one weaselly nod and mama's boy Heini could send us to Dachau."

"Of course. We'll lick his boots, too. That's how it works."

"He must know we're not really cowboys."

"I've brought the Ḥakhan's papers. So he'll know we're Karaites."

"Yes, it's more convenient to die here than to have to travel all the way to Berlin to do it."

"The papers are supposed to help us."

"Ask Indians how that usually works out. Anyway, we could just leave with Gerry and Mike instead."

"I've still got to go to Switzerland—and not just to yodel."

"Why don't you forget that and just be safe? We'd go together."

An officer opened the door and spoke to one of the guards posted outside.

The guard saluted and turned to them. "The Reichsführer is ready."

"Whatever we decide, we'd better do a bit of cowboy first," Esther said.

Chinless Himmler sat at a table, brocaded and laden with insignia. He was a weasel in rimless glasses, his roadkill moustache, a strip of balding mouse-hide, his receding hair revealing the waxen territory of his head, a delusional land of murderous functionaries and Teutonic cartoons. Himmler the petty emperor of a gas station or roadside fruit stand, he aspired to Genghis Khan greatness, attempting to compensate for his weak physiognomy through cruelty.

"Right proud to meet you, sir," Motl said, tipping his hat. "The heart in my brisket is swole big as a saddle blanket. You're ace-high with us cowpokes."

"We're powerful glad to make your acquaintance," Esther said with a combination curtsey and buckaroo nod. "*Heil Hitler*."

"*Heil Hitler*," Himmler said, and they all saluted. "Now sit. We were pleased by your performance. We value discipline. We value diligence. And my SS officers were entertained. A drink for the performers."

A waiter placed whiskey before them.

"When I was a boy in Munich, and my *schöne* mama read to me, I thought cowboys to be our Teutonic Knights. Strong, courageous, steadfast and loyal. They, like us, cleared territory for their people to live. We value such warriors." Himmler pursed his lips primly. "And now we are at war with America. Who are your people?"

"The Reich."

"Of course. But you are not Americans."

"We . . ." Motl began, then reached for the bag slung behind him. "We have papers." He slid the sealed documents onto the table as if laying out a poker hand. Five aces.

The Reichskommissar for the Consolidation of Germanness regarded the folio.

"Our Ḥakhan wished for us to deliver this to you, Reichsführer."

"Jews." It was as if the room had darkened. And darkened Hebraically, right to left. The soldiers in the room straightened.

"No, Herr Reichsführer: Karaites," Esther said. "We are a Mosaic religion, but not Catholics. Not Jews. Respectfully, your commission has determined that."

Himmler raised his hand. A pause and then a soldier strode forward and placed a *Totenkopf* Nazi death's head letter opener in his hand. With the slightest twitch of acknowledgement, Himmler cut open the seal and then the envelope. He removed the document as a sword from a sheath.

"Yes," he said. "From your Ḥakhan. He is known to us. He has provided information in the past." Himmler's face was as emotionless as an empty sink. "A list of who is a Karaite. Who is posing. Very helpful, don't you think, *meine* cowboys?"

He poured some water from a jug into a glass on the table before him and took a precise sip, then touched a linen napkin to his lips, as if reverentially kissing it. A stylized eagle balanced atop a swastika, the initials *H H* on either side, was embroidered on the corner.

"This document you have delivered provides such information. And it arrives with a letter."

Esther and Motl did not see any indication of an order from Himmler. But it seemed that the invisible tilt of a single Reichsführer-SS molecule was sufficient cause for the four soldiers in the room to move forward, silently gathering around the table.

Himmler held up the letter and a soldier took it from him.

"His Excellency Hajji Seraya Khan Shapshal . . ." the soldier began.

"*Your* Ḥakhan," Himmler interjected, staring at them with intent.

"Writes that 'upon receipt of this letter and the list which accompanies it,'" the soldier continued, "'the two messengers delivering it . . .'"

Himmler took the letter from the soldier and continued. "'. . . masquerading as Karaites, are entrusted into the care of the Reich and, specifically, the SS, as a sign of the good faith and loyalty of His Excellency Hajji Seraya Khan Shapshal, in order that his most esteemed and respected Reichsführer Heinrich Himmler may attend to them in whatever manner he deems most appropriate for those determined to be Jewish *Unnütze Esser*— useless mouths—life unworthy of life.'

"Well," Himmler said. "As it is written on the gates of Buchenwald, *Jedem das Seine*. To each his own. Do you not think so, Sturmmann Müller?"

"Yes, Herr Reichsführer. *Die Juden sind unser Unglück*," the soldier Müller said. "The Jews are indeed our misfortune."

The four soldiers pulled their Lugers from their holsters like gunslingers and pointed them at Esther and Motl.

"*Die Meisterslingers*, no?" Himmler said.

A knife tore through the canvas wall and Mike and Gerry were borne into the room on a wave of sinister ululations and fearsome whooping from a Wild West film. They had tomahawks but also guns. The uncanny appearance of a scene from a storybook massacre bewildered the soldiers, who didn't understand their role in this or what to do.

"Go!" Gerry shouted, and the four of them—Mike, Gerry, Motl and Esther—disappeared through the rent in the tent wall, Mike grabbing the letter from the table as he ran.

Behind them, they could hear Himmler, apparently also bewildered by the raid, shouting foul-mouthed reprimands and contradictory orders at the soldiers.

The ringmaster was waiting outside.

"Follow," she said.

They ran to the boxcar, near the tent where performers were stretching, drinking, adjusting, animals pacing restlessly around the limited world of their boxcar cages, before the second half of the show began.

"Here," the ringmaster said, stopping them at the tiger cage. She gave a sharp look at the trainer, who unbolted the door, slid inside and offered a palmful of meat to the vast cat.

"In," the ringmaster said, indicating that they too should enter the cage. Was it to be death by Fritz or feline, better to be gnawed by cat or executed by Krauts?

They sidestepped along the side of the cage, pressing against the bars on the supposition that even a few extra inches of distance from the tiger would be that much more safe, would provide seconds more life if it were to spring. A door at the end of the cage, painted with a scene of dense subcontinental vegetation, hanging snakes, tigers bright as flame against the shadows of the mango-strewn, bird-busy trees, opened onto a secret compartment. It might be *de rigueur* to hide behind bookcases, in basements, cellars, orphanages, attics or holes in the ground, but the Germans would never think to look behind the tiger. Who seeks refuge in fire when they leap from a pan?

By the time a squad of spirited Nazi soldiers came running into the area with their guns drawn, the trainer had bolted the door and was standing outside, murmuring to the tiger, intermittently snapping his whip as if preparing the animal for the upcoming act. The ringmaster had joined the performers in the green room and was deep in consultation with the contortionist.

A small opening in the roof of the boxcar allowed a thin column of light to reach the fugitives. Their pupils were dilated the size of dimes. And not only because of the dimness. While their escape had been an ironic adventure-story rescue, replete with storybook Indian warriors and an excess of feathers and whooping, it had also been very narrow, in the way the edge of a razor is narrow.

"We were almost dead Karaites in there," Motl said.

"Or non-non-Karaites."

"I'm alive, though at the moment I'm not sure what I am."

"Not eaten by a tiger."

"In any case, thanks."

"Look," Mike said, waving the pages. "The letter from the Hakhan. It doesn't say what Himmler said it did. It says to offer you safe passage."

"I always thought Himmler wasn't good for the Jews."

———

They huddled in the tiger cage. They were sure that the performance would be over by midnight. By dawn, the big top would be torn down, the circus packed and the train headed for a field in the next village. If they encountered Nazis there, at least it would be different Nazis. They waited.

"What if they forget about us here?"

"They won't."

"How long would it take before we ate each other?"

"Raw?"

"Would you eat a Nazi if there was no other choice?"

"I don't know. Are they kosher?"

"Definitely *treif*. Most of them have cloven hooves."

"What's the blessing—the *bracha*—for eating Nazi?"

After they'd been hiding for only fifteen minutes, they heard a voice from the ceiling, someone muttering through the hole in the roof. An angel, but it was too early for angels. If they came, they'd come after the Nazis had found them and then only after they were executed. Jewish angels with cloud-white rabbi beards and goose-feather wings.

"Listen," a girl's voice said. "Ringmaster sent me. She'll help two of you escape to Switzerland. Two of you. The Jewish ones. The others should stay on the circus train. Then do their vanishing act when it's rendezvous time." She explained the plan, then dropped some makeup and clothes through the hole.

There's only one of the Ten Commandments that applies to circuses: the show must go on. And so, five minutes after the girl left, the trainer came to lead the tiger into the tent for its act, and Motl and Esther, as instructed, walked out of the empty cage, dressed as clowns. They'd painted their lips red and huge like sausages, and smeared their faces white; they wore ruddy and bulbous noses like the nipples of giants. Straw-haired dogs had curled then died upon their heads. Like tramps, they wore mangy oversized suits and floppy-soled shoes like slapsticks.

While the show continued and the officers gulleted peanuts and beer, the soldiers continued to prowl outside the big top, searching for the vanishing Indians, the wandering Jews. And Esther and Motl teetered to the centre of the ring with a squad of other clowns.

The ground beneath them was the deck of a writhing ship, the shaking surface of a jelly. The contingent world on which we mortals stagger.

"We make the *minyan*," Motl said to Esther, observing the numbers of their new troupe, the necessary Jewish ten in order to pray. "Who knows who they are when they're not clowns."

One clown hit another on the noggin with a mallet. A different clown clutched his head. Still another fell down. In this circus, as with war, a single cause had bewildering effects.

Himmler had returned to his seat in the centre of the front row, his legs crossed, his hands resting on a walking stick, as if no incident had troubled him during the intermission. He smirked. He was amused. He enjoyed groups in ridiculous uniforms contriving to please him with their antics.

Esther fell down. No one had hit anyone with a mallet, but she was improvising. Then the first clown hit another clown. The effect before the cause.

Motl looked at his clown hand and made his fingers into a gun. He spun the imaginary cartridge, Russian roulette–style, then shot himself in the head. Three other clowns collapsed. Esther stood up. She looked at her hand. She made her fingers into a gun. She pointed it at her head, considering if she should shoot.

Then she pointed it at the audience and shot. Three clowns stood up.

Then all of the clowns made their hands into guns, and one stood against an imaginary wall, ready to be executed. Another clown gave the order, and all the clowns fired. They all fell down, except for the condemned clown, who remained standing.

Then Motl stood and pointed his gun at Himmler. All the clowns got up and held their hands against the sides of their heads, arms akimbo. "Oh, no!" they mimed.

Motl raised his other hand into the air, a rodeo rider holding on to rope, breaking a bucking bronc, the other gun hand steady toward the Reichsführer.

Then he fired.

Simultaneously:

Everything went dark.

The sound of a real gun.

The *ungh* of someone being hit.

Then, after a long minute and invisible confusion, the lights came on again. Himmler and his surrounding posse had disappeared. Motl was on the sawdust, clutching his shoulder.

The audience stood in a bewildered hubbub of carping and speculation. The clowns circled around Motl, lifted him up and then ran for the wings.

"Good Ladies and Most Gentle Men," the ringmaster announced from the now-empty ring. "Within this round and sawdusty O, we expect all to be circus, that no shadows will fall. But today this war and its assaults and contusions have entered this tent. The dangers you see in here—our leaps and bullets, roaring mouths, our ballets in the sky—these are made for amazement and inspiration, not for thoughts of strife or mortality. The world has here pierced a performer and so, for tonight, our circus is at an end. Tomorrow and the next tomorrow, the circus will continue. Our clowns will clown, our acrobats will fly, our tigers will roar. We will again raise the big top and find reason for joy and belief. But for now, it is time for you to find your homes safely and without delay."

And she bowed deeply to the empty tent and strode quickly away.

17

A lanky clown in yellow suspenders and a red fright wig appeared with bandages, tongs, vodka, matches and a knife. The standard circus emergency kit.

"Time for bullet hunting. Drink this," he said to Motl, and tipped the bottle into Motl's groaning mouth—anaesthetic via vodka-boarding. Motl struggled to gulp and not breathe the fire-water, to avoid being non-metaphorically drowned. Then the clown tore his jacket and shirt and tipped the bottle over his shoulder, hooch pooling in the wound. Motl would have leapt up and run a vicious circle around the circus, hollering, except a gang of the big-shoed held him down.

"Esther," Motl moaned.

"We put her in a dressing room so she can calm down—she thought you'd been killed," the clown said.

The gang had more work to do after the clown went in with the tongs and the knife, spelunking for lead.

The bullet had disappeared.

They turned him over. There was a hole in his back. The bullet had come and gone, entered and left.

"Should've thought of that," the clown with the tongs and knife said.

"Hold him up and you can see clear through," another clown observed.

"He's been daylighted."

The clown poured vodka in the wound on Motl's back. "Hold a glass up to his front. Let's not waste it."

The clown lit a match and touched the flame to the wound. The vodka flared with a cauterizing sizzle. Motl screeched and then passed out. They turned him over again and repeated the process, the scent of Motl-flesh filling the air.

The ringmaster arrived with Esther, who had been declowned and was now dressed in a tweed civilian jacket and dress, like a civil servant on her way home.

"Motl," Esther said, rushing over, kneeling down and embracing him.

"The shoulder!" the clown warned as Motl woke with a gasp.

She kissed his forehead, his cheeks, then his lips. "Motl."

"I've explained everything to Esther," the ringmaster said.

Esther wiped the clown face from Motl and helped him change into a nondescript suit.

"That is the person," Esther said.

In the tent's shadows, a man, scrawny and harmless as a broom but, like a broom, deadly when used in the right way and at the right time. The perfect operative.

"The ringmaster made arrangements," she said. "The man's a toxic weasel, but he'll take us to Switzerland. We have no choice except to embrace such fiends."

"Hard to do while holding our noses."

They began walking to the tiger cage, hiding behind tents and other boxcars, attempting to remain unseen.

"This is the story. The Nazis have been laundering stolen gold—*Raubgold*—in Switzerland. Himmler dropped by to arrange a little private deal of his own—a secret the ringmaster couldn't help but overhear because, as she told me, 'It's true—no matter how much you whisper, you can have no secrets under the big top.' So, we're going to help Himmler, and he's going to let us. He's arranged everything. The only thing is . . . Mike and Gerry have to be sacrificed."

"How can we do that?"

"It's terrible, but there's only room for two on the plane. And the plane is what saves us. If we warn them, though, it gives them time to escape and maybe they can make Gerry's rendezvous."

"It's not right."

"It's a chance for us to have a life. Together. To survive."

"Yes, but . . ."

"Gerry is a soldier. He'll understand. He'll know what to do."

"My mother. Your father. Everything else. Now this. How much can we hold inside before we're corroded, before we're hollow and can't breathe?"

The tiger had been returned to the cage after the show and was prowling the narrowness of its world with barely repressed malevolence. Esther leaned close to the bars near the hidden compartment and whispered to Mike and Gerry.

"There's a plane for us to Switzerland. Motl and I must go. But the Germans have been told where you're hiding. You have to leave. Now. For Gdansk."

They heard the ruckus of a troop of soldiers coming toward the cage.

"Quick," Esther said to Motl. "We're to meet behind the dog kennel." They crossed around the far side of the tiger cage and then hurried toward their rendezvous.

They both could hear the tiger's cage door rattling. Howling. Shrieks. The tiger furious. There was no mistaking the sound of a big cat attack. Roaring.

Unintelligible cries. From which mouth? What was the language? Gunshots.

Who had been attacked? Who had been shot?

18

"Now I'm a real cowboy. I've betrayed Indians who befriended me. Indians who saved me," Motl said.

Motl and Esther had climbed in the back of an army transport truck that had been waiting for them, and settled between piles of large sacks as the transport rumbled over a dirt track across the field.

The operative held on to a strap on the wall. He caught their eyes and motioned to the canvas mounds all around them.

"The dead can possess nothing. What they had belongs now to the living. To their country. Gold in the mouth at death? Only the living are entitled to their teeth. Why should it be buried with them when it can benefit the Reich? The teeth of the Jews are rich in gold. They are bent dwarves with gold inside. Crooked-lipped vermin with glittering mouths."

"These sacks contain . . . teeth?"

"They were dipped in acid and dissolved. Sent to a foundry along with wedding rings and turned into gold bars. You will transport them to Switzerland for the Führer. It is needed to win this war."

Like so much else, they knew this was a fiction. It was code for

"Himmler is a thief stealing from thieves but we will pretend there is honour there."

There were Swiss accounts in the name of Max Heiliger waiting to receive this stolen gold. An ironic joke. *Heiliger* is "holy" in German and so the gold from teeth, glasses, wedding rings was melted and deposited as bars along with plundered banknotes and jewellery.

Motl and Esther balanced on the bench against the truck walls, holding on to the straps as the truck rattled toward the plane, surrounded by gold from the mouths of Jews. Silently speaking to them. Pleading with them. Accusing them. Asking for witness.

The operative did not speak again until they trundled onto the landing strip.

"You are no longer Karaite, but Swiss. New names have been assigned to you. You are Denis and Sofia Genoud. Here is your documentation. Destroy your other papers. You may be searched after the plane lands. This is a highly confidential operation."

And he motioned to them to climb from the truck and board the plane for the West.

Denis and Sofia. Motl and Esther, a married couple. Their new life would begin as Monsieur and Madame Genoud.

Motl regarded Esther, his not-really wife, wondering if their union could become true should his return to the mountains be successful.

The sacks, filled with gold from rings and hitherto grinning or grimacing teeth from mouths now finally closed, were loaded into a Junkers Ju 52 transport plane, an Aunti Ju, an Iron Annie. It had no other cargo except for the newly Swiss couple returning home for the first time to make a deposit at the National Bank, and the two pilots in the cockpit.

Luftwaffe Captain Fritz and First Officer Fritz, his co-pilot.

Monsieur and Madame Genoud climbed the rolling stairs and into the shadowy green glade of the Junkers's belly. They flipped down two seats and strapped in. The guttural trill of the three engines, their propellers juddery as the plane heaved forward.

Motl held Esther's hand. Together, they'd leap from this cliff, fall up into the air, survive that moment when the craft no longer touches the ground, earth and its gravity left behind like ballast, like forgetting, and the air takes you into its arms like an embrace. That moment when the teeth rattle.

A porthole in the side of the airplane. Other than dreams, the first time Motl had ever been in the air. He watched. The lights shining from the plane made the view uncanny.

Clouds as a continuous fabric of spirits. A killing field obscuring the ground, thousands of feet below. The countless breaths of the dead a white plain.

Dimensionless sky above. A vacant eternity.

Sorrow in a place so vast, it might well have evaporated into nothingness. Infinitesimal. Like a dove, an insignificant speck above a loss-flooded world.

If this was an image of Heaven, Heaven was empty or huge beyond conception. Beyond the human.

A rumbling as they passed over cumulus. Motl imagined a limitless herd of invisible bison running the breath-white prairie, a stampede's turbulence.

There were wisps above the cloud cover.

Shrouds that had floated free, risen from the clouds, buoyed by voices below.

Yisgadal v'yiskadash sh'mei rabbaw.

The voices of the dead. Praying for each other. They were remembering.

Y'hei sh'mei raba m'varach
l'alam ul'almei almaya.

They were singing for the living.

The melody reached into the future. Sorrowing. The melody rose into the present, like mountains visible above the clouds. Consoling.

The gold from teeth was behind them, clanking, and they were flying above the clouds. There were wedding rings making the passage over mountains.

"Look," said Motl. "Do you see?"

"The clouds—mashed potatoes made of air?" Esther said. "Poland and Germany and Lithuania, the war—somewhere behind us? The sky, like it was cleaned by the colour blue? Escape?"

"No, over there. See the peaks of the mountains?"

"Yes."

"See that valley where there's snow?"

"Yes."

"See that glacier?"

"Yes."

"Do you know what's waiting for us there?"

"What?"

"Our future."

⊰ PART THREE ⊱

The future is dark, with a darkness as much of the womb as the grave.

—REBECCA SOLNIT

I

SWITZERLAND

The airport had a wide tarmac road beginning nowhere then, without warning, arriving there. Beside it, an incongruous Arts and Crafts—style house, its roof mollycoddling a profusion of gables. Rocking chairs beside its exposed-wood porch contained contented Nazis taking an *Einsatzschloff*, perhaps counting sheep that couldn't get over the fence they patrolled. As the travellers descended, the German soldiers woke up and then ran onto the runway, marshalling the plane with a hurried "all clear" *Sieg Heil* and then additional arm waving, apparently suggesting the pilots slow the plane down.

One of the Nazis drove a small truck up to the plane and began unloading.

In the terminal, there were no customs agents.

"What do you have to declare?" Motl imagined one of the soldiers asking.

"Teeth," Motl would say.

"Incisors or molars? Brushed or not? Jewish or non-Jewish? Do you floss?"

Instead, they were approached by a banker in a money-scented business suit that spoke of conspicuous ironing.

"Monsieur and Madame Genoud, I am Monsieur Denaud. I welcome you to Switzerland on behalf of the National Bank. If you will be so kind as to wait outside, I will request my car."

Motl to Esther: We don't believe in borders, just in fencing.

Esther to Motl: Wash and Fold. Delicates or Whites. Banknotes, jewellery, stolen gold. We launder it all.

They went out onto the porch.

"Switzerland. It's all around us," Motl said.

"It's a clever design," Esther said. "For a country."

For Motl, not the William Tell apple split from a quivering son's head but Tzara's between-the-legs bull's eye of his own apples, lost in snow.

His quest. Finally reachable. Retrieve these hairy grails so life could begin anew.

His mother, his sister, Hannah, his family, lost. Esther's family: grandfather, brother, father. Gone.

A child.

They'd have a bairn, a wean, a sprogget, a kiddiewink. A lamb, a foal, a newling. Something to rekindle life itself.

A begetter, he'd make of himself an ancestor, a circumcised forefather with this bedwetter, this baby, an angel of history flying like a dove into the now-possible future.

Motl. Thrustless stallion by proxy. Procreator. Breeder.

Father.

And Esther, a mother, her world become a womb. A wound healed. Consoled. Salved. She could whisper her father's words in its tiny pink ears, delicate mollusc shells, the child protected by their hope, their love.

The wisp of souls lost to them, gathered in diapers, in this bassinet of their embracing. A thousand years before, when their people squinted into time, they imagined this coupling, this mewling, this little Jewish piglet.

A black limousine appeared from behind the airport house. A chauffeur stepped out and offered them an open door. The banker was already inside, sprawled back against the seat, legs spread, a cigar like a bulrush clamped between his teeth, his exhalations turned to blue exhaust. He gestured to the black leather across from him.

"The truck with your capital will follow us to the bank," he said.

There was no mention of Nazis, of nationality. Monsieur and Madame Genoud were simply customers who wished to make a deposit.

They were expecting to arrive at a grand marble bank fronted with Corinthian columns and baroque scrolls, to be greeted with the precise politeness of bank officials handing them flutes of champagne as they entered.

"Monsieur Genoud. Madame Genoud. Welcome home. We thank you for trusting us with your deposit."

Then a brief ceremony where they'd sign papers and gloved officials elegantly removed the sacks to somewhere in the vaulted interior of the bank and then the two of them together would walk down the many white steps to the pavement where they would begin their new life free of teeth, obvious Nazis and fear.

Instead, they were transported in a cigar-blue cloud through postcard-green fields spotted with chalets and bell-wearing cows come down from the hills. They travelled as the dog flies, at least in dreams, meandering from one vague scent to another, a yarn-tangle of a route, untrackable, the truck with the gold following them. Eventually they stopped in a small village in the crook of a valley, with a church, a school and a small bank building.

The chauffeur opened the door for the banker, who handed him the stub of his cigar then motioned for Esther and Motl to follow him into the bank. It would have been the perfect place for a heist, mild-looking tellers standing behind their wickets and a lineup of a handful of locals waiting to deposit their market earnings. "This is a stickup. Everyone on the ground." Motl waving a pistol, Esther pointing and guiding people to the tile floor.

"Your money or your life," Motl says to the teller.

"You want my life? It's much more exciting to be a bank robber."

But instead, the bags of loot were carried into the bank by the chauffeur. "Monsieur and Madame Genoud would like to make a deposit," the banker said to the nervously bowing branch manager, a man apparently made of loose change, obsequious sheep and a metronome. Bent as a sixpence and as thin, silver dollar–size lenses askew on the minuscule alp of his nose, he scurried before them the way one would kowtow to a grenade rolled through the door.

"Sir. Yes, sir. This is a welcome pleasure and a delightful surprise. We're honoured to assist you. Certainly. Most certainly. We're truly grateful for your business, Monsieur and Madame Genoud, most appreciative. Honoured indeed. We want only to serve."

Perhaps his wife and children, both his testicles and his little dog had been taken as collateral to ensure he accepted the gold as legitimate and asked no questions.

Two tellers hefted the bags through the wickets and carried them into the vault. Their contents were not counted or assessed, but a small leather passbook was offered to Motl and Esther, already filled out. There were also previously prepared deposit forms for both Monsieur Genoud and Madame Genoud to sign, which they did with a fountain pen and the awkward flourish of the newly flush and recently renamed.

Another flurry of servile appreciations and skittish bows from the branch manager. Surely his twitching chipmunk of a heart would soon quaver itself into bursting, spewing fragments of paperwork and sycophantic quisling sugar like volcanic ash settling over the inlay of the bank floor.

They left the bank and returned to the open door of the waiting limousine, the chauffeur handing a lit cigar to the banker.

"Perhaps in the interest of safekeeping and prudence, I could be trusted with your passbook," the banker told them, and then slipped the slim book they surrendered into his breast pocket.

2

The moon a bullet hole bleeding light visible through the window of the *pension* where the limousine had taken and deposited them after the bank. Motl on their bed, Esther sliding his jacket and shirt off his bandaged shoulder. A Nightingale intimacy of unwrapping gauze, then a damp handkerchief circling the wound's edge.

Motl winced and said, "Give m' hoss to the nipper. Tell him to heed the wind an' don't look a buffalo in the eye coz then you're too close and will be made pemmican in the stampede. And give m' gun to the clowns. These times, a red nose could use more than a barrel-imitating finger."

"I'll give them your bullets too," Esther said. "Saying 'bang' isn't enough, even with a real gun." She smoothed his temple. "But rest, Monsieur Genoud, rest."

And Motl, shirtless, lay back, taking Esther with him.

"With the hole right through you," she said, "you could work as a key fob."

"Better than a hitching post."

Out the window, the sheen of moon over mountain snow. The divided sky. Starlight harrowing Poland and Lithuania. A repose of stars on the slopes of Switzerland.

"We're only here because of who isn't," Motl said.

"That's how history always works."

"Sure, the past betrays, but we shouldn't."

"What can we do? We're here."

"The war. Our families. Mike and Gerry."

"We warned them."

"We almost literally fed them to the lions."

They listened to the wind and the distant sound of trumpets, some incongruous nocturnal emission involving tubas also.

They slept.

Motl woke, his arm around Esther. "Madame Genoud."

"Monsieur Genoud."

She was naked. He kissed her. Her small shoulders. Her greying hair, thin fingers, broken nails. He ran his hand over the small nubs of her spine, the fine hairs on the back of her thighs.

When he was a boy, Motl had once found himself with a girl in a storage room of the synagogue. He held her hand. Kissed her once. They had stood together awkwardly until they heard voices, then he hid while she slipped away. After twenty minutes, he emerged sweating. He had seen her the next day but was too overwhelmed to speak.

She had died in an accident when she was still a teenager. This Yuli, this lanky girl. He thought of her, his only kiss until Esther.

"*Mon petit chou,*" Esther said.

It was as if he were swimming without water, without any knowledge of swimming. Or water.

She moved his hand. "Like this, Monsieur Genoud."

What had he expected? His heart shaking, his hand nearly numb with fear and expectation.

The fine reddened veins of Esther's eyes. She rocked on the bed. He thought he might feel like leaping, a stallion or man broad-chested, sun-leathered and strong, but instead he felt electric, miniature, whirring like a train set, pins and needles prickling through his body. And though he knew it ridiculous, an image conjured by anxiety, he imagined his hand reaching through the curtains on the bimah, reaching for the Torah, hidden, powerful, charged. The ringing of the tiny bells in its silver crown.

Which reminded him of a story. A rabbi lived on the slope of a hill above the shtetl and because it was a mitzvah, a sacred good deed, to celebrate the immanence of God through the coupling of married bodies, because it was propitious to procreate on Shabbos, to *shmintz* with one's Faigel, he tied bells on his bedstead and opened his windows so the entire community could hear the silver ringing as he and the rebbetzin passed shards of divine light from one vessel to another.

"Oy mine God," the rebbetzin would say.

"I'm good, mine Faigeleh, but I'm not the Almighty Himself."

Then, "*Gevalt*," the rabbi would say. "Think I just smashed a tablet."

But the congregation would hear only the divine jingling like Van Gogh starlight over the town and know that the rabbi and rebbetzin were making the priest with two backs, making up for lost tribes.

Motl's nervous hand between Esther's legs. Esther rolling on the bed. Esther shuddering, weeping, shuddering. Then moving his hand away, holding him, kissing him. The two of them turned silver by moonlight.

"I wish I could . . ." he said. "I can't shoot . . . not even blanks."

"A cake that doesn't rise is still sweet," she said. "Especially on Passover—did our ancestors shlepping around the desert have time for it to rise? Besides, doesn't it say somewhere in the Torah that everything doesn't have to work for it to work? Or was that my bubbie?"

She brushed the hair back from his forehead, her other hand beginning the wandering toward, as she said, "the promised land."

"And besides, there's pleasure," she said.

"What'll that do?"

"Relieve some pain."

"And what'll that do?"

"Sometimes even cowboys bite the bullet and accept a little joy," she said.

He reached for her hand, and they lay there, hands intertwined, two tangled spiders at rest.

"After we find them in the mountains and we take them to a doctor . . ." Motl began. "And they defrost and he . . . Esther, I was hoping for this . . . I mean, Esther, would you consider . . . would you be willing . . . would . . . would you bear my colt?"

"Bear your colt? That's so romantic."

"It's because . . . I feel so awkward."

"Imagine me."

"Right. So a child—could we have a child? We're not too old. My mother was your age when she had her first child. Me. We'd be father and mother. Parents. Together."

"It usually works something like that."

"We'd make a new life, a new world. We'd start again. We could go to America."

"But first . . ."

"First, we search the glacier."

"Yes. For your two little lost Abrahams, like kittens, they must be so cute. Twin fathers of the Jews."

"Unless together we're the great patriarch Moses, bringing the tablets down from Sinai."

"Well, I've already been on fire."

3

Morning. They strolled into the farmlands outside the village, walking small paths through the fields. It wasn't only that the air was fresh, but that they could breathe differently. On the other side of the border they'd have travelled to the end of history. Here, it would be like a wake behind them.

Esther pointed out a verge of blue flowers.

"What you reckon—cornflowers?" Motl asked.

"Gentians, I think. If you asked what colour I feel inside, I'd say I was filled with that blue," Esther said. "Blue like the brightest of nights."

"And crowded with bees. Look." They crouched to examine the blooms more closely.

A fat one—if bees can be said to be fat—disappeared into the blue trumpet of a flower. It was a long time before it returned, covered in pollen. It took off, following a zigzag path, tacking over a fence toward its hive.

"Maybe I'm the blue of a gentian inside, but I'm also that bee. All this stuff sticking to me," Esther said.

"We've been deep in the same sad flower."

"And sticky with what? What we've left. What's gone. Who's gone."

"And grief. Grief made lacerating by guilt."

"That's some sweet honey, way beyond clover."

Wildflowers in the meadow. The drab joy of cowbells. Mountains and picturesque gables. Warm sun. They walked, their outsides, at least, charmed and lulled by this music, their insides gentian blue.

"Last night," Motl said, "I was talking to the concierge, and he told me Göring was injured in the Beer Hall Putsch and so, according to *Der Stürmer*, his beloved little Edda wasn't his. They say her father was a syringe. Göring was furious about the article. He didn't want anyone to know their Reichsmarschall was all *Luft* and no *waffe*."

"Bet he wishes the Putsch had taken place in the mountains."

"Anywhere but between his legs."

At the end of a field they came to a fence with a stile and legged it over. The steady dun eyes of cows considered them philosophically from under their long, tender-hearted lashes. The motionless Bessies appeared like features of the landscape—hillocks with udders—as if the rolling field had eyes and a constant, unassuming temperament.

Calves were clustered around their mothers, waiting to grow as large as leather sofas.

"Look at those droop-eyed rusties," Motl said. "The little wind-bellies. If I had a horse . . ."

He held his hand out as if feeding sugar to a pony, though all he could offer was sweat salt, palm lines—heart, life and love lines to be read by their wet snouts—and an expectation of reward.

"Here, little buttermilk," he crooned. One nonplussed calf regarded Motl warily and shuffled in his direction. Apparently it didn't know that Motl was well-read in both the major arcana of the cowpunch—the ropes, guns and ten-gallon hats—and the minor ones—the whiskey, Texas hold'em and boots—of the range-riding buckaroo.

Whether the calf's mother knew of Motl's burgeoning appreciation for the profound and abiding relationship of Indigenous people with the land and of their dire experience with colonial expansion was unclear, but this Swiss Minnie turned rumination into action, potential energy into hot-footed joules, and charged at them with abandon.

Esther was able to jackrabbit up onto the stile, while Motl, being in greater proximity to the calf, was the target of the meat-tenderizing hooves of this protective Daisy. She ran at him over the short grass, blasting spurts of cow breath from her dilated nostrils, glistening pink caves of burbling phlegm, while seemingly propelled by the methane-bleating detonations of her muffler end. If her eyes had previously regarded Motl philosophically, now they had the askew strabismus of a meat boulder intent on rendering Motl's corporeal materiality into a sack of insubstantial flesh. She ploughed into him, flipping him Schweiz over schnitzel, but it is difficult for a stampeding bovine to reverse and so this Henrietta had to make a circuit of the field in order to try again to pulverize her prey. This gave Motl time to drag himself over the stile before she fired up her beef engines and charged again on full power.

Motl fell onto the earth, looked up at the sky. He had not been made flat as paper, but had been broadsided and run over.

"Anything broken?" Esther asked.

Motl said nothing, only laughed. He had escaped the genocidal hankering of the Reich only for a cow to attempt to grind him into matzo meal and grits.

Then he stopped laughing. His ribs hurt and his entire body felt tenderized.

"Your shoulder?" Esther asked.

"The only part of me that doesn't hurt is the bullet hole," Motl said.

4

Esther helped Motl lower his cow-pressed Jew-jerky onto a seat on the Bern-bound train.

"Think of me as manna," he said, "flattened by my fall from Heaven."

When they arrived in Bern, they transferred to the train headed for Zimmerwald.

"Roadkill. You can say so much in two dimensions," he said, but he slept most of the way to Zimmerwald, his body using all of its energy in an effort to reinflate.

Half-awake, he'd mutter variously:

"Man is born to trouble as the sparks fly to the star-spurred dark."

"Soon we shall multiply and our children will be spared the sword, the six-gun and the murderous banditry of one-balled Dolphie."

He was saddle meat twisting within Esther's embrace.

"I remember you, old friend, Theodor Herzl, I remember your patchy swayback, your fly-crossed eyes. I remember playing with you in the scrub of the chicken-filled yard."

They'd arrive late in the evening and so would need to sleep one night at a *pension*. Early the next morning they would travel into the mountains, assuming Motl had regained his former health.

The local *pension* turned out to be the home of the Russian count where many years before Motl had attempted to perforate the bourgeoisie. Burned to the ground, it had risen from the revolutionary ashes, newly phoenixed as a small hotel. Like everything else, there was little that had remained the same. Motl recognized the stone walk cobbling up to the once-classical steps—which had been rebuilt in the porridge style, clotted and uneven—but the rest of the home had been reconstructed in an entirely new design.

As they entered, they heard the posh haw-haw of English, audible from what must be the drawing room amid the clink of glassware. "Gosh, it's simply ghastly. One does so pine for a decent horse."

"The English? Here?" Motl said, surprised.

"British supporters of the Reich," the front desk clerk said. "A major general, a bank director, a baroness and a viscount. They're friends of the Mitford family—you know, Unity Mitford, Hitler's English girl who stood with him as he announced the *Anschluss*?"

Then came the explosive mewling of a baby from behind the dining room door.

"Polly, please remove little Dolfie. It is rather a struggle to join one word to another when he cries so."

The receding squalling of the baby as the sound of plummy chatter and clinking resumed.

"He natters quite as Unity does now, doesn't he?"

"Rather. Just like Bobo herself. But soon he too shall be giving speeches, I'm sure."

Though his knowledge was imperfect, Motl had apprenticed in cowboy English and these upper-crust Brits were both horsey and mostly intelligible if filtered through the rarefied pomp of their imperious vowels. He was able to glean the gist.

"The baby," they kept saying. "The baby."

Motl and Esther climbed the stairs to their room.

A nanny came scurrying toward them from out of a bedroom, still bearing the child, a ruckle-haired cherub in knickerbockers and suspenders, thick as a gnome. The nanny was costumed in classic maid: black dress, white cotton pinafore, downcast class-aware eyes.

"Sir. Ma'am," she said as she slowed to move past Motl and Esther.

"Such cheeks," said Esther. "May I see the child? It would cheer me up."

Esther made goggle-mouth baby sounds, and the child stopped kvetching and turned his mashed-potato face toward her, grinning.

"A strange time for his parents to take him on holiday," Motl said.

"No, sir, his parents are not with him. There's quite a kerfuffle back in England," the nanny said. Then she added in a conspiratorial whisper, "He's going to meet his father . . . for the first time."

"Being conceived is messy. And it doesn't get easier after that," Motl said.

"And what does your mama think, my little Fritzchen Nudelprinz?" Esther asked, and chucked one of his dumpling cheeks.

"She's at a convalescent home in England," the maid said as the child not unexpectedly said nothing. "Wounded. But his father . . . They say his father is . . . his father is an important German leader. Maybe even the Führer himself."

"We'll have to wait for the hairs on his upper lip," Motl said. "Then we'll know. Also, if it turns out he wants to clear the land of Jews."

"Please don't say anything, sir. I should not have spoken of it," the nanny said.

Footsteps. Germanic huffing on the stairs. The nanny and the Führerling disappeared quickly back into the child's room. A gor-bellied Nazi rose from the landing. First his balding, brilliantined hair, the binocular shine of his spectacles, black moustache like the hula skirt of a rat, his turnip cheeks and chin, then the tumes-cent heft of his torso surmounting broomstick legs.

His uniform was an overwrought suitcase, overrun with straps and buckles, insignia and badges, swastikas and the double light-ning scars of the SS. He regarded Motl and Esther as if vermin had crawled up his nostrils.

"*Guten Abend.* Good evening," Motl said.

Deep inside the vault of the officer's sinuses, the vermin had begun to burrow, their scabby, scrabbling feet causing the carti-lage of his nose to twitch. He showed no other sign of acknowl-edging Motl and Esther's presence, and they were relieved when he twisted the doorknob and bellied his way through the doorway into the child's room.

"I was never upstairs when this house belonged to the Russian count," Motl said, "but I feel it burning with shame."

They walked the hall to their room and sat on the bed.

"Tomorrow, we shall run into the mountains and find my conk-ers and at last I'll have something to give life instead of being filled with nothing but what a ghost is filled with."

"What's a ghost filled with?"

"More ghost."

Esther turned to Motl and lowered him onto the bed, kissing him.

"Ghosts are never anywhere except where they're not," Motl said. "They're edgeless, like a sack of air with the sack gone."

Do they speak with each other about Hitler's child? They do not.

5

The garden pink in the just-after-dawn. Once, it had been a circuit board of bushes and flowers, paths leading between topiary pruned into simple shapes, a battalion of clippers and gardeners employed to snip the world into compliance. Without the count and his maintenance of a moneyed Eden, it was more a roiling sea of stubby hedges, stunted trees and the occasional punctuation of flower. Motl and Esther picked their way along a gravel path, sharing a bagful of bread and cheese and a pot of reheated coffee they'd filched from the kitchen.

"Last time I was here, I legged it like a rabbit chased by kiotes. I'd no idea where I was going, but I've played it over so many times since, I think I know the direction."

"Are there dowsing rods for this kind of thing?"

"I'll pay attention to any twitching in my pants."

"As any of us would."

Travelling through a landscape from the past by memory was like dowsing—crediting, if not marvels, then ghosts.

A hedge at the end of the garden. Beyond it, a meadow, abruptly sloping up the long green cape of the alp. They straddled a bald patch in the hedge and began walking up the slope. Cows.

Small flowers. The golden pink of the sun rising into the mountain-scalloped sky.

"I've never climbed a mountain before," Esther said.

"The best way to go is up."

"Thanks. I'd never have figured that out."

"It's in the Torah. They do everything important on a mountain."

"So it's like we're looking for the Ark and two of everything to begin the world again. It figures the Torah is all about men climbing mountains when really it's the women in the valleys who get things done."

"We'll do plenty in the valley. Besides, I'm not so keen on mountains. Remember: Abraham and his knife, Isaac and his almost-sacrifice, and then, of course, circumcision. Like my father used to say, 'As far as God is concerned, less is more.'"

"It's one way to learn about your body: by losing some."

"Tell me about it," Motl said.

The tilted meadow ended in forest, and Esther and Motl slipped into the brindled dark, the aisles between the trees quiet, cool and expectant. Motl reached for Esther's hand. When they could, they walked side by side or else Motl led, his arm stretched behind so he could hang on to her.

In a small clearing by a stream, Esther and Motl sat on a lichen-blotched boulder to rest. They shared the remains of the cold coffee, the bread and cheese.

"We'll be a family," Esther said.

"Yes."

"When we have the child."

"Yes."

"We will start again."

"Like Noah."

"Two of every memory."

"Yes," Motl said. "Maybe they'll cancel each other out."

"I don't know if it works that way."

"Maybe not. You know, I never married."

"I know," Esther said.

"I was a cowboy. All alone. Well, my mother was always there."

"You were a nice Jewish boy."

"A nice Jewish cowboy."

"Sure," Esther said. "And your mother was the bean-master."

"The cook and coffee maker. Yes."

"Do you think there can be marriage with this war?"

"There can be children."

"So, you mean yes?"

"Yes."

"Yes, there can be marriage?"

"Yes," Motl said. "Esther?"

"Yes?"

"The forest is a kind of temple."

"A kind of synagogue."

"Yes. So maybe it is a place where we could marry."

"Yes," Esther said. "Are you asking me?"

"Yes," Motl said. "I am."

6

They walked for several hours through the forest. When Motl and Esther emerged from the trees, Motl expected they would be standing on a frozen tide. But the glacier was not where it was supposed to be.

Motl and Esther climbed onto a rocky outcrop to survey the slope, searching for where the glacier had slithered. For twenty years it had crept steadily back; now the cold creature crouched behind a small undulation in the mountainside, waiting, as if to pounce or else in trepidation. Perhaps the glacier feared the ruinous depredations of the future. Motl nodded, a subtle indication of recognition, of—if this can be said to a glacier—warmth, as if greeting a friend from a past life. They walked over and climbed onto it.

"It was over here that they rolled, I think," Motl said, indicating a fissure.

Esther scrabbled over the cold surface with her hands, digging at a shadow barely visible through the translucence.

"Uhh," she said. "A squirrel." She extracted the frozen thing and held it up.

"I was nineteen. Mine were not so hairy," Motl said.

The glacier was a map, except everything had moved. Motl walked about the frozen wave, attempting to recognize its ruts and hummocks, its fractures and knobs, while Esther continued to dig beneath the pearlescent surface.

"Motl," she said, and opened her hand. She had a palmful of bullets and casings.

"None of them look familiar," he said. "Of course, it was more how they felt than how they looked that I noticed at the time."

Several hours later, they had a collection of animal skulls, stones, teeth and wood fragments. Also numb fingers, despite using the coffee pot as a shovel and passing it back and forth between them. Motl had also found a pocket watch. It wasn't working, unless its function was to mark 4:43 in the night or day of some undetermined week and month and year. And as they say, a stopped clock is right twice per day, just as you always find something in the last place you look, unless you don't understand the principle of looking. Or finding.

They continued looking but not finding.

Late in the afternoon, they came upon a small hut with the cockeyed posture of the resplendently inebriated, as askew as their own shadows, tucked against some trees.

"Maybe we can camp here for the night?" he said.

"Can we get room service?"

"We'll ask the rats."

They left their few worldly goods in the cabin and followed the glacier to the edge of a near-cliff-steep slope. They sat and looked at the view. Far below, they could make out meadows filled with cows, the *pension* and the rest of the village, with its postcard of gabled houses.

"Reckon those British Nazis down there have room service?"

"Hot and cold running evil."

"And the little Führerleh has a tiny plastic Europe to teethe on."

Motl leaned back on his arms. Had he rested, just looking at scenery, since he had left Vilnius? Had he ever rested?

It had all been books and worry. After the destruction of the Temple, this had been the Chosen People's chief recreation, their chief job.

"Ahh," Motl said. His breath a visible spectre before him.

His hands sank into the snow, melting it with their heat. He felt something against his palms. He closed his fingers around it.

Mouse heads? Matzo balls? Apricots? The fetuses of mountain goats?

He was afraid to look. He feared they were something they weren't.

The possibility of a thousand babies? A new village of Motls? A city of his children and their children and their children's children down through the ages?

Motl and Esther would survive.

And when they were old, their children would bring them soup and they would live in a home while their children spent their money and sold their valuables and argued over their heirlooms and property and they would die happy.

Motl held his hands out. "Guess which one?"

Esther looked thoughtfully at the back of each of his pale hands in turn, as if she could read what was within. After a minute of dramatic chin-holding and deeply thoughtful face-squinching, she announced, "This one," and tapped the knuckles of his left hand.

Motl smiled and turned his hand over, opening his fingers in ostentatious display.

And dropped the testicle.

They watched with dread as it toppled from the cliff, then buffeted from crag to crag. It didn't take Motl and Esther's warmer route through the forests and meadow, but instead followed the colder route of the glacier. Rolling, it began to collect snow.

Though it became more and more distant, its size remained the same, for it became larger as the snow collected around it. Then larger still, until it was rolling over the snowy crags above the village.

Take the snow of a mountainside and roll it like a carpet. Take this entire carpet, a vast crystalline cabbage roll, and compact each end, turn it into a ball, a frozen somersaulting cherub, a scoop as large as a house. It was an icy comet hurtling toward the village. A torpedo released from Motl's hand high above had attained near-limitless mass, incalculable velocity, and became a snow angel of death, its frosty scythe like an eyeball looking both everywhere and nowhere.

The snow had mobbed around Motl's single clacker. And it rolled. Fat Man. Little Boy. Dame Fortuna. It rolled.

And in its wake, the snow on the crags began to unsettle. To dislodge. By the time the immeasurable colossus of this murderous snowball with Motl's earnest and unaware single jibbly at its centre thumped blindly into the village, it was followed by an avalanche. His scudding boychik body-slammed the buildings. Chimneys, gables, the roofs, windows, walls, stairs, its *pension* and small outbuildings all crumpled, toppled over, destroyed. And then the torrent from the mountains buried the village. A mining disaster. A rock slide. A tsunami. A Biblical flood.

Motl regarded the devastated, snow-engulfed village.

"And that's why we're born with two."

───

He had not lowered his other arm. His hand was still held out, his fist closed.

Esther touched it gently. "Is there something in this hand too?"

"Yes," Motl said. "I'll be more careful. One is more than twice as rare as two."

He packed the coffee pot half-full with snow and then lowered his hand inside. "Night night, little one. It's time for bed." He placed the testicle on the bed of snow. Then he filled the rest of the pot. "Sleep tight. Don't let the snow fleas bite. You have big days ahead," he said, and closed the lid.

"I wanted to see," Esther said.

"Soon enough," Motl said, and kissed her.

The mountain below was honeying with the lowering sun, the distant clouds rosy with the coming dusk.

"We'll shelter in the hut until morning, then decide what's next," Motl said.

There was no lock on the door, but it required Esther's battering-ram shoulder to open it. Inside, the place smelled like a cross-country ski, the wax tarred on, pungent cedar with the depth of dark. Several grey blankets were balled in the corner of a narrow, sauna-like shelf. A small stove, pot-bellied like a cherub of iron, had some logs piled beside it along with a box of Alpenhorn matches.

Esther lit the fire with the long, red-tipped matches and kin-dling scraps while Motl secured a safe place for the precious coffee pot in a snowdrift nearby. Once they sat, they realized how deeply the cold had penetrated. They eased off their shoes, took off their jackets and lay back together under blankets, leaning against the wall, watching the flames like the writhing of orange mountain ranges.

"A day of ups and downs," Motl said.

"But even the downs were ups," Esther replied.

They slept.

7

Motl woke alone, the blanket fallen, moonlight the colour of sour milk through the half-open door. The fire in the stove had burned to embers. Where was Esther? Even the goats were asleep.

She must have gone to find a place to whiz in the woods.

He went to the door to look out, but there was no sign of her outside. He walked to the nearest crest of the glacier. Nothing. He hadn't expected disappearances once they'd crossed the border.

A keening. Maybe the wind? There was no wind. Had she fallen? Was she hurt? An animal crawling out of the forest—a wolf, a bear. Motl rushed as best he could toward the wailing.

Movement at the edge of the trees, nothing more than flailing shadows. A body. Esther twisting in pain.

But something more. A creature thrashing. A wolf, a black dog attacking. No—a man on top of Esther. The officer from the *pension*. Heaving. His officer's hat set beside them as if it were only waiting patiently for an appointment to be over.

His hand covered Esther's mouth, her arms—wings beating wildly—her legs hammered against him. He had torn her dress. His own dark clothes pulled aside. The shine of a gun in a holster now at his knees. Esther screaming into his hand. The dull thudding of his body against hers.

"I knew I could find you," the Nazi said. "The nanny confessed she'd told you about the baby."

Esther's smothered roaring as she writhed to throw him off.

"First, I fuck you, then I shoot between your pretty eyes," the Nazi said. "And then I shoot your husband."

And without thinking, Motl, who had crept up behind him, reached for the officer's gun, raised it and fired. A mute click.

Then he realized. The safety. He pulled the lever, pressed the gun to the Nazi's head, closed his eyes and fired again.

The German shuddering. The German convulsed.

In death.

In climax.

Esther pushed him off her and rolled away from the blood pooling beneath the Nazi's head. Motl dropped the gun, said nothing, gathered Esther into his arms.

I

TORONTO,

1984

"God must beeeee a cowboyyyyy . . ." Motl, my grandfather, sang, not at the top of his lungs but at some location where he was able to produce maximum wobble with maximum volume. This particular location was the boys' washroom at the Wandering Spirit Survival School. I didn't have to worry about him frightening the boys. He already had. None would risk getting near such hideous, ear-cleaving ululation. Particularly in the stall of the jakes.

"You okay in there?" I asked.

"I should not be okay? It sounds good in here," he called. "You know that song? It's on the radio."

"Yes, Zaidy. I've heard it."

"Almost finished riding the porcelain horse, almost dropped the last chestnut filly into the stable."

"I need to know this, Zaidy?"

"What, you're not interested in your grandfather?"

"Also, you probably shouldn't sing about cowboys here. Home on their range and all."

My grandfather, in the ornery middle of his eighties, had come to the school to talk about the Holocaust to Anishinaabe kids. Because I lived with him, it was my job to wrangle this singing *alter kaker* western enthusiast, grandfather, survivor.

My mother, Bella, liked to say she was conveniently born on her birthday. Though she was nearly not born at all.

Who she might have been had rolled down a mountain and destroyed a village.

Or was carried over the sea in a coffee pot.

Motl and my grandmother Esther had found their way from Switzerland to the port of Marseille, from whence they sailed for Canada, Esther becoming increasingly pregnant. First she wasn't, then she became more so. Until she noticed. And then Motl noticed, still carrying the coffee pot filled with a constant supply of ice begged from the kitchen and with what could have become my mother. If she hadn't already gotten a soft pink toehold in the world, her two waterlogged fists ready for a fight once she was born. And then every day after.

When they arrived in Toronto, the very pregnant Esther was admitted to Our Lady of Mercy Hospital, until the previous year called the Mercy Hospital for Incurables.

"There's always a cure," my mother said. "Sometimes, though, it's death. That tends to fix things. Permanently."

Thanks, Mom. Always helpful.

The hospital had been rechristened in time for her emergence and Bella came out soaked in history, her DNA souped up by intergenerational collywobbles. Born and raised in a family of survivors, barely surviving, she did kvetch with operatic gusto until she found drink at fourteen, whereupon her complaints were declaimed with the angry zeal of a banshee.

After she was born, Motl left Esther in the hospital and took his glacial companion, his faithful sidekick, in its coffee pot and walked past the Sunnyside Amusement Park and the Flyer ("the dippiest-dips on the continent") to the shores of Lake Ontario. He removed his shoes and socks, rolled up his pants and waded up to his mashed-potato knees. He opened the lid of the pot and then, *Yisgadal v'yiskadash*, flicked its contents into the water.

No Lady of the Lake reached out of the waves to clutch his precious treasure. What once had been one of the golden apples of his quest now floated like a duck's egg toward Hamilton. Or like *tashlich* on Rosh Hashanah. Casting pieces of bread onto the surface of the water. Casting off sin.

Motl stood on the rocky lake floor, coffee pot in hand, watching as a ring-necked gull swept from the sky, beaked his boy and flew away. It landed above the *H* of the Red Hots' restaurant sign to eat its catch.

How many children of Nazis are the right amount? None is too many. Which was also the Canadian government's policy toward the immigration of Jews during the war, though Motl and Esther were two of the none that managed it. They had a Nazi's child. And here in Canada, when Esther gave birth, they became her parents.

"I remember what Rabbi Zaltzman said at my bar mitzvah. 'With each child the world begins anew,'" Motl said to Esther. "And judging by what was in his beard, he'd been around since the first beginning, so he would know. Our girl is no Nazi. She's a half-pint turtle, a dumpling, one of my lost boychiks with a milky face and a sweet little blintz belly."

My infant mother scrabbling at Esther's breast, finally settling, feeding, sleeping. Wrapped in a blanket, fists held up boxer-style, tiny brow tufts furrowed, a delicate network of blue veins under opalescent skin.

"I look at you two and I see a goose and her gosling. A nursling and her mother. A dayling. An hourling. I see how we climbed mountains, escaped together, crossed an ocean. Survived."

2

A lanky teacher strode toward us, tweed jacket over his Buffy Sainte-Marie T-shirt, his hair in a long braid.

"Waubgeshig Harper. Call me Waub. Sorry I wasn't here to meet you. Urgent call from my husband." He held out his hand to Motl. "You must be Mr. Isaakson."

"Mr. Isaakson? I hide when I hear that name. It can't be good news. I'm Motl to anyone who knows me and still puts up with me."

"Motl, then. Welcome to the Wandering Spirit Survival School."

"*That* name I like. We Jews are also always wandering. And we're interested in survival. I survived."

"That's why you're here," Waub said.

Motl shuffled to the front of the classroom. Forty ten-year-olds were sitting expectantly at their desks.

"Natives and Jews," he began. "We're like a rash. Try to get rid of us, sure, but you never can. We refuse to die. So, you and me, we're genocide buddies."

His croaking chuckle, a violin buzzed by flies.

He told them about the Nazi plan for the Jews. And for everyone else. Roma and homosexuals, the disabled, the mentally ill,
all the others. He didn't tell them about his testicles. Neither the
European nor the North American. Nor the other stories he'd told
me. They weren't for ten-year-olds. The kids would instantly turn
old, hair sprouting from their ears, all the freshness gone from
their bodies. He did say he had been a cowboy.

"But a Jewish cowboy isn't a regular one. He's more like you
First Nations, because he knows something about being rounded
up, about not being able to live where you want. About being run
off by the cavalry. Hunted by regular cowboys. Though they were
wearing brown shirts and jackboots.

"But no matter how we're filled with holes—even if we're just
one big hole under a Stetson—we keep riding. Or being dragged by
our horse. We round up history, drag that little doggie behind us."

He looked around the classroom. Pointed a crooked finger at a
shelf of books.

"I hear you kids like stories about the end of the world.
That's not science fiction, that's history. That's the news. Once
I was told by a Lakota that the world had already ended. For
us. For you."

So this cowboy—this Jewish cowboy—saddled down in the
teacher's chair behind the teacher's desk and hacked a handkerchief full of black mire from his esophagus, and he continued.

"You know what those three dots in a row are called? Ellipses.
They mean something's missing. If you erase them, you have to
put them back in to show you've erased them. We're like that.
We're the absence of absence. We didn't have a future, but we're
going there anyway."

He adjusted his handkerchief, folding the ooze into the centre, and hacked again. Then he origamied the sumpy cloth and stuffed it in the breast pocket of his cardigan.

"I knew an Oneida during the war. A professor in Poland studying Indianers. Where else do you expect to find them? But in the middle of the Holocaust—he couldn't wait? Last I heard of him, he escaped a tiger. And why not. After all, tigers are the same as Nazis, just with more stripes."

The kids were captivated by Motl. He had the charisma of being committed to his own eccentricity—not to mention his furious engagement with phlegm—but also a commitment to the stories themselves. And ultimately, behind it all, the wish to connect. He was going deep. With his coughing. With his obviously heartfelt feelings.

After the presentation, Waub long-legged it straight toward us. I was ready to pull a bright bouquet of shame and apologies out of my sleeve.

"An Indigenous professor," Waub said. "An Oneida. In Poland? With a tiger? How many could there have been? I think it was my father."

"Did he have a mole, right here?" Motl thrust a finger at his left cheek.

"Not that I remember."

"Then it was him. The guy I knew didn't have a mole either."

And so it turned out Waub's father was Mike. Mike, who Motl had abandoned in a tiger cage during the war.

"Mike and Gerry. For forty years, I worried that I'd left them to be lunch for a tiger, and after that, something worse," Motl said. "Who knew it'd choose freedom over fresh meat?"

As Waub told it, Mike and Gerry had padded quietly past the cat. By the time it roused, they'd swung the cage door open and were down the stairs.

"Must have thought they were white meat, letting them go by just like that," he said.

The tiger had then leapt from the train car, making a break for the Polish jungle rather than holding up for an Indigenous nosh.

"Sometimes I wake feeling like I'm drowning. Like memory is drowning me in piss and shit," Motl said. "Sometimes I haven't been able to sleep because of your father. I'm glad to know he's alive."

Waub peered into the past, which hovered in the air just over our shoulders, then explained how his father had died of a heart attack after his youngest sister had disappeared and her children were taken away. "It was happening to everyone. After all he'd seen in the war, and all that education . . . and he couldn't do anything. He gave up and I think his heart just stopped.

"But I haven't given up. It's why I'm teaching at this school—to do something positive. For our kids. And to teach them to do something for themselves, too.

"And there's also this," he said, and pulled up his sleeve. A rough tattoo of numbers was carved into his forearm, the blue-green of algae.

"But . . . you weren't in a camp," Motl said.

"Same thing. It's my Indian status number," Waub said. "I had it done after I saw an artist who did it too. Once, I tried to get a phone number the same as this number. Not quite enough numbers, though. But if you add a one at the end, you get a sex shop in Sacramento. Figures."

Waub led us to the staff room. "Coffee?" He indicated a battered percolator. "I heard that a guy who used his camp number won millions," he said. "So I use the numbers in the lottery when I can."

He poured us all weak coffee in mismatched cups, arranged them on the mug-battered table.

"Way I see it, my job—all our jobs—is to help each other not die now that, as you said, the world has ended one time already."

We walked across the black rivulets of tar-repair in the parking lot and found my grandfather's car. He'd named it Theodor Herzl because, though it'd been many years, he remembered his beloved shlumper of a steed, the horse that seemed to always head toward some hoped-for homeland.

We got into Theodor Herzl. I rode shotgun, and Motl squirmed into position behind the steering wheel, refusing to put on his seat belt despite the increasingly desperate carillon of the dashboard.

"What—I'm going to die young? Besides, at my age there's more past than present. It surrounds me like quicksand. Or a huge fart. But though you have my mother's name, knowing you were born in the future helps keep me here."

"The future? Maybe that explains why I can never figure anything out."

"Okay, so *my* future. But one day you'll be like me—a dried-up crick. Only irrigated by the damp of drool."

Motl heaved the gearshift forward and performed some kind of Litvak grand jeté with the pedals. The car gambolled like a filly across the parking lot.

"You'll tell me if there's anything you think I should avoid," he said.

"Usually, I'd say death, but driving with you, I'm not sure that that's possible."

3

My mother was four when Esther died. No one was clear—or was willing to be clear—about exactly how she died, not even my storytelling grandfather, though I was able to, as he would say about the TV, "read between the lies."

It was late autumn. My mother remembers the sound of cars fissling through the leaves on the road and the morning sun, itself the colour of autumn leaves, pouring like syrup into her bedroom. Esther taking her by the hand down the stairs for a special breakfast of pancakes, whipped cream and strawberries. Motl was outside, fussing in the yard. Esther was dressed in long skirts, her neck wrapped in a surfeit of blue and orange scarves that looked like the autumn world outside. The family dog, Fritz, was slumped under the table, chin on his paws, waiting with sad eyes for scraps to fall, or a surreptitious hand to reach down with a splendid and greasy gift. Usually it was Motl, a wink shared sidelong with his little Bella.

On this morning, Esther played a game with my mother, a nursery rhyme where she circled her fingers around my mother's palm ("*Meezhelah mayzhelah, boyt a hayzele*") and then ran them up her arm to tickle her underarm ("*Kutchelah, katchelah, kutchelah, koo!*"). It was the most content and cozy of mornings.

Then Esther walked her daughter through the neighbourhood to nursery school. They kicked leaves as they went, kept an eye out for acorns and chestnuts, watched the squirrels scuttle up the sides of trees. Esther took my mother through the door of the synagogue to the school, unbuttoned her grown-up purple coat, hung it on its designated hook and then brought her into the playroom. She hugged my mother, waved goodbye through the door and turned to leave. But she turned around once again and went back through the door, hugged my mother and then, waving a final time, disappeared.

Esther went back along the golden street and then out to the yard behind their house, where she told Motl she was tired and unwell, and asked him if he would retrieve my mother from the nursery after work. She climbed the stairs to her bedroom, lay down on the brocaded covers to sleep and did not wake again.

There were sleeping pills. There were other medications. But no one was able to speak of what happened. A mother of a young child. A wife. A survivor. Until she was no longer any of those things.

Remembering, Motl's eyes became unfocused though they seemed inclined to sorrow.

"We lived through much. We escaped it together. She was a star shooting through the darkness. It was still so soon after the war, not everyone had even found their way home. We were both so happy that—no matter how it happened—she was able to become a mother, that we were able to have a child, that we were a family."

How could a mother who had endured so much, who had escaped so much, who had a future again, how could she not continue? How could this mother who'd seemed so happy, so content, who'd seemed to finally have created a new life after the old one was broken, how could she have such pain inside?

"Sometimes a war continues long after it seems to be over.

Sometimes the past is a time bomb ticking until its appointed and sometimes unexpected explosion," Motl said.

But he continued this family, this family of two. Motherless. Wifeless. Only partially surviving.

And somehow, so far, Motl himself had survived. If everywhere both inside and out is a minefield, if bombs pock the way forward and back, pit your brain and your guts, courage is just keeping still. Just standing on the ground as steady as you can. And loving your child.

Theodor Herzl, deep in its combustible Ford Pinto heart, must indeed have been consumed with zeal for aliyah—for a return to Zion—since in Motl's hands it didn't necessarily follow the painted conventions of the road but rather veered on a path of its own desire, fording traffic medians and encroaching on curbs.

"My philosophy is, 'As long as we get where we're going,'" Motl said.

"You mean the hospital?"

"I was thinking," he said. "Those ponies at the Survival School, wet behind the ears, looking at me as I told them stories. If I can talk to them—well, maybe it's time to visit your mother. But first, lunch."

Before I could say anything, or even collect my thoughts, Motl straddled the dotted line, cut across oncoming traffic, sparking an irritated gaggle of car horns, narrowly avoided a streetcar and jauntily assumed two parking spots.

"You think I don't know they honk? They figure it's because I'm an old man, but the world is crooked, and I'm just trying to drive straight through."

"Motl," a woman behind the counter at United Bakers Dairy called as he shuffled in. *"Vos makhstu?"*

"How am I? You tell me—you've got a better view."

"In one word, 'good.' In two words, 'not good.'"

"It's true. Even my aches have aches. And the aches are the parts that hurt least. But you know my granddaughter, Gitl?"

"I wouldn't have recognized. How old?"

"Twenty."

"So grown-up. And thanks Gott she doesn't look like you."

Seconds after we made it to a booth, the waitress arrived, hair piled high on her head like a haystack. "Don't tell me what you want, I already know what's good."

She soon returned with two full platters. She did know what I wanted.

Almost everything.

She put the platters down with one hand and, with the other, tilted a coffee pot expectantly over our cups.

"So, Gitl, you'll come with to see your mother?" Motl said.

I gazed down at my blintzes, moving the slurry of cherries back and forth over their pale bellies.

"Yes," I said.

"Coffee or your mother?" the waitress asked.

"Both," I replied.

"Good," she said, and poured the coffee, deposited a handful of creamers and then left to become involved in the lives unfolding at the tables beside us, brandishing the coffee pot like a dark beacon.

My mother lived and worked on an equine therapy farm outside Fort Macleod, Alberta, near the famous Head-Smashed-In Buffalo Jump. Youth lived in residence, helped feed and curry, saddle and water the horses, and learned to ride. Certainly, none of the horses were named Herzl, but maybe Sigmund Freud, Carl Jung, Elisabeth Kübler-Ross, R. D. Laing. Who knew where they might veer?

My mother had her own issues, but she was good with horses. "A horse just looks at you and understands," she'd say.

Once, Motl told me a story from when my mother was young. He'd sent her to school, her pony-emblazoned lunch box packed with the requisite sandwich and juice.

On the playground, a boy approached. "If you give me your lunch, I'll bring you a horse tomorrow. A real horse."

She gave him her lunch.

"But why?" Motl asked her later. "You knew he wouldn't really give you a horse."

"I know," she said. "But I hoped so much it could be true."

"This story says a lot about your mother," Motl told me. "When you have such hope—when you even hope for hope—it's not long before you have it no more."

To get to my mother would mean thirty-six hours of driving together in a Ford Pinto, Theodor Herzl turned to memory machine, to story hatchback. Exhaustion, distraction, boredom and the long road would turn the car into a confessional, a witness stand, an isolation booth, a speech balloon, and Motl would tell me his stories. Though we'd spent long hours together—playing chess, going to the library, listening to music, watching TV, even many "I need you for your brain" times when he called me over to move things for him—he'd never spoken to me, to anyone, about the war years. The visit to the Survival School was the first time.

"Last night," Motl said, "I saw this television show where Japanese glue broken dishes back together with gold to make a new dish. It's *meshuga*, but I like it. Between your mother and me, I don't know who's the bowl and who's the glue—maybe you are?—but it's time to fix it."

Motl's plan was to head south from Toronto and drive through the US—from Michigan through to North Dakota and Montana. We'd travel up to Head-Smashed-In Buffalo Jump, where the foothills rose from the prairie over the squinched bottom of Alberta.

"Always wanted to see it," Motl said. "For eleven thousand years it was where buffalo were run off the cliff, so their bones built up like the graveyard of a lost city. But the name isn't about buffalo heads being smashed in, though of course they were. A Peigan boy stood underneath for a better view. Never mind raining cats and dogs. It's his head that was eggs.

"It makes me think of being broken open and everything floating out, sticking a hat on my head so nothing essential spills out and then walking away. And while I'm thinking about being empty, remember to bring some vittles. Some places, there'll be nowhere to stop for miles."

We didn't tell my mother that we were coming. Who knows how she would react? It was better to surprise her, her father and daughter driving into town, two mysterious characters from the East climbing out of the stagecoach, looking left and right at this new place they have arrived at, stopping at the local saloon to ask her whereabouts.

4

Motl had me call into the pizza place where I worked and launch into a soliloquy about a family health crisis requiring me to urgently leave the province, the day of my return uncertain and contingent on intimated metaphysical concerns including death. When I'd called in pretend-sick before, I'd made my voice weak and wavering, coughing intermittently, doing my best to wheeze in the middle of clauses. Really, I was attempting to represent my inner state, my wheezing-in-the-middle-of-myself emotions, which were the cause of most of my frequent mental health sick days.

It was more difficult to mimic the carpet-pulled-from-under-you worry of this kind of emergency, though Motl and his insistence was a kind of health crisis. His driving alone was cause for concern. If I did nothing else on this trip, taking the wheel as much as he would let me and, when he was driving, watching out for cars, ditches, moose, buildings, cliffs, semi-trailers, lakes, rivers and six-lane lift bridges raised in front of us was in fact avoiding a family health crisis, namely, my zaidy and me becoming chunks under a tzimmes of pulped Pinto.

It's not that an old coot like Motl couldn't necessarily wrangle a car without destroying himself, oncoming traffic, and any nearby witnesses and their possessions, it's just that he had entered that gristle and earhair stage in the life cycle of old men where the world irritatingly refuses to be in the correct place, to progress at a reasonable speed and to consider his perspective as primary. As a result, inside his skinny spotted chest, he had grown the compensating, self-protective heart of a mule. He would drive the way he dressed: if his decisions had been good in 1950, they were good now.

Why was I going? To keep him safe, of course. But also, his previous journey—though he had never spoken of it beyond the barest facts—had the aura of legend. We might travel that legend now. He might tell me stories.

And like binder twine, Motl and his eccentric western cosmology might rope us together. Not so much a repaired Japanese bowl as a hay bale of a family. If not happy, then we might at least glean what was left over.

And my mother.

Sometimes she was most present when she was gone, most distant when she was with us. We were closer when she wasn't here to make it more painful, though she made it painful most of the time.

South to Sarnia, then across Michigan.

There was an undulating rhythm to our driving. Coffee bought at one rest stop, sipped one-handed as we drove, then consigned to porcelain at the next rest stop, where more coffee was acquired. It was a dialysis of the double-double, creating the nervous enervation of the long road where we were both alert and sleepy all day.

Grand Rapids then the ferry across Lake Michigan to Milwaukee.

Motl horking dark red into tissues, balling them up, collecting these snowballs in his pocket until it bulged. He didn't throw them away.

"Are you starting a collection?"

On the ferry, he stood at the gunwale, dropped them one by one into the choppy drink. They churned on the surface for an instant, became sodden then sank below, large burgundy-and-white petals trailing behind us, Hansel and Gitl in a soggy cherry blossom horror film.

The apparition of Motl's roseate sputum
Petals on a wet, black bough

I couldn't help being reminded of Ezra Pound. I didn't just abandon a degree in English to guarantee myself a place in the lucrative and fast-paced world of contemporary poetry by refusing the institution. I needed to know enough, but not too much, through reading.

"Once, for her birthday, your mother and I went riding," Motl began as soon as we had driven off the ferry and were on dry land again. "We were in a line of horses, following a sandy trail across the open fields. I was at the tail end, nothing but dappled and chestnut rumps to see, your mother right behind the guide at the front. The horses tramped over a rock where the path veered into forest. Her horse tripped and fell on its side. A horse isn't made to topple. A couch isn't meant to fall over. Or a bed. I could do nothing. Horse traffic was bumper to bumper, and I could see your mother's little body half-covered by a sofa-sized mare. 'Bella!' I shouted. 'Bella,' but she was silent. I slid off my mount, almost made kindling of my legs when I got tangled in the stirrups, and scrambled over to your mother. She was beneath the horse, patiently lying in the sand. Between horse and the path, a hollow, and your mother's legs were safe there. She was murmuring to the

horse, telling it not to worry, that they could just rest until someone helped them."

"Are all your stories about my mother to do with horses?"

"When Esther died, your mother cried for ten days."

"And you?"

"I cried with her. I hadn't cried since I was a boy. Even during
the war. Even when the two-bits were plugged from under my
Lone Ranger in the war before that war.

"Which reminds me. Lone Ranger and Tonto are prancing
about on the range. Over a hill, a thousand Indigenous warriors
appear, shaking spears, guns, fists, treaties.

"Lone Ranger says, 'We're in a real pickle here, friend. What
are we going to do?'

"'What do you mean *we*, paleface?' Tonto replies."

Motl's laugh was a burbling hurdy-gurdy deep within his chest,
and he thumped himself as it transformed into hacking.

"An old joke. But a good one, Zaidy," I said. "I remembered it
when you were talking about Jewish cowboys. *We*'re palefaces."

"Not pale, but on the other hand not *not* pale, either. Pale-of-
Settlement faces."

"Guess it depends on who the warriors are."

"You mean if they're Nazis?"

"That'd make anyone's face pale."

As we drove through Minneapolis toward North Dakota, Motl
began telling me of years before, when he and Esther had travelled to Canada.

"I was sick much of the time on the boat from Marseille. I
remained in our windowless cabin below deck, not so much a

stateroom as a cubby for bilge-water immigrants, their pockets empty except for lint and hope, though it was often hard to tell the difference, hope so often comprising only the fluff of what is left over. I staggered out of the cabin, bent over, clutching the railings, looking for ice for the coffee pot—I've told you about the coffee pot, yes? After I got the ice, I'd hobble back to bed, trying not to have my insides become my out. I slept with the pot beside my bed, like a baby in a bassinet, trying to quiet the sloshing waves of my inner sea. Esther, however, became the table tennis champion of the ship. She learned how to shuffle cards one-handed, like a poker-room shark, after watching a pinstriped nabob puffing on a thick cigar perform the trick with his stubby, diamond-ringed fingers. She acquired a small world of English. *Hold. Captain. Deal. Fold. Seasick. Whiskey. Dollar bill.*

"During the weeks of our ocean voyage, her belly humped, and she felt your mother quickening.

"Your mother twisted and punched, wriggled and hiccuped, booted the soft walls of the stateroom of her womb with zeal. Your mother Charlestoned and polkaed, did the dog-paddle of an exuberant Labrador retriever. Esther sang to her. She whispered stories and spells, rhymes and songs. And when my insides were not deluged by the surge and slosh of my own quickening, I leaned close and told her of the brave old new world we were travelling to. Its mountains and prairies, its firewater, rivers, buffalo, turkeys and skyscrapers. Its movies and locomotives, cowboys, immigrants, tycoons and Indigenous nations. We had seen death and now we were joined by this life, this child that we would raise far from the cemetery that had been our home.

"There were nights when Esther and I stood together on the deck of our boat, an island beneath wall-to-wall sky, the broadloom of stars, the prairie of the heavens. We remained still while Europe floated away, the flotsam of years behind us, Canada, like a vast life raft covered in moose and snow, drifting east to greet us.

"We knew we would land in Halifax, and then we'd take a train, but we didn't know how far we would continue to travel. A drowning swimmer only thinks of the shore. A stampeding buffalo thinks only of the buffalo in front of him.

"One night I held Esther as we stood close by the railing, blustered in the salt air, the seagulls yawping high above us. My arm was around her, my hand embracing her belly. Behind us we heard the rasp of metal against metal, a repeated chafing. Chhtt. Chhtt. Chhtt. A squawkless gull, able only to hiss. It was the unmistakable snick of scissors. We turned to see a young man in shirt and suspenders cutting at the air with a pair of barber's shears.

"'I'm keeping in practice,' he said. 'I snip like a violinist. Like Heifetz. I apprenticed with an uncle since my bar mitzvah and when I get to Toronto, I intend to open my own barbershop.'

"His name was Harry. He was travelling to meet a girl from Radomsko. They'd been betrothed since before the war, and she and her family had an apartment on Bathurst Street.

"'Come with me,' he said. 'Toronto is the Warsaw of the West, but on a lake big as a sea. My girl's family will get you work. They'll find a place for you to live. You can't take chances, not with your wife in her condition.'"

The highway sign said *FARGO, 100 miles.*

"For years I'd dreamed of the Wild West," Motl said. "Like where we are now, but full of possibility. Prairies, buttes and coulees. Box canyons, wild sage and sierras. Herds and cowboys, Native tribes, chiefs and warriors. The chance to grizzle and broil, peer out from under the dusty brim of a ten-gallon, six-shooters ready to make stories from men and their blood in the middle of Main Street. To be Knight of the Not Yet Entirely Doleful Continent.

"But because of this barber, I rode an iron horse from Halifax, squinted my way down the streets of Toronto, where Esther and I raised our child. My perilous quest commenced in Vilnius with a barber and, on the shores of this Native world, it so continued.

"And now I reckon it might well be time to christen this current Jewish expedition to your mother with such a visit. A shave, and the hairs of my ears and nose pruned, my head once again made sleek as a saddle and reflective of the sun above, a beacon for your mother."

5

A telephone booth in the parking lot of a diner, portal to another world, unassuming under the large sign: *Don't go far for dinner, dine at FARGO'S DINER*. In the booth, two telephone books hung like hunted geese left out to age, feathers ruffled, bodies limp. Was the gander the yellow and the white one the goose? We fluffed open the sallow wings of the gander and scanned for nearby barbershops. Two Bits Shave & A Haircut was close. Cutthroat's closer.

The sign outside Cutthroat's was a dapper Brylcreemed 1950s man drawing an outstretched index finger over his throat in the universal sign for death.

"You trust this place?" I asked my grandfather.

"A cutthroat is a variety of straight razor. Besides, what have I got to lose?"

"Blood."

Inside, we were welcomed by the barber, an Indigenous man, tall and smiling, long hair falling around his skinny shoulders. He made a maître-d' motion, upturned palm sashaying an invitation to the large barber's chair. Motl shuffled over and was bethroned.

"You remind me of Shmuel the Shaker, a barber from my youth," Motl said. "Old Shatterhand we used to call him. Only

Vlad the Impaler was worse. But you look like Winnetou, from the westerns I used to read."

The barber, Sol, flicked a bright barber's cape open and spun it around Motl with a flourish, a magician removing the cloth from a table laden with dishes. Without ceremony, I sat in the second chair and watched in the mirror.

Motl settled in as if for meditation, his eyes closed, elbows on the armrests, his hands held in yoga beneath the cape.

"Shave and a haircut," he said.

Sol exercised monk-like fortitude and did not answer, "Two bits," instead only nodding silently.

"Every time you cut me, I take a dollar off the price," Motl said suddenly. "I've been shaved by Nazis, and worse."

"To make skin into a lamp, you got to be careful to take it in one piece," Sol said. "I'm no shaking Eichmann."

The haircut went quickly. As Motl predicted, it was all ears and nose with some limited topiary of the prairie of his head. "Shaved it when I was a thinning young man, hoping it'd grow in thicker. It never did, though now I could braid my back and tuchus," he said.

Sol adjusted the chair. Copious spurts of shaving cream turned Motl into an ancient sage lost in the thicket of his own chin's curls.

Sol winked at me and with a delicate movement of the blade made the tiniest nick on Motl's cheek.

"That's a dollar," Motl said.

The next scrape of the blade over Motl's whiskery cheek also ended in a calligraphic flourish and a minute red line. Sol winked at me again.

"That's two dollars," my grandfather said.

Motl began to say something else, but Sol moved the razor, a silver plough over a field of Jew, and Motl fell silent. Sol squeezed Motl's nose with great tenderness and drew more blood from his upper lip.

"Three dollars."

"Don't know why the blade is so unsteady today," Sol said. "We Indians are usually unshakable. But then again, we're also inscrutable."

Another tiny flick and the pink of blood turning the shaving cream to strawberry sorbet.

"We're so inscrutable, we don't even know ourselves."

"Four dollars," I said.

Sol dabbed at Motl's cuts with a styptic pencil and said nothing.

"I didn't mean to insult," Motl said. "I know you're no Mengele. I just like a bargain."

"Cut rate. I understand," Sol said, deadpan.

Motl nodded with great respect, as if Sol had just quoted some obscure wisdom from the Mishnah.

"My granddaughter and I are going to visit my daughter," he said, and motioned in my direction. "Her mother. It's been years. So maybe I'm nervous."

"I haven't seen my mother in a while either," Sol said. "She could visit. I'd shave her for free—it'd be a big job, but I'd do it. On the other hand, my daughter works in the bar down the street. See her every day."

"Good," Motl said. "That's good. Like my granddaughter over there. Lives with me. I keep her around to take the garbage out. To cook sometimes. Mostly at mealtimes. And to help me find my teeth when they're lost."

"It's not too hard, Zaidy," I said. "Since they're not dentures."

"You know, barber, that reminds me," Motl said. "Some men go to the saloon to confess, to learn what to do. But we Jews, we don't drink."

"Why not?"

I knew what was coming. The joke was old as Esau.

"It dulls the pain."

Sol nodded and raised the blade, ready to address the underside of Motl's chins.

"Instead, we Jews, those who don't cultivate a beard and schmooze their rabbi, hairy cheek by hairy jowl, we go to the barber's. That's where we talk. That's where we think. That's where we make decisions. Unless we go to the deli or the poker table, or the golf course, or the shvitz. Okay, so we're always talking, but once I was a cowboy at the barber's, and I began my life again."

"And now?" Sol asked. "Have you decided anything?"

Motl rubbed his face. "Not to go under the knife when you're on the other end."

"On the bright side, you're getting a discount."

"Is that what a pound of flesh sells for these days?"

"Not much market for scalps, lately."

The scritch of Sol's blade as it traced Motl's chins. Then he wiped the remaining shaving cream and covered Motl's face with a hot towel.

"Finally, some quiet," I said.

"Mmm," Motl said. "A hot towel is the old man's meditation."

After a few minutes, Sol removed the cooling white cloth and revealed Motl, sleek and red as a saveloy sausage.

"So—inner peace?" Sol asked as he raised the chair.

And Motl, sitting up, grinned like a Tzaddik, a Jewish sage

with an invisible Cheshire cat for a beard, the smile the only part remaining.

Sol had a golden cash register baroque as the throne of the Grand Duchy of Luxembourg and the size of a small pig. It would not have been out of place in a grand saloon, women on stairs girded with crinoline and petticoats, flounces and bustles orbiting their fuchsia undercarriages, polkas pounded from out-of-tune pianos, the clack of whiskey glasses on poker tables within a velvet universe of curtains and oakwork.

Sol depressed a key and a number appeared on a gravestone-shaped card in the little window. Motl handed him a grimy sandwich of folded-over greenbacks, and as Sol pushed another key, the money drawer shot open with a jangle.

"I deducted for the bloodshed, but gave you a tip because I didn't die."

"Yet," Sol said.

We left Cutthroat's through a jingling door. As soon as we were on the sidewalk, Motl began to hack again, spitting more blood pudding into his handkerchief.

"Zaidy," I said. "A hospital?"

"Hospitals are for the sick. If I were sick, I wouldn't have lived this long."

I took the wheel since Motl was still engaged in hauling his lungs into the daylight.

"Don't drive me to the hospital," he said. "I've only swallowed a hair."

"Maybe, but by the looks of it, if we run out of road, you've enough tar inside to pave the way ahead."

We'd be in Montana by late afternoon, driving directly into the sun. I put on my sunglasses and the world turned to honey, golden light over strip malls and roadsides, drive-thrus and bus stops, and then, finally, the fields and river valleys.

Motl tilted his seat back like he was still at the barber's. "Gitl, I'm not sleeping. I'm just resting."

It must have been difficult for him to get any rest with all the snoring—a huge territory of his insides was invested in the juddering.

6

Gitl. I carried Motl's mother's name if not her blood.

And even before we had begun our drive and he began to talk, I carried her memories. Motl's, too. Memory in the way we lived. How we breathed. Each morning, I'd wake empty-headed and my mind would flood with their grammar. Great-grammar and grandpa.

And Esther. Because she never left. In Motl's world, everything was a translation from the original Esther.

In school I was "Git" or "Stupid Git." And, as everyone knew my kooky granddad's penchant for the western, "Gitty-Up." Throughout the cold slush of Toronto winters, old-world Jew that he was, he'd pick me up from school clad in the duds of a wrangler. Snap-button, yoke-backed shirts with flowers, a Stetson, boots with spurs. ("Training wheels for ice so's I break the bronco back of winter and don't fall.") My few friends called me Jill.

My mother was rarely able to muster out of her pill-and-booze-fuelled mental health crises to make it to the schoolyard, or to pack me the standard grade school lunch of mac and cheese, Alphagetti or baked beans. Motl became Master of the Microwave, Boyardee of the Range. He made "Surprise Eggs," not only because the egg's yellow eye would peek from beneath a

medallion cut from toast, but because we were surprised if breakfast was not burnt and did not taste like a coal mine.

I never knew who my father was. My mother said she didn't
either.

"I want to know. What if he was a Nazi?"

"Been there, done that," she said. "We've enough Nazi fathers
for one family."

The details of my conception were obscure, but I was grateful
for Motl. He raised me with idiosyncratic dependability and the
steadfast certainty with which he would have cared for a horse,
keeping me shod, curried, trimmed. Throughout my childhood I
was largely worm-free, my teeth were strong, and I was provided
sufficient oats to grow. A stable childhood, let's say.

I had not lived another life, did not know that my grandfather's
sorrow, his compulsions, his living in two places and in two times
but yet mostly shying away from talking about it, were not most
parents'. My mother's rages and fears, tears and intermittent affec-
tion, were not how most families were. Motl did what he could to
help her, though much of the help she needed was to help her
want to get help, to want to heal.

She would lash out, often at random strangers on the street or in
the grocery store. After one incident ended with some court-ordered
therapy, I overheard her tell Motl, "I used to have a problem with
violence. Now I only hit people when I'm angry with them."

And she was angry at a lot of people. But she did most of the
harm to herself. Drinking. Drugs. Disappearing for days. Being
with raging and violent men. Getting hurt.

She was always angry with Motl. And except for the occasional
outburst of bewildered mothering she directed my way, it seemed
like she hoped that if she ignored me, I would go away, that she

only need concentrate on looking back over her shoulder to her father and absent mother and not forward to me.

Spooky action at a distance. That was my family.

Motl had managed to doze off after his coughing jag, and now woke with a snort and began to dream aloud. "Used to dream I was a roly-poly pink baby, juicy like the soft heart inside me. I was perched on a great white horse, riding west under the scorch of the sun. Then I shrivelled into a chicken roasted on the spit of my own spine, until I was more barbecue than baby and all my juice was sucked into the cracked-dry dirt. I was one of those bog men, flat leather like an old glove, and I was ancient. Then I parched some more and became older still, and my horse was hard and knotted like black walnut, and I was nothing but bones and thorns in a cloak of dry jerky."

"And just now—what d'you dream?"

"Chinese takeout."

We passed through the North Dakota capital, Bismarck, named after the blood-and-iron chancellor of historic moustache and eyebrows as well as of the German Empire. We were north of the Standing Rock Indian Reservation, making our way across territory once part of the Great Sioux Nation until it was dismembered in the Great Sioux War. This was all part of the Battle of the Little Bighorn, also known as Custer's Last Stand, since it was where he last stood in his stovepipe boots before a Lakota named Big-nose allegedly shot him in the head and chest. They say the head wound may have been inflicted after he was already dead. They say always kill someone twice. You don't want a witness to the first time.

Farther west into Montana, we could visit a memorial to Custer and his Seventh Cavalry.

"Imagine a monument to Nazis," I said.

"The families who aren't there are the monument."

"I guess I'm kind of a monument too."

"The good kind. No one looks like me," Motl said. "No one who is left."

If we headed into South Dakota, we'd end up at the site of the Wounded Knee Massacre where hundreds of Lakota—mostly women and children—had been killed by US soldiers. The majority of the warriors had given up their arms. I remembered a song by the Native American band Redbone that ended: "We were all wounded by Wounded Knee."

It wouldn't be much farther to the gold rush town of Deadwood, on whose infamous thoroughfares once mosied Wild Bill Hickok, Wyatt Earp and Calamity Jane, gunslinging cherubim guarding the gates of Motl's erstwhile-imagined western paradise. Or maybe Hickok and Calamity Jane had been more Adam and Eve, shooting apples from a forbidden tree, living in a place before law or modesty, Deadwood in a gulch near the Lakota's sacred Black Hills, though to the settlers and prospectors nothing was more sacred than gold and personal enrichment.

We crossed the Missouri River then, and hours later the Yellowstone as we entered Montana. We had reached the Badlands. We had about eight hours left to drive to get to my mother, so we stopped for the night at Glendive.

"You know what I always say, Zaidy. 'There are no badlands. Just bad people.'"

A long sigh from Motl, suffused with more sorrow and regret than was usual. I had accomplished much in my few years, but this was a singular triumph I would not soon forget. A dad joke squared. A granddad joke. Intergenerational.

7

We woke early the following morning. Or, I should say, too soon after I was finally able to fall asleep in the serrated cough-storm, the tractor pull of snoring from the bed beside mine. There was a soggy cairn of pink-streaked tissues on the nightstand.

We had planned to drive to Makoshika State Park to the lookout view of the Badlands, but Motl said he was too tired. "Someone kept me up, coughing all night."

Breakfast was Corn Pops or Froot Loops tumbled from a Plexiglas chute into a Styrofoam bowl, soused with milk from a spout and eaten with a plastic spoon. There was a brackish-coloured fluid to which we added a sachet of white powdered oil. If the fluid had actually been brackish water, it might have tasted better. Fortified with this range food, we climbed aboard Theodor Herzl and headed toward Circle, the next town on our route.

"You drive," Motl said to me. "I need the time to cough."

And as soon as the car doors slammed closed, Motl began. I could feel the chassis of the car roiling. A car and a human are one. A car and a human and the black phlegm of Motl are one. We drove.

"Zaidy . . ."

"Don't take me to the hospital. Coughing is the only exercise I get."

"You're not getting better."

"I've almost gobbed it all up. It'll be gone soon."

"That's not how it works."

"It's like being possessed by a dybbuk, but soggier."

"Does Dr. Hodenbruch know about this?"

"It's good for your mother and you to see each other," Motl said, looking out at the stipples and creases of the Badlands. "A year and a half is too long."

"We could stop so you could get checked. It wouldn't take long."

"I don't want to see a doctor. I know what I need."

More wadfuls of Motl's alleged dybbuk innards as he choked in the seat beside me.

"There's nothing like big sky, fresh air all the way to the horizon. It's good for her here. She's going to be glad to see you," he said in a momentary pause from coughing.

I doubted that. Last time we spoke, we didn't speak. And the time we spoke before that, it was shouting.

I'd quit university in Ottawa and had come home. It was eleven in the morning and my mother was beached under a comforter and an empty bottle of vodka. One fuzzy pink rabbit slipper and one bare foot stuck out. Between the rabbit and my mother, I'd have said that the fuzzy rabbit was more alert.

"Mom, you okay?"

"My mother killed herself and my father was a Nazi. How are you?"

I sat down in Motl's reading chair, clomped my feet on the coffee table.

"How am I? My mother is also going to kill herself. It's just going more slowly."

"I'll try to hurry it up, then."

She shimmied and lurched upright, tottered across the room then staggered up the stairs. I heard clinking as she waded through empty bottles and then her bedroom door slammed.

On the road toward Circle. A horse and buggy plodded on the shoulder of the road.

"Amish?" I asked.

"Mennonite," Motl said. "I saw a church in Glendive."

We waited for the oncoming traffic to pass so we could scoot around the clip-clopping driver. A rabbi except for the Jesus in his beard-camouflaged heart.

As we went by, Motl watched the man in the side-view, holding the long leather reins, elbows on his knees, his patient, calm expression. Time moved at the speed of him and his horse.

"When I see the space shuttle on TV," Motl said, "it feels like it's already the future. When I was a boy, we rode in wagons like the black hat there. We had the original Theodor Herzl to pull our cart—this was long before there was Israel. I was seven before Mr. Ford made his every-colour-as-long-as-it's-black Model T, though it was years before anyone other than the rich and rim-worthy had one."

"Remember you called me inside to watch the moon landing on our little black-and-white TV? It was so grainy—like NASA was doing video surveillance at a convenience store and a couple of astronauts walked in. I remember looking up at the moon that night, thinking if I squinted hard enough, I'd see the astronauts like gnats on the surface of the moon."

"Another frontier, I reckon. Least there wasn't anyone there to get rid of."

"As far as we know, Zaidy. Maybe there were aliens?"

"Or the lost tribes. I never thought I'd live long enough to see man on the moon. Or to see a grandchild. I'm getting to be old, Giteleh. Old as hills."

"Hills stick around a long time."

"From my perspective, it's all downhill."

"Don't think you're ready for *Yisgadal v'yiskadash* yet."

"Nah. But don't wash all my clothes. Might not need them."

"Okay, Zaidy. Just the underwear, then. I insist. So you can at least be buried in a clean pair."

From when I was old enough to notice, I'd thought Motl had been fuelled by bad jokes and obstinance. Remaining here was a stubborn habit. Is the coffin half-full or half-empty? Doesn't matter as long as it's not yours.

We'd arrive late in the golden afternoon, drive through the ranch gates and meet my mother at her little cabin on the property. Would she be on the porch, her feet propped on a railing, reading, or in her garden, watering flowers, pulling weeds?

From somewhere in Minnesota, Motl had phoned the office to let them know we were coming. How did he think my mother would greet us? Motl kept those cards close to his vest. A Full House, a Royal Flush? The Hanged Man and the sloshed Empress slumped over her throne sharing big cups of bitter wine? Or maybe the Hierophant would be inhaling a spliff big as the three of swords. Motl had told the person on the other end that this was a special surprise, that we had news to share.

What news? That you can travel more than three thousand miles and still not shake your family? That you can't escape your past life and the past life of your family? That your child and your father have you surrounded? That Motl had staged the biggest dad joke of all?

I didn't want to just roll up to her cabin and knock on the door. She wouldn't likely really be on her porch engaged in literary activities or out on the soil bent in domestic agriculture. The least we could do was to give her some notice. So she could hide the bottles, brush her hair and try to be brave as she waited for us.

I guessed Motl thought surprise was an essential part of the strategy, or else she'd chicken out and take off. Like Germany breaching the Molotov–Ribbentrop Pact and stomping across the Lithuanian border while Stalin had his pants down, taking a despotic dump in the little autocrats' room at the Kremlin.

Motl's plan was family therapy along the lines of breaking in a horse by bucking it out. For me as well as for my mother. But he was the man who'd travelled across Europe to retrieve his cobblers from a snowbank twenty years after they'd been remaindered. Was my mother the left and I the right?

If the world was a book, Motl wished to write its ending, having lived through several already. For him, my mother and I were a sequel. Not a final chapter, despite how it might look. His westerns had thought their Indians were final chapters, too, but it was the westerns that were over.

Here were Motl and me near the Canadian border in his Ford Pinto, and he put on the radio. What we heard was not "Mammas Don't Let Your Babies Grow Up to Be Cowboys" or even "Man of Constant Sorrow," but "Don't Fence Me In," the singer asking for a plenitude of land under the pearly snap-button stars, being willing to be sent off for eternity as long as whichever entity follows through on the promise of the song also follows through on the promise of this song's title and enables what we long for over yonder to in fact become true.

"I reckon it a near plumb-perfect thing," Motl said, "but not a real cowboy song."

"Are any of them?"

"As real as some cowboys. But this is Cole Porter. Though he did buy the lyrics from a guy born not far from here. In Helena."

We arrived at the town of Sweet Grass on the US side of the border. We'd cross through to Coutts and then head toward Fort Macleod and Head-Smashed-In Buffalo Jump.

Near the border crossing, I slowed as I approached the line of Canadian flag–emblazoned booths. A six-lane road filled with hatchbacks, pickups, cube vans, semi-trailers, and trucks bearing hatchbacks, pickups and cube vans on their double-decker backs. Lineups of trucks always remind me of a procession of dinosaurs: slow, heavy, ponderous, and likely to emit sudden rumblings and snorts.

We got our blue Canadian passports out of the glove compartment, little books that supposedly confirmed who we were. A few rubber stamps of work and holiday destinations over half-tone images of national heroes and mug shots that made each of us look like, after the trip, we would continue our rich life of torturing squirrels, though still not enjoy it.

"A passport is like a licence for ourselves," I said.

"When does it expire?" Motl said. "I'd like to know."

The border guard had a moustache. Across the world, it seems that a disproportionately large percentage of male border guards had moustaches. Perhaps a symbolical protection covering the border between upper lip and nose. I reached out and gave the border guard the passports.

"Citizenship?"

"Purpose of your travel?"

"Residence?"

"Anything to declare?"

Motl began to convulse, heaving and spluttering, filling handfuls of tissue with dark effluvium. When he was able to talk, he said, "This is something I got in Canada. I'm not importing it. I don't need to declare it. All this stuff"—he indicated the crimson tissues—"came with me from Toronto."

The guard, likely fearing contracting whatever contagion Motl was emitting, quickly returned our passports and waved us on.

"My mother would have given him bread," Motl said. "With money in it."

"She'd have been arrested."

"Not if there was enough inside."

8

Highway 4 took us through Milk River, Warner and Lethbridge and then on to "historic" Fort Macleod. The downtown looked like an old western town, but we didn't stop. We crossed the Old Man River—Motl tipped his cap to it—"From one old man to another," he said. "We both understand erosion"—and took the 785 toward Head-Smashed-In Buffalo Jump.

"Maybe we can go there with my mother," I said. "It'd be good to have something to do."

"As long as she doesn't try to push me off. She's not my easiest daughter."

"You have another one?"

"I can only hope."

"If you two get into it, I might jump."

"Take me with you, then."

Eventually, we arrived at the gates of the ranch. We could see the ridge of Head-Smashed-In Buffalo Jump in the distance. Several horses grazed in the scrub, a halter-hitched lead rope tying them to the fence.

"Let me out," Motl said, pulling at the door.

There was a long driveway leading to the buildings, too far to walk.

"Let me out," Motl insisted.

As soon as I stopped, he began to cough, shaking his mortal body loose from his bones, his insides from his out. Then he climbed from the car.

"Shh," he said, and, one palm up, slowly approached a beautiful red roan that nuzzled close to the fence. "Shh," he said as it touched its nose to his hand. He stroked its muzzle. "Shh."

I was surprised how gracefully he climbed the fence and slipped onto the horse's back.

"Zaidy," I called.

He leaned forward, unhitched the rope and rode bareback across the field.

"Zaidy!"

An old, sick man should not be venturing into the darkening fields, especially with no saddle or reins. If he had a coughing fit, he might fall. He might fall anyway. And he would get lost. Motl clutched the roan's dark mane, urging the horse on with his knees. The horse cantered along the curve of fence until I could hardly see them.

"Zaidy," I called again. I opened the driver's door and stood on the floor's lip, craning to see.

Motl rode out toward the sun as it sank low over the distant Rockies, colouring the grasses in pinks and roses. The air cooled, a spectral chill curling toward me. The mist or fog was like a vast herd of bison crowding the crimson prairie. The beasts were a twilight cloud, ghost buffalo no longer of this world. They were shadows on great hooves, creatures of smoke as if the plains themselves were smouldering.

The lead buffalo raised its huge head, a shaggy boulder on a torso-sized neck. It detected the scent of horse, of man. Its steadfast eyes reflected this diminutive Jew in blue polyester slacks, a beige cardigan and a checkered button-down, his face fissured as badlands stone. He rode in an arc around the herd, so that they were between him, the coulee and the fence.

"Oy," Motl shouted, kneeing the horse to a gallop back and forth in front of them. "Oyyyyy," he said, raising his arms, shaking his cardigan before them like a spear.

What was he doing? It was delusion. The buffalo spooked and began to run, their pelts rubbing together as they hurtled side by side over everything in their path. In peril, the animals were a tide of pure fear, a vast muscled rumble, a dark, unbroken wave of encroaching night.

Motl dropped the cardigan, slipped off the horse and stood before them, his arms wide open as they ran toward him. His shadow was the branches of a huge tree painted in darkness against the ground, stretched impossibly long by the sinking sun. The bison were the shadows of thunder.

I had not understood. Motl intended to be trampled beneath their hooves, turned to chopped liver and sour mash. He'd galloped into the sunset, dreaming of a deluded and epic death.

Had he known he would do this? The coughing. The slurry of black-red blood. He had been dying. But he had always been dying. As Sancho Panza said, "I have never died all my life," but now Motl had chosen it.

The bison. What had been extinguished, what had once been lost, had once been here, had now returned to engulf him.

I gunned the car. I would drive the shadow buffalo away. I pressed the horn, a clarion call, a klaxon. I pressed it again and again as I drove. It was the blast of the shofar. A cry like the blaring ram's horn of the great temple, which would shock the buffalo and they would look inward and repent of their route toward Motl. The car scraped against the rocks as I buffeted forward. I could hear Motl shouting over the buffalo's quake but could not see him. Then a wheel swerved down into a ditch, and the car lurched to a crooked stop. I pushed the accelerator, but the engine only revved. I shifted into reverse but was wedged into the ground. I'd have to run.

The driver's door was jammed, so I squeezed out the passenger side. All was dim, and I could no longer see Motl, the buffalo or their long shadows. I ran stumbling forward, calling out his name. "Zaidy. Motl. Zaidy." I heard nothing. A distant thunder. The buffalo had retreated. I stood in an empty field.

Sancho Panza again: "Until death it is all life."

Yisgadal v'yiskadash.

Sh'mei rabbaw.

Motl was gone. I felt at the end of a story, here in the fabled evening redness of the west, walking back from where he had disappeared into the sunset, just as he had always hoped. Our old Ford Pinto, Theodor Herzl, bashed and askew in a ditch, the dim outline of the fence before me. Motl had left me and my mother to carry on. By ourselves. *L'dor v'dor.* From generation to generation.

I arrived at the locked gate of the farm and the intercom attached like a mezuzah to the doorpost. It was the same kind of intercom we had at our local *shul*, which I'd noticed the few times Motl and I actually attended. There was a video camera so they could see who's talking, who to buzz in. Almost all synagogues have this arrangement now. Never know when someone will gussy themselves up with epaulettes, insignia, righteousness and a semi-automatic then attempt to manifest what they think of as destiny and Ribbentrop-the-living-Molotov out of the congre-gants. Making living room by making more dead.

But here the locked gates were to keep people in as well as out. A reservation. A ghetto. A camp. The Garden of Eden with an electronic angel wielding a fiery sword guarding the gates.

Motl used to tell this Henny Youngman joke:

Guy comes up and asks to bum a couple bucks for a cup of coffee.

"But coffee's only a dollar," I say.

"So maybe you'll join me?" he says.

Perhaps it'll be like this with my mother, but instead:

"Couple bucks for a cup of coffee?" I say.

"Coffee's only a dollar!" she'd answer.

"Think of it as paying me back for yesterday."

I pressed the intercom and explained who I was. The gate buzzed. Open.

Acknowledgements

"Now it seems to me the heart /must enlarge to hold the losses /we have ahead of us." Since I first encountered them as a teenager, I often think of these lines from Marvin Bell's poem "Gemwood." To me they mean that while we must be ready for what the future brings, we must also be ready for the extent of the losses of the past and present as we continue to learn. Like the universe itself, both past and present never stop expanding.

I have learned much from many; their insight, learning, courage, empathy, their stories and their capacious yet thankfully non-medically enlarged hearts have helped me to explore the difficult histories told in this book.

When I got married, there was a videographer who surprised the family, including my grandfather, Percy Zelikow, with mostly cheesy questions. ("Gary, why do you love your bride?") After some typical shtick ("I would like to address the nation,") my grandfather, aware that he was speaking at an important moment in the history of the family, stared into the camera with an intensity I'd never seen from him, and spoke of the horrors of the Holocaust in his birthplace of Lithuania and of his family, his neighbours, whole communities, and of an entire world that was extinguished. This single moment has haunted me ever since.

This book weaves broad research with stories I learned directly from my family, including my grandparents, my parents, my in-laws, our family friend, Erwin Koranyi, and my great-uncle Isaak Grazutis, a painter, who as a child, literally walked himself to safety. He was an exceedingly warm, generous and positive man alert to life's joys, humour, and beauty, and I greatly value the time we were able to speak together of his life. I am, of course, deeply grateful to them and to the survivors and researchers for sharing their stories and knowledge.

I thank Drew Hayden Taylor for advice and for several anecdotes that he generously allowed me to use, including some from the making of his fantastic documentary, *Searching for Winnetou*. I refer to a Mohawk-Jewish artist's work and indeed that artist, Steven Loft, gave me important guidance at an early stage of writing. I learned much about Lakota Code-talkers and some great stories from online interviews with Clarence Wolf Guts. A conversation with Antanas Sileika provided an important perspective about Lithuanian history. I closely read the poems of resistance fighters Abraham Sutzkever and Abba Kovner and adapted elements from their lives. My favourite tiny Norwegian cowboy, Tor Lukasik-Foss, offered some useful leads and inspiration at various stages. Ally Fleming provided some great lines and kind enthusiasm, and Martha Baillie shared her intense belief in the possibilities and important tasks of fiction. Amanda Lewis, who edited *Yiddish for Pirates,* continued to be a help in the early stages of this book. The passion and commitment to address difficult stories, not to mention research acumen, of Marsha Forchuk Skrypuch was a model. Cherie Dimaline shared some of her invaluable irrepressibility, insight, and the remarkable quip, "We're genocide buddies." I recalled her power-ful talks often during the writing.

I have learned from long discussions with my daughter, Rudi Bromberg-Barwin, about everything, but particularly about geno-cide, Judaism, North American and Indigenous society and his-tory, and I'm grateful for her commitment to thinking about what would make a just world.

The wry kindness and wise counsel of my agent, Shaun Bradley continues to guide me. Sarah Jackson offered essential editorial suggestions, copy editor John Sweet improved the book with his eegle-eye (yes, John, I know there's two e's there: stet) and Andrew Roberts created the remarkable cover (wow!).

I am extremely glad for the absolutely vital clarity, wit, com-passion and good judgement of my editor, Anne Collins, whose wisdom and trust allowed this novel to complete its own eccentric quest and find its own jewels.

I thank the supporters of public funding of the arts for grants from the Canada Council and the Hamilton City Enrichment fund. A series of Writer in Residence positions were not only energizing but invaluable in providing me time to write. Thank you faculty and students of University of Toronto (Scarborough) and McMaster and Wilfrid Laurier Universities, and the staff and patrons of the Hamilton and London Public Libraries.

I thank my parents, in-laws, siblings and children for their continued support, enthusiasm and curiosity. And my wife, Beth Bromberg-Barwin for the whole of our life (there—take that, cheesy videography guy!).

Permissions

GARY BARWIN is a writer, composer, and multidisciplinary artist and the author of twenty-three books of poetry, fiction and books for children. His recent national bestselling novel, *Yiddish for Pirates*, won the Stephen Leacock Medal for Humour as well as the Canadian Jewish Literary Award and the Hamilton Literary Award. It was also a finalist for both the Scotiabank Giller Prize and the Governor General's Literary Award for Fiction. *For It Is a Pleasure and a Surprise to Breathe: New and Selected Poems* was also recently published to much acclaim. A PhD in music composition, Barwin has taught creative writing at a number of colleges and universities. His prose and poetry has been published in hundreds of magazines and journals internationally—from *Reader's Digest* to *Granta* and the *Walrus*. Born in Northern Ireland to South African parents of Ashkenazi descent, Barwin lives in Hamilton, Ontario.